A.E. NALLE

EVERNIGHT PUBLISHING ®

www.evernightpublishing.com

Editor: Lisa Petrocelli

Cover Art: Jay Aheer

ISBN: 978-0-3695-0777-8

A.E. NALLE

DEDICATION

This is for the Jill's of the world. Your past will never define who you are.

The hardest of times often lead to the greatest moments of your life.

Keep going you beautiful badass.

A.E. NALLE

The Wicked Series, 2

A.E. Nalle

Copyright © 2023

Chapter One

I wish I had a crystal ball. I think everyone at some point in their lives wishes for the same thing. The visceral need to see the future before it happens. Maybe they could have changed their own outcome. Stop themselves before they made a decision they would later regret. They say everything happens for a reason. Unfortunately for me, I have yet to know the reason.

****

Sixteen Years Ago

"Hey, beautiful," a silky voice said against my ear. The smell of vanilla mixed with a heady musk assaulted my senses. If he hadn't been so close to me, I never would have heard his intimate whisper over the raging music that thumped through the three-story frat house I found myself in on this Saturday night. All around me, bodies gyrated to that stupid "Sexy Back" song everyone overplayed. I looked at my roommate, Jenna, with wide eyes as his arm snaked around my middle, pulling me back to a big muscular chest. I sighed to myself, *here we go.*

I winked at her, giving her the all-clear to leave us before I turned in his arms, giving him what I hoped was a stern look. We had been playing this cat and mouse game for months and he was evermore bold with his chase.

"Jason, what did I tell you about touching me?" I tried to keep my bitch face intact as I looked up at his enormous frame.

He was one of the best defensive linebackers at UGA and definitely built for the part. He was at least 6'5" and built like a brick shithouse, easily towering over my small stature by a foot. He put all the piddly little high school boys of my past to shame. Although, normally I wasn't picky about who I dated. As long as they treated me with moderate respect, it was all good in my book. For some reason, Jason got it in his thick skull that I was going to be another one of his conquests. His playboy attitude was legendary around campus. He strutted around like everything was owed to him because he was attractive—reason number one why I wasn't interested—but the boy just didn't seem to take the hint.

When he had first approached me with his football buddies, the one thought that ran through my mind was to climb his ass like a tree. But then he opened that gorgeous mouth and proved that not all beautiful people were indeed smart. The idiot actually bragged about all of the "poon" he had been pulling this year. Right in front of me! Like talking about all the sex he was getting from randos was supposed to make me drop my panties for him on the spot.

When his bragging had finally ceased, I knew what was coming next. Before he could get the first syllable past his perfect teeth, I held my hand up. I simply could not listen to him talk for one more second.

"The next words out of your mouth better be 'I'm sorry I wasted your time, Jill.' Please tell me you did not go through your list of weekly skanks before you attempted to ask me out. If you even so much as think I would be interested in a short dick, color-outside-the-lines, man-child such as yourself, you must truly be daft. I would probably get a better orgasm from riding my pillow than I would ever get from you. Next time you want to talk to me, rethink it before you embarrass yourself again." I gave his big chest a couple of slaps, then promptly showed him my back as he stood there with a slack jaw and his friends laughing behind him.

I had gone back to my dorm and called Kate. We both had a good laugh over it.

Now, normally you would think that after you wounded a man's pride like that, he would simply leave you alone. But, that wasn't the case with Jason.

For the last three months, he had only gotten bolder with each passing day. I couldn't get him to leave me alone. He would wait outside my dorm complex and try to walk me to my classes. After about the second week I finally stopped trying to walk faster than him. If he wanted to waste his time chasing something he could never have, who was I to stop him?

He tried to talk to me more and more every day, to show me there was more to him than what I saw on the surface. Even intellectually knowing him, I still thought he was an idiot. Although, slowly but surely he had started to grow on me.

I got used to our daily walks and even found myself enjoying some of our conversations. I still wasn't stupid enough to date him but I had found a somewhat easy friendship. That was when he was keeping his hands to himself. When he progressed to trying to hold my hand, I had shut that shit down with a hard no. I told him I could try to be his friend, but I would never let it get further than that. He had just smiled and shrugged like my refusal hadn't bothered him in the least.

Now here I was, standing off the side of the dance floor, drinking cheap booze and trying to shrug off his unwanted touch. When Jenna asked if I wanted to go to a party with her, I should have asked where it was. Of course, it was at his frat house. I thought briefly about going home early with a glance at the door.

Jason smiled down at me with his pearly whites and his dimples that always made an appearance on his stupid face. "I know, I'm sorry." He held his hands out like he couldn't help himself. "You're just so sexy and I have a hard time not touching you," he said in a low voice as he gave me bedroom eyes and stood a little closer.

I crossed my arms over my chest and glared back at him. Letting my body language do all the talking for me. He looked down at me and rolled his baby blue eyes, holding his hands up in surrender. "Fine, I'll back off. You know you don't have the right type of body to be such a prude, Jill. You really shouldn't dress like that if you don't want the attention," he said as he towered over me.

I squinted my eyes and stepped closer to him. I would not let him try to intimidate me. So what if my dress was a little on the short side. That didn't give people like him the right to touch me if I didn't ask for it. I cupped my ear and leaned in closer, standing on my tiptoes.

"Say that one more time for the bitches in the back?" I said, putting venom in each word. If he was stupid enough to say it one more time, I was going to rip his balls off his body before he could blink.

I would be lying if I said I didn't begrudge the fact that he had the common sense to back down from me. I grinned a little as I headed toward the door. I got about two steps away when he grabbed my wrist to halt my retreat. I looked at my wrist that he held firmly in his hand and then up at him. I'm sure my face was saying, "Are you fucking serious?"

He saw me shooting daggers at him and released me, holding his hands up again. "Look, I'm sorry, okay. My only excuse is I find you incredibly attractive and it's frustrating that you won't give me a chance. You're the most interesting, smart person I know, and I just like myself a little more when I'm around you. I haven't even fucked anyone else since I started walking you to class, Jill," he finished with a loud sigh.

I rolled my eyes. "So what? Am I supposed to reward you for not sticking your dick into everything with two legs and tits? I don't give a shit who you fuck, Jason. Because this"—I gestured between us—"is not happening."

I made to turn toward the door one more time and he stopped me by rushing in front of me. I balled my fists up, becoming increasingly irritated by the second.

"Move!" I ground out between clenched teeth. He shuffled closer still, crowding me. He was brave, I had to give him that.

"Please," he begged. "Just stay for a little while. You were having fun before I came up to you. I was watching you dance with your friend. Just let me get you a drink and we can talk, like usual. I promise I won't touch you anymore," he finished with puppy dog eyes.

I huffed and stared at him. In the last three months I had never heard him say he was sorry for anything and he sure as hell never said "please." I couldn't kid myself into thinking that he hadn't been wearing me down a little over time. He could be charming when he wanted to be and he had the looks to go with it. And he was right, I was having a good time until he tried pushing me.

A wide grin spread over his gorgeous face when he saw my resolution waver the slightest bit. I pursed my lips, trying not to let my smile show through. "Fine," I conceded. "But watch your hands," I said, waving my finger in his face.

He threw his head back in a delighted laugh before looking back down at me, humor apparent in his eyes. "Come on, let's get you a drink."

The rest of the night passed in a blur. The music seemed to get louder and the people right along with it. Jenna had joined us again as we took shot after shot of cheap tequila. The beer in my hand was constantly being drained until it turned into strong mixed drinks. The thick haze of marijuana smoke clung to the air. Jason and I sat on the couch and passed the joint back and forth in-between drinks. I lost track of the number of drinks I had consumed at some point but didn't care. I was floating on cloud nine.

Until I wasn't.

My memory of that night gets a little shoddy after that. At one point I was on the couch between Jason and Jenna, the next I was in the middle of the dance floor surrounded by sweaty bodies. All of us writhing against one another in alcohol and drug-induced ecstasy. Looking to my left, two girls from my civics class were making out. To my right, a couple of frat guys drinking out of one of those funnel things. I remember holding my hands above my head with a half-empty cup, hips swaying to the thumping music.

Hands snaked around my middle, pulling me

back to a hard body. Eyes closed, I let my inhibitions free as I leaned back into strong arms. A hand crept up my body until they were grabbing my drink and pressing the remainder to my lips, helping me tilt my head back to ingest the contents. Hooded baby blue eyes watched my throat work as I swallowed the last gulp. Somehow Jason ended up in front of me with his hands cupping my behind.

That wasn't right. I tried to weakly push his hands away but he held firm.

"I told you..." my slurred voice trailed off. My tongue felt so thick in my mouth it was hard to talk.

"You don't know how badly I want you," Jason murmured before he brought his lips to mine with brutal force.

I tried to push his chest away from me but fell short. I couldn't get my arms to work the way they were supposed to. Everything was so blurry. One minute he was shoving his tongue in my mouth, the next he had me in front of him at the top of the stairs, pushing me along. How did I get up here?

I tried to turn the other way but he grabbed my waist and herded me along. He held me tight to his front as he opened a door. He pushed and pulled until he had me behind a door, then he locked it.

"What're y—" I slurred. Why couldn't I talk? I know I had a lot to drink but something was off. This wasn't normal.

Jason grabbed me and crushed me to his body. It felt as though his hands were everywhere at once, roughly grabbing my breasts and my ass. He tried to lift my dress and I tried to get my arms to work. I grabbed for his hands, halting them before he touched my panties.

"Jason, stop," I finally managed.

I was so woozy and the room wouldn't stop

spinning. He pulled back long enough to look down at me with a frigid gaze. I felt the cold stab of fear hit me in the gut as I saw the look in his eyes. I fumbled trying to get my hands off his arms. Forcing my feet to work, I took a wobbly step toward the locked door. Jason hauled me back to him in a rough jerk, bruising my arms with his big hands.

"You should be passed out by now. That fucker sold me some weak shit," he snarled.

My heart rate picked up as panic laced its way through my blood. I opened my mouth to shout for help. Before I could draw in a breath, Jason slapped his hand over my lips so hard it rattled my teeth.

"Shut your fucking mouth!" he hissed in my ear. All I could manage was a strangled whimper as he pushed me and my world spun out of control.

My back hit a lumpy mattress with a dizzying force before my body stilled. Nausea rose as the smell of musty sheets assaulted my senses. I willed my body to move. Nothing was working as it should. I was to the point where I couldn't even move my arms anymore.

I was a prisoner inside my own body. I could feel the cold air spreading across my lower belly. My dress had ridden up, exposing me. I couldn't even pull it back down to cover myself from his lustful eyes. All I could do was look up at my attacker as he stripped off his shirt while he leered at me. My breathing was so fast that I was afraid I'd pass out. He unbuckled his belt with clumsy fingers as he watched me. Need plain in his expression.

"You have no idea how long I've wanted to do this," he murmured almost as though he was talking to himself.

I whined again as he shoved his jeans off his hips, his erection coming into view. I willed my lips to work.

"Please, don't," I managed with slurred speech. Whatever drug he had used on me had taken full effect now as my vision faded in and out.

He was descending on top of me one moment and the next he had my dress shoved up to my neck. Hot pain bloomed as he roughly pinched my naked flesh with fast, hurried motions. I heard a tear as he ripped my panties from my body. Tears streamed down the sides of my face as he fumbled with my most intimate area.

I must have whined a little too loud when he forced himself inside of me. My body was not ready for sex, but he didn't care. He used one hand to cover my mouth and the other to hold my arms above my head, as if I could use them to fight back anyway. His big hand covering my mouth was blocking most of my nose so I could hardly breathe as he invaded me. I could hear the screams in my head that I wasn't able to vocalize. I squeezed my eyes shut as agony ripped from my core.

All I could do was lay there and cry as he did what he wanted to my body. I was a bystander to my own assault. There was no gentleness in his movements or his eyes as he looked down at me with a harsh gaze. It felt like hours as I lay there taking his cruel punishment. All the while he murmured things to me, demeaning things I couldn't defend myself against.

He called me his "dirty little whore" and kept telling me I loved what he was giving me. That nobody else would ever fuck me the way he could. I was a cock tease and was finally getting what I'd asked for.

I took it all, recoiling inside myself, just waiting for it to be over. Finally, his damaging thrusts became erratic and he grunted his release. He removed his hands from me and I gasped for air, my head rolling to the side. He pulled out of me, leaving a sharp ache behind. I still couldn't move as he stood and dressed in front of me. I could feel bile burning my throat before I wretched all over the pillow under my cheek.

"Fuck! All over my bed! Goddamnit, Jill!" he yelled as he looked down at my used body in disgust.

I had never truly hated someone until that moment. I could feel myself practically vibrate with rage. He had the arrogance to be disgusted after he just raped me. I didn't doubt that it was rape. Even If I had dressed in a short dress and drank excessively, that didn't give him the right to fuck me without consent.

"I'm glad you waited until we were done to do that." He smirked at me. "You should sleep it off for the night. I'll take you home in the morning. You can have the room. I gotta go tell the boys I finally got into Jill Brookes's panties. They bet me it would never happen, but I have these"—he held up my ripped panties—"as proof. Daddy's about to get paid!" His voice faded as he exited the room.

And that's how he left me. He didn't even bother to pull my dress back down. I lay there covered in my own vomit, naked, bruised, and broken. It was two hours before I regained the use of my extremities again. Another hour before I could stand and make it to the door. The house was quiet as I stumbled down the stairs. The soft threads of early morning light seeped through the windows. Sleeping bodies littered the random furniture around the main floor. I didn't see Jason as I left the house. Somehow I made it back to my dorm where I called Kate. She found me crouched in my bathroom, sobbing my eyes out. She sat with me, two-year-old Lindsey on her hip until I could stomach going to the hospital.

****

I wish I had a crystal ball. One that could have told me what was going to happen that night, or how those events would change me. Maybe I would be the same carefree girl I used to be. Maybe I wouldn't have become so tainted by the evil in this world.

Chapter Two

Present Day

"And how does that make you feel?" The concerned voice of my therapist broke through the haze of my thoughts. I fought the urge to roll my eyes at her. She knew damn well I hated that question but she kept asking it. I looked at the pretty doctor sitting in front of me and tried to keep a straight face.

Dr. Lisa Yorker had been my long-term therapist ever since my ... incident. The older gray-haired woman always had warm eyes and an even more inviting smile. She was always willing to hear me bitch about my problems. She had known me long enough now that we were more like friends than mere patient and doctor.

After Jason, I had gone to the hospital with Kate and was immediately admitted. Having to succumb to a pelvic exam and a rape kit so soon after being violated like that, was not something I would ever wish on anyone. Not saying the nurses and female doctor weren't great. They were amazing and completely comforting. It's just that having to show strangers your greatest shame so soon after a huge trauma left a person feeling even more vulnerable.

The months that followed flew by in a blur. After Mom and Dad found out what had happened, everything spiraled out of control. Mom had cried a lot during that time and Dad looked like he wanted to murder someone.

It wasn't hard to find a lawyer willing to take the case. It had been what they called a "slam dunk case." I was told more than once that I was lucky I was able to remember what had happened. Can you imagine that? Telling a rape victim they were lucky. What a crock of shit.

The drug Jason had slipped into my last drink of the evening was called Rohypnol. The drug was supposed to knock me out cold and/or make me forget about the experience altogether. Apparently, the one Jason had given me was way past its expiration date and wasn't as potent. Although it had worked in making it impossible for me to get away, it didn't work by making me blissfully unaware of what was happening to me.

The rape kit had shown obvious bruising and swelling as well as tears along my vaginal walls from the force he used on me. That, coupled with his obvious DNA, made my lawyer's job fairly easy.

Jason was expelled immediately from UGA and promptly arrested for his crimes. My father had a long-standing career as a politician for the State of Georgia, and a gag order was released so nobody could speak about the case with anyone who wasn't directly involved. We wouldn't want to sully the Brookes family name with my unfortunate scandal.

Jason had come from a fairly prominent family as well, but they washed their hands of him after they heard the evidence. They left him to clean up his own mess, withdrawing their legal help and forcing him to use a public defender. My lawyer had dragged his ass through the mud. When it was all said and done, he was left with time in prison as well as forced to pay restitution in the form of a $1.5M check made from his inheritance. In the end, everyone was happy about the outcome except for Jason and myself.

I may have been richer but no amount of blood money could have healed the gaping hole left inside of me. I felt like someone had ripped my soul out of my body and replaced it with something broken and ugly.

I spun further out of control when I returned to school that following fall. I drank a lot and partied too much. I skipped classes and my grades slipped so far that I lost my scholarship. Not that it mattered anymore.

The only way I felt I had control anymore was when I used my body. I had stopped being so picky about who I let between my legs. If I could control who I let fuck me, it gave me some sense of false stability. I refused to let Jason taint my need for human touch. I had almost always enjoyed sex before, why couldn't I still enjoy it … just with more partners?

I was never with one for more than a night or two, refusing to let myself feel anything more than the physical oblivion that came with a good orgasm. For a while, I ran through lovers like I was collecting baseball cards. When I say I have been with every shade of the rainbow, I am not exaggerating.

As much as I liked to say my life leveled itself out after a while, that just wasn't true. As hard as I tried to forget about that night, everything about that place reminded me of it. I couldn't go more than a day without seeing one of Jason's football buddies or one of his frat brothers. They would look at me warily as if I was the one that caused all of this to happen. I couldn't even walk past his old frat house without having a panic attack.

I felt like I was completely alone in the middle of the ocean just trying to keep my head above water. I could never figure out why it was such a shock to everyone when I tried to end it all after I came home for the summer.

My biggest regret is that Kate was the one that found me bleeding in my bathtub that day. She had known I wasn't right in the head at the time and felt the overwhelming urge to come to my parents' house that day. Call it divine intervention or whatever that pushed her to come see me, but she saved my life that day. I'll never forget the panicked look in her eyes as she tried to stop the blood flowing from my arms. I remember telling her I was so sorry over and over again. I decided to get help for not only myself but also her and Lindsey. I never wanted to see that look on her face again. It was the same look I had while Jason violated me.

I transferred schools and started seeing Dr. Yorker after that. Talking with her and leaning heavily on Kate helped me get through the worst of it. Watching Lindsey grow up and having a huge part in her life also helped. I had picked up some coping mechanisms along the way, obviously. Like my *slight* OCD. Everything had a place and I only freaked out a *little* when my routine was thrown off-kilter. I had a schedule that I followed and didn't like to veer off course. I ruled my life with an iron fist and refused to apologize for it. I still drank, but never excessively. I would never allow myself to spiral out of control again.

I still enjoyed the occasional one-night stand, but I was a little more selective than I used to be. I wanted to wake up still respecting myself in the morning. I saw Dr. Yorker regularly. It was always good to be able to fully express myself in a safe space without the judgment that sometimes followed. Doc had helped me just as much as Kate had when I had been going through my dark shit. I had a lot of respect for the woman and always felt at ease around her.

But not today. Today her questions were grinding on my damn nerves.

"It makes me feel pissed off!" I stood, pacing back and forth, unable to sit still any longer. "That fucker knew that was my client and *still* tried to go after him." I panted while pointing my finger at thin air like that prick Derek was standing in front of me.

Derek Vincant owned the rival publishing

company in this part of the state. I swear the fucker got half his clientele just by stealing them from other companies. I was waiting for the day when I could punch that permanent smirk off his stupid face.

"In what world is it okay to fuck with someone else's business?" I continued on my rant, still pacing.

"Jill, why don't w—"

"I mean seriously, like why doesn't he hire more people so they can draw in fresh business for him? It's not that hard to understand."

"Jill, can—"

"I bet he's got a little dick. That's probably why he went out and bought that shiny red Porsche. Trying to overcompensate for something, buddy?"

"Jill—"

"I bet you that wife of his is cheating on him. That's probably why he's such a miserable sack of sh—"

"Jill!" Doc's loud voice finally cut through my ranting. "Will you please take a seat before you wear a hole in my rug?" she asked with a calm smile.

I took a deep breath and stilled my movements, bringing my hands to my sides and clenching my fists. "Sorry," I said as I took my seat again.

"It's fine, you're obviously frustrated about something. The question is, what's really bothering you?" she said with that knowing gleam in her eyes.

After all these years of seeing her, it still amazed me when she saw right through my deflection. You would figure after this long I would just tell her what was wrong in the first place. What could I say, I was a stubborn bitch.

"I told you, Derek is a limp dick ass—"

She cut me off with a wave of her hand. Sitting forward from her plush chair, she shut her iPad case and regarded me with stern eyes.

"Cut the shit, Jill. I've been seeing you for fifteen years now. You honestly think you can get anything past me?" She paused, giving me a chance to speak. When I didn't she continued. "For one, you called me two weeks ago to push up our monthly appointment. Two, you're jumpier than a squirrel trying to cross the road. And three, you're rambling on about crap that you and I both know you don't care about. Now tell me what the real problem is so I can help you."

She was right on all three counts. After the panic attack that ended with me passing out in my car, I called her the next day. I had been off my anxiety meds for years now, but I was wondering if I needed to renew my prescription as of late. I was full of anxious energy that I couldn't seem to get rid of. Even running for an hour every night on my treadmill wasn't helping me wind down.

And it was true, I didn't give a shit about Derek. I knew Brookes Publishing was the top firm in the area. He could try all he liked, but he would never compete with me.

I took a deep breath, holding it for a moment before releasing it in a rush. Then I spilled my guts about everything I was feeling. Rambling on about how I wasn't sleeping much anymore. My dreams were filled with gunshots and musty sheets.

Gunshots from when Kate's crazy-ass ex-husband shot me a few months ago. He went "coo-coo for Cocoa Puffs" and tried to kill us both because Kate had gotten a chunk of change from her late father that she didn't share with him. But that was a story for another time.

I always awoke soaked in sweat, still able to feel the hand covering my mouth. Still able to smell the scent of vanilla. I told her about the "break-in" that was more than likely a stray rock that got thrown through my window by the neighbor's mower, but my panic-addled brain immediately went to the worst-case scenario. I told her about passing out in my car after calling the authorities. I omitted the fact of who I truly called. I still couldn't get the panicked look in those chocolate eyes out of my thoughts.

I told her about how the cops aka Damon, had to bust the window out of my car in order to get to me and see if I was still breathing. I could still feel the way his hands had gently held me steady as he brought me back to the present.

I was rattled and didn't know how to drag myself back out of the hole I found myself in.

"On top of all this, I feel like I'm going crazy lately. I swear, I will put something up where it belongs one day and the next it's in a completely different place. It's like my sleep-deprived brain can't keep its shit together anymore and I just forget that I moved it," I blurted quickly before releasing an exasperated huff. "I don't know what to do anymore. Do you think I should go back on the Xanax? I know it makes me kind of numb to everything, but that has to be better than this."

I felt as though a weight was lifted off my chest as I finished rambling. Doc was the only person besides Kate that I could be completely vulnerable around. And with Kate being in her new marital bliss, I had refrained from telling her anything. She had put up with enough of my shit over the years. I didn't need to keep piling it on.

Doc regarded me with squinted eyes and pursed lips. That was the face she always got when she was trying to work through a problem for me. "What are you doing to relieve stress right now? I know you canceled your gym membership. Have you found something else to fill that time?" she asked. She opened her old-school

Rolodex full of business cards.

I scrunched my face. I canceled that membership because my trainer was annoying as fuck. It seemed like he would use the thinnest excuse to get his hands on my ass. Claiming my form was off during squats or trying to show me how my muscle was supposed to flex. I had finally snapped when he thought it was appropriate to slap my ass at the water bottle fill station. I had promptly shown him how much I appreciated all his manhandling with a swift kick to the nads. Maybe he would think twice next time before laying his hands on some other female.

"No, I haven't found another trainer I like yet," was all I offered.

She nodded her head like she had expected that answer. She finally found what she was looking for and handed me a card with big bold lettering.

"Krav Maga?" I asked. When I looked back up at her she was smiling at me.

"Yes, Krav Maga. Hugh is an old client of mine and he runs a studio downtown. I think you'll enjoy it. It's very physical and it will help a lot with that anger you've been carrying around. I would rather you give that a try before we put you back on any medication. You need to keep yourself busy, Jill. When you give yourself too much free time, you don't relax like other people. You sit and you dwell, you pull further into yourself." She paused as I fiddled with the card between my fingers. "When was the last time you had sex?" she asked seemingly out of nowhere.

I huffed a humorless laugh. "It's been a while," I mumbled. She was always so intuitive, sometimes it scared me how much she knew me.

"I'm not going to sit here and tell you to go have sex with the greater half of downtown, but I am not going to pretend that you don't need to give in to your urges sometimes. You know that I view sex as a healthy way to deal with some of your emotions—in moderation. Is there anyone that has engaged that part of you lately?" she asked.

Brown eyes and olive skin filled my mind's eye. I squeezed my thighs together to stop the sudden ache that always accompanied the fantasy of him. I shook my head, trying to clear my thoughts. She took that as my answer.

"Well, maybe it's time to start finding someone who can help you out in that area." She gave me a knowing wink before she tapped the card in my hands. "Give him a call, try a couple of classes. If that doesn't work, then we can discuss other methods." She stood and I followed. My time was up for the day.

I tucked the card into my pocket and gave her a short hug before exiting her office. The day was late and I was exhausted, I would check out that studio tomorrow after work. I climbed into the car and prepared myself for the long, quiet drive, begrudging the time it gave me to listen to my inner thoughts.

Chapter Three

The sun was setting as I drove home in my rental car. Mine was still being fixed from when Damon had knocked the window in. I couldn't get in this damn car without thinking of him, and thinking of him always made me a little hot under the collar. Thoughts of his callused hands roaming across my skin assailed me. His plump sensual lips, with the most delicious amount of stubble around them.

I loved the way he ate at my lips like he didn't own a watch and wouldn't be held to any time constraint. He had taken his time exploring every nook and cranny with his skilled tongue. The way he kissed me made me think of other things he could do with his mouth. I knew he would go slowly, starting at my breasts, stopping to suck each of my hard-pebbled nipples. He would look up at me with those chocolate eyes as he licked around the peak, making sure I saw what he was doing before he sucked it inside. He would use those lavish lips to kiss and suck his way down. Stopping shortly to dip his wicked tongue into my navel, making me squirm before he moved further south. He would grin up at me with that crooked smile as he pulled my panties down...

A loud horn jarred me from my fantasy with a violent jerk. I jumped and jammed my knee into the steering wheel.

"Mother fu—" I cursed as I rubbed my knee. I pushed down on the accelerator and the car lurched forward. Normally, if someone honked at me, I would give them my happy middle finger but seeing as I was stopped at a green light, I figured I'd better let it slide.

I raked my hand down my face with an exasperated sigh. What the fuck was wrong with me?

Had I resorted to having a sex dream in the middle of traffic? Maybe Doc was right. I needed to get laid. I was clearly so horny I couldn't even safely drive home without my deprived brain blanking out.

I tried to tell myself that it had nothing to do with Damon. In the short time I'd known him it was like he wormed his way into my mind like some sort of sexy parasite. That wouldn't be such a bad thing if I thought I'd be able to just jump his bones a couple of times and fuck him out of my system. No, if I was a betting girl, I would say that man would chew my ass up and spit me out. I just knew I wouldn't survive the experience. Sure, the sex would be hot, but I didn't know if it was worth my sanity.

What I needed was a Ken. It didn't matter what his real name was, they were always a Ken. The type of man you didn't have to worry about after a night with him. There were always plenty of Kens at your local watering hole. Most men were like me, they wanted a good orgasm and then they wanted to get the hell out of Dodge. Hell, I held the door open for them most of the time. Now, if Ken was really good at what he did, I would take him for one more ride, but that was it.

I wasn't so oblivious to think I was good enough for decent men. I don't think I would be capable of putting any honorable man through what I referred to as *Hurricane Jill*. Even if I wanted a long-term relationship, I honestly didn't think it would ever work out. I knew who I was and I made no excuses. I didn't know very many men that were okay with a woman with such a strong need for stability. I had to have things in my life a certain way.

Although, I would be lying if I said that I loved my life the way it was. I would adore nothing more than to be able to just ... be, for once. It was extremely exhausting to keep everything in meticulous order all the time. If my brain would allow me to give the reins to someone else for a change, well, that would be a freakin' miracle.

I used to be just fine with the status quo, until recently. I think watching Kate with Heath and Reid opened my eyes a little. My bestie had gone and found her happily ever after months ago with not one, but two men. If there was anyone in this world who deserved those two amazing men, it was my Kate. The only bad thing about being around their joy was that they were so happy it made me see just how miserable I was. Don't get me wrong, I loved Kate and I was so happy for her. It's just that when someone in your life was so freaking happy all the time, it left you feeling a little jaded.

I shook my head to clear out my thoughts. I needed to get the wishes of happily ever after out of my head. Nobody would want me once they saw how ruined I truly was.

Maybe a good romp in the sheets would help me get my mind off a certain someone I couldn't stop fantasizing about.

Sighing, I turned off on a side street, going in the direction of my favorite "Ken Den" as I liked to call it. I usually had good luck finding someone to take to the suite for a night. Was it bad if I reserved a fuck pad nearby that I paid a monthly fee to keep for when I needed it?

I didn't ever take any of the Kens to my home. That was just another way I was able to control the outcome of the hookup. If Ken never knew where I lived, he couldn't come knocking for more.

The drive there was a short one. In no time at all, I was pulling up to what felt like my reserved parking spot. I pulled my vanity down after placing the car in "park." Bright blue eyes stared back at me. They were deceiving, they looked innocent and happy. It was a good thing people couldn't see the tarnish that resided on my soul.

I pursed my plump lips and dabbed on some gloss, fluffing my long auburn hair before I fixed my mascara. I settled and looked over the image I made in the mirror. The woman who stared back at me was beautiful. It wasn't arrogance or pride that made me think that, it was simple biology. I had a face most found attractive and a body that was equally as alluring. My constant need to have some form of exercise as an outlet insured that much.

I often begrudged the fact that I was "pretty." Maybe if I didn't look like this, Jason would have never happened. Maybe I could be a normal thirty-five-year-old with a husband to come home to every day. Maybe I would have 2.5 kids and a dog.

Closing my eyes at the sudden burn I felt, I took a deep breath. Opening again I stared at those blue eyes, hating the woman who looked back at me.

I slammed the mirror shut, not able to look any longer, and exited the car. Pulling on that fake confidence I so often wore, I walked through the door to my Ken Den and slapped a sultry smile on my face.

****

They say if you never try, you'll never succeed. I say that is a load of genuine bullshit.

I used my foot to slam my front door as I walked into my quiet house, stuffing my face with fast food fries. It was just after midnight when I gave up the hunt at the Ken Den and booked it to a burger joint with the golden arches that lit the way like a beacon for a starving man. I normally wouldn't eat this late, but fuck it. Lord knows I wasn't going to get much sleep tonight, so chances were

I'd be running it off on the treadmill before too long.

I slid my heels off my aching feet and put them in their respective slot in my hall closet. Color-coded, obviously. Fiona ran between my feet, purring as she greeted me. I looked down at the feline as I grabbed what was left of my burger out of the greasy sack.

"How was your night?" I asked the white beast. "In case you were wondering, mine was this good," I mumbled as I shoved the rest of the meal past my lips.

I had sat in that godforsaken den of ill repute for three long hours. I sipped on a few vodka-crans slowly throughout the night. I knew better than to have too many. I had twirled my straw around my glass and made eyes with a few possible suitors. Now and then I would take the straw and slide it between my teeth, teasing it with my tongue. The move always drew them in eventually.

The first victim that had approached me was what I would call a sexy nerd. He had dirty-blond hair with light-green eyes he hid behind thick-framed glasses. He was a little on the scrawny side but that was okay with me. I was short so it was always easy to find a man that could still make me feel delicate even when I knew I was anything but. He had cute dimples when he smiled that would make most women swoon. He would have been perfect. But then he opened his mouth.

I tried, really tried to shut down all the comparisons that ran through my mind as he talked to me about the latest PlayStation game he had just downloaded. Normally, I didn't care about anything other than how a Ken looked. But this time I couldn't stop myself from comparing as I listened to him drag on and on. I just kept coming back to how Damon would be talking to me about his interests. Or how when he looked at me his eyes told a story of everything he wanted to do to me.

In the end, I couldn't take it any longer. I excused myself and went to the other end of the bar in search of a new target.

The rest of the night had gone just like that. Whether it was the Motorcycle Ken with a dark beard and hard eyes or the Ken with the long black braids and skinny jeans. Or even the Lumberjack Ken with the deep baritone voice and scarred hands. All of them fell short in one way or another.

I even tried to speak to a handsome Latino man while I was there. Maybe I could trick myself into thinking I was getting what I really wanted. But as soon as he smiled at me and it wasn't that crooked grin I fantasized about, the illusion was ruined and I gave up.

So now here I was, seated at my big empty dinner table while my cat snoozed at my feet. I tilted my fry box into my mouth and scarfed down the remaining contents. Pathetic.

I finished my second dinner and walked down the hall to the master suite. I thought I should try to take a hot bath so I could maybe relax enough to sleep tonight. One glance at the clock and I vetoed that plan. I would have to settle for a scorching hot shower instead.

Fishing the Krav Maga card out of my pocket, I flipped the card between my fingers before placing it on the nightstand. I stripped out of my clothes and sorted them out by color into their appropriate baskets. Padding into my huge bathroom, I turned on the shower.

I turned to grab my towel from the rack I always hung it on to find it missing. I huffed loudly as I looked all around for it. This was what I was talking to Dr. Yorker about. I swear shit moved around by itself in this house. I always placed the towel on this rack, but now I found it clear across the room. I swore I was going insane. I grabbed the towel and walked back to the steaming water pouring out of the showerhead.

I had made sure this house was up-to-date with top-of-the-line appliances and luxuries, so it took less than a minute for the water to reach the hellish temperature I craved. I stepped into the scalding water with a hiss.

I was so mentally done for the day. I didn't even have the energy to shut down daydreams about things I shouldn't be thinking about. As I sudsed my hair with meticulous strokes, I let my thoughts wander freely. I finally let myself think of Damon Santos as I moved to wash the rest of my body.

I pictured his callused hands were the ones rubbing the soap down my body. I moaned lightly as I let my hands travel over my achy breasts, wishing he was the one touching me.

Damon stood behind me gloriously naked and wet, in my mind's eye. My back was flush against his front. I could feel the tickle of his dusting of hair that spanned his cut chest and ripped abdomen. His huge, hard cock was pressed against the seam of my ass as his hands roamed my torso.

"You feel so good, Red," he murmured against my ear.

I felt my smile as I listened to his term of endearment. Nobody had ever given me a nickname before and it left a warm feeling in my belly. I could feel a gush of arousal flood my center as he kissed the side of my neck before his hands came up to cup my breasts, running his thumbs across my tightened nipples.

"Do you want me to make you come, amor?" he rasped as he pinched and rolled my tender flesh.

"Yesss," I heard myself say.

He chuckled as he let his hand slide down my

body, growing closer to where I needed him most with each second. When he came to my core he slid his roughened fingers between my labia, across my throbbing clitoris, and into my drenched pussy. I gasped as he pumped his fingers into me as he rubbed his excitement against my ass. Reaching my arms back, I grabbed onto his long hair and pulled. He groaned deep in his chest at my rough treatment before pushing his palm onto my swollen nub.

"This pussy is mine," he nipped my ear. "Say it," he demanded roughly against me as he twisted my nipple with his other fingers.

"It's yours!" I yelped as the sharp discomfort turned to delicious heat.

His fingers kept pumping, and his palm kept grinding, building me higher. I was about to crumble in his arms, but I knew he would catch me.

I couldn't stop myself as my hips started to grind against his hand of their own accord. I moaned loudly as he told me to raise my leg. I followed his direction, placing my foot on the lower shelf in the shower. Making more room for him to finger-fuck me. There was no gentleness in his rough grasp as he squeezed and flicked his fingers over the tight peaks of my breasts. He held me tight.

"That's right, baby. You take your pleasure. Fuck my hand with that little cunt," he growled harshly in my ear again, making me pant.

I normally didn't like rough treatment for obvious reasons, but when it was Damon it felt right. It felt hot. My hips undulated themselves further. My mouth was wide open as I moaned and wailed.

"Yes, come for me, Red," he commanded and my body listened.

I came hard in an explosion of sensation. I

screamed my pleasure as I felt a large wave of hot liquid run down my inner thighs.

My chest was heaving as I leaned further back against his chest, only to be met with cold tile. I opened my eyes and broke the illusion that he was ever here at all. For a while, I could pretend it was his fingers bringing me pleasure instead of my own. I swear I had felt his warm breath as it spanned across my neck. Shamefully, that wasn't the first time I ever masturbated to the thought of him. I felt a pang of regret in my chest as I found myself always wishing it had been real.

I shut the shower off and stepped out with wobbly legs. I mentally kicked myself as I went through the motions of preparing myself for bed. I should have stopped myself before I had even gotten started. It was stupid of me to be fantasizing about someone that I was likely to never see again in the first place. And even if I did see him again, it could never happen. People like him didn't belong with people like me.

I'd hoped that maybe at least the orgasm I had wrung from myself would have worn me out enough to finally get some sleep, but my restless energy was saying otherwise. I laid down under my plush comforter and huffed a frustrated breath. I knew I should shut my thoughts of him down before they even started again. But I obviously had a long sleepless night ahead of me, so I let my mind drift. I closed my eyes as I remembered when he came to my rescue like some kind of Latino knight in shining armor.

Chapter Four

Two Weeks Ago

Everything was blissfully silent until it wasn't anymore. The sound of a muffled voice was starting to cut through the fog that clouded my mind. Then, it got quiet once more and I breathed a sigh of relief. My body was heavy and I didn't have the urge to move. This felt like the best sleep I had gotten in months. Before I could sink further into unconsciousness, the sound of glass being shattered jarred me and I came crashing back to reality.

You know that feeling you get when you just step off a super-fast roller-coaster ride? Where you get tunnel vision, become dizzy, and you're not sure if you're going to throw up. Add massive confusion to that list of symptoms and you get how I felt being thrust back to consciousness, after passing out due to a panic attack.

My head wobbled back and forth as I looked around the inside of my car. Everything looked like it should for a moment. Polished leather interior, pristine, dust-free infotainment center, and clutter-free organizational caddy along the center console, all intact. The one thing I couldn't wrap my brain around was all the glass that was on my passenger seat. That wasn't right. I reached over and started to wipe the shattered glass onto the floorboard. I would have to get out my Dustbuster later and clean it up properly.

Before I could get more than two handfuls of glass brushed out of the seat, the driver's-side door jerked open roughly. I swiveled my head around so fast vertigo set in and I had to lean back and close my eyes again. Holding my hand to my mouth, I tried to keep my stomach contents in check.

Big hands grabbed my upper arms and pulled me from the car in a fast, panicked motion. That didn't help with my dizziness at all.

I hadn't even seen who had taken me from my car before I was pushing away to vomit in the bushes. I heaved what was left of my dinner into my azaleas while I tried to stay upright. My legs were no more than wet noodles as they started to wobble and fail me. I lurched forward and prepared for my knees to crash into the pavement of my driveway.

But, before I could fall, strong arms grabbed me around the waist. They held me tight, refusing to let me go as I wretched the contents of my stomach. A soothing hand rubbed my back before gathering my hair and pulling it back from my face. If I hadn't been in the middle of being sick, I would have swooned.

When I was done, I used the back of my hand to wipe my mouth and tried to stand upright. The arm around my waist held me up while the other that was holding my hair joined it, holding firmly along my hip.

Still dizzy and confused, I leaned back into the hard body that held me. I sighed as my head rolled back against a broad chest. Warmth surrounded me as I closed my eyes again. A girl could get used to being held like this, I thought to myself with a slight grin on my lips.

"Hey, Red, are you going to get sick again? If so, I need to get you inside so I can call an ambulance."

The deep voice startled me and my eyes sprang open. I knew that voice. I sucked in a quick breath and spun in his arms. My confusion had finally worn off and I needed to get the hell out of his arms before I made a fool of myself.

As I spun out of his grasp, my heel caught on a rock, and I went careening to the side. I squealed as I waved my hands wildly, trying to get a grasp on anything. Before I could hit the hard pavement, Damon caught me once again.

His hands caressed the small of my back as he stood us upright, chest to chest. I sucked in another breath as the smell of him washed over me. His own spicy scent and leather. The smell reminded me of sex— hot, sweaty, carnal sex. I had to crane my neck to look up at him. My mouth went dry suddenly as I swallowed past the lump in my throat while looking into his chocolate-colored eyes.

I ran my tongue along my parched lips, his dark gaze following the movement. The feel of his hard abdominal muscles under my palms made me want to trace every divot and crest as I traveled down. His heart felt like it was beating just as fast as mine as he slid one of his hands further up my side. I clenched my thighs together as his thumb grazed the underside of my breast before he removed his hand to brush back the hair that had fallen over my eyes. He tucked it behind my ear before traveling lower. His fingers came to rest on the pulse point on my neck where he made tiny circles with the pad of his thumb. He was still staring at my lips when he opened his mouth.

"Are you all right?" he asked in a hushed tone.

As if his talking had broken a spell, I shook my head to clear the lust that hazed my every thought.

"No…" I murmured. "I mean, yeah … yes, I'm fine. You should let me go," I said, clearing my throat.

I pushed away from him and his hands reluctantly fell to his sides. I stood and crossed my arms across my torso, suddenly cold. I felt a fine tremble course through my body as I regained my bearings. I looked around at the state of things and let the events of the night filter back in.

Damon put his hands in his pockets and rocked

back on his heels. The movement only added to his charm.

"So, are you going to tell me why you called me in a panic and scared the shit out of me? I thought you were being attacked. God only knows how many traffic laws I broke on the way here." He looked down at me with a scolding expression.

I winced as I recalled the events of the evening. I'd come home from helping Kate move. I remembered how tired I felt as I walked through my front door. I was putting my keys up and felt a breeze rake over my knuckles. That's when I noticed my broken window and freaked the fuck out. I'd run out of the house like my ass was on fire all while poor Fiona went along for the ride.

I scrunched my eyes closed and brought my hand up to my forehead, rubbing the ache that suddenly appeared. God, I was such an idiot. Why did I have to call him of all people? This was completely embarrassing.

"Would you believe me if I said it was a slight slip in judgment?" I asked with my face still pinched.

His eyes hardened as he glared down at me, not saying a word. I deflated with a sag of my shoulders. I gave in and spilled my guts. I told him all about finding the busted window and locking myself in the car. I voiced how I had called him in the middle of a panic attack that had resulted in me hyperventilating and eventually passing out. I used my hands in wide gestures as I explained that I was evidently not in the right state of mind when I decided it was a good idea to call him. The whole time I spoke he stared down at me, listening intently.

When I was done he stepped toward me like he was going to gather me in his arms. Alarm bells rang in my head as I felt every muscle tense in fight-or-flight mode. I held my hands out to stop his approach which did little to halt him as he grabbed my right wrist. I tried to jerk my hand out of his grasp but he used his other hand to grip me at the elbow. Before I could protest he turned my hand over to inspect my palm.

I gasped at the sight of my shredded flesh. I had angry red cuts all over my palm with blood seeping out. I must have not felt any of the glass cutting me as I tried to clean my front seat earlier.

I sucked in a sharp breath as he brought attention to the wound like it hadn't hurt until right now. Damon shook his head and started to walk me to the house.

"Um, where do you think you're taking me?" I asked with an indignant tone. I dug my heels in to halt his forward motion.

He stared back at me with a look that could have frozen hell. "We are going inside so I can clean the glass out of your hand. Unless you would like me to take you to the hospital?" he challenged.

I scrunched my nose. "I think I'm capable of cleaning my own hand, Detective Santos," I retorted.

His eyes flared before he crowded me. I'd never backed down to a man before and I wasn't about to start now. I stepped forward, our chests a breath away from touching as I stared him down. Or *up* was more like it. I smiled when he backed up but it was quickly wiped from my face when he squatted in front of me. He put his shoulder against my belly and tossed me up and over like a sack of potatoes.

"What the fuck are you doing?" I yelled as I tried to squirm out of his fireman's hold. "You are such a child, put me down right now!" I shrieked as I tried to spit my hair out of my mouth.

He said nothing as his powerful legs carried me up the steps to my front door.

"Are you fucking deaf? I said put me down!" I tried again.

I pounded on his strong back with my good hand in a weak attempt to get him to release me. He stopped and I thought I had won until he brought his flattened palm down on my ass cheek. I yelped and stopped squirming. He chuckled as he stepped through the threshold, into my lit foyer.

My face flamed as I tried to squelch the sudden arousal that coursed to my core. I had let a couple of men spank me before during sex but it never had done anything for me until now. I went from pissed off to turned on in five seconds flat. Something about Damon being the one who doled out the warning had done it for me. I could feel my nipples tighten under my t-shirt and my panties were suddenly damp.

For someone who had never been inside my home before, he acted like he knew his way around. After he stopped shortly to inspect my broken window, he flipped on the lights and found his way to my bedroom without instructions. When he stepped up to my king-sized bed, he flipped me back down carefully, sitting me on the edge of the bed before walking into my bathroom.

I sat there in shock as he rummaged around in the drawers. When he came back he held a disposable cup containing blue liquid, a box of tissues, rubbing alcohol, tweezers, and bandages. He slid over a small trash can that sat in the corner of my room and got down on his knees in front of me.

Something about having him kneeling before me made my mind go to naughty places. Of course, everything about him made my mind go to naughty places.

He held out the cup of blue liquid for me and I

realized it was mouthwash. I glared at him while I took the offered cup. I thought about tossing it back into his face for a moment, but then again, I could still taste my earlier sick.

I held eye contact while I tilted the minty contents into my mouth and swished. He watched my mouth work the liquid back and forth with humor in his eyes. I continued to give him the stink eye as I spit back into the cup and snatched a tissue he offered me. After I wiped my mouth, I pushed the tissue into the cup and threw it in the trash can.

He just kept looking at me silently, waiting for something. The silence stretched for long moments. Neither one of us was willing to be the first to back down from this weird staring contest. I rolled my eyes. This was childish, so I conceded.

"Okay, I will be the grown-up here." I huffed. "I'm sorry I called you for nothing. I will admit that I haven't been sleeping a lot lately and my nerves have had me a little … jumpy lately." I made an excuse. He just kept looking at me with a small smirk on his lips. "Clearly, there is no reason for you to be here. You can go now," I finished, hoping he would take the hint.

He shook his head and held out his open hand. I looked at it like it was poisonous before meeting his eyes again. When I didn't move, he let out a huff of a laugh and grabbed for my wounded hand. His warm, gentle touch made a shiver run up my spine before I snatched my hand back.

"I can take care of this, you don't need to clean it."

His eyes hardened again. "Jill, give me your hand," he demanded coarsely. I glared at him again.

"I said I can take care of it. Seriously, you ca—"

"Do you ever just shut up and let someone take

care of you for a change? I said. Give. Me. Your. Hand."
He said each word with a chipped tone.

I felt goose bumps rise on my arms. Nobody ever talked to me the way Damon did. He took charge and didn't put up with any shit. Honestly, I found it a little refreshing. I also found it infuriating. I rolled my eyes and held my palm out for his inspection.

"Fine, have at it. Could you try to hurry? I would like to be done with this day," I murmured in an annoyed tone.

I watched him as he carefully looked over my shredded palm. He was surprisingly gentle as he used the tweezers to extract a broken piece of glass from my hand. I took that time to look over his features while he wasn't looking at me. His long dark-brown curls were mussed like he had run his hand through the soft locks more than once today. I would bet that's what he did when he was frustrated by something. The silky strands hit right at the top of his shoulders, begging for my fingers to run through them.

He had the cutest little crease between his eyes that spoke of long moments of concentration. His lips were plump and moist. I knew from our last kiss that they were perfect to nibble on as he took his time devouring me. He had the start of a beard growing, unkempt along his sharp jaw. I couldn't help thinking about how the rough hair would feel rubbing against my inner thighs.

Dangerous territory, Jill, move on. My gaze traveled further up again to look at his deep cocoa eyes surrounded by lashes that most women would kill for. The whole image he made was one of masculine beauty.

He fluttered his eyes up to meet mine as if he knew I was staring at him again. I don't know what he read on my face but whatever it was had his eyes darkening. I sucked in a breath and tried to pull away my gaze but I couldn't. I was enchanted. But, he broke the spell by looking away first.

"So, what is it that has made you so jumpy lately?" he asked as he put the tweezers down. "Why haven't you been sleeping?" He arched an eyebrow before returning his attention to my hand.

After grabbing the rubbing alcohol, he dabbed my palm. I hissed at the burn but didn't pull out of his hold. I continued to observe him as he cleaned my hand.

"Oh, I don't know. Maybe because I got shot three months ago, in case you forgot," I responded, sarcasm dripping from my voice.

He looked up long enough to glare at me "Believe me, I remember," he scolded in a hard voice before he returned to his task.

I sighed as I continued. "For half my life, I have needed to hold a certain degree of … control. When I got shot, it kind of threw me into a place where I had none. I think I'm just having a hard time getting it back." It was so hard to explain to people who didn't understand what it felt like to have no choice in what happened to them. "As for sleep…" I trailed off.

Damon glanced back up to me as I mulled over what to divulge with him. The thought crossed my mind to make him jealous. Tell him I was seeing someone and that's why I wasn't sleeping. But one look in his concerned eyes had me telling the truth.

"Nightmares."

He nodded and resumed examining my palm. "What do you dream about?" he asked.

I snorted before answering as if the answer to his question was obvious. I watched him as he started to bandage my hand. "Things I can't control," I murmured.

Now that the blood was all cleaned up, I could

see it wasn't that bad. It would heal in a few days.

When he was done, he looked back up at me. "Why do you need to control every little thing in your life, Red?" I could tell his question was genuine and held no condescension.

Because bad things happen to me when I don't, I thought to myself.

I didn't talk about what happened to me with anyone besides Kate and Dr. Yorker. I wasn't about to share my shame with someone I barely knew. Especially not Damon. For some reason the thought of him knowing about my past made me feel even dirtier and more unlovable than normal. I shook my head and turned my face away from him.

"I just do," was all I offered as an answer.

He grabbed my chin and forced me to look at him before he leaned in closer to me. His other hand traveled up my thigh and held firm. I licked my dry lips and watched as he followed the movement with his gaze again. I thought for a second he was going to kiss me before he spoke.

"Have you ever thought about giving some control up in a couple of aspects in your life? If you give someone else some of your responsibilities, maybe you wouldn't feel this way," he said in an intimate tone that raked across my flesh.

I shivered again and felt my nipples tighten further into aching peaks. I stared at his lips as I answered him. "I don't know if I could. What aspect are you referring to?" My voice came out far more breathy than I had intended.

He leaned in even further until his lips almost brushed across mine. Both of his hands held me now on the outside of my thighs. Tucked firmly where my legs meet the side of my ass. He squeezed and kneaded, nearly ripping a moan of pleasure from my lips. It had been so long since I had felt someone's intimate touch.

"When was the last time you didn't have complete control over your next orgasm?" he asked against my lips.

His question jarred me and I tried to lean back. Before I could, Damon pulled me toward him. Making a place for himself between my spread legs. He crashed his lips down on mine. I moaned against him and wound my arms around his neck, bringing my chest to his. He thrust his tongue inside my mouth and groaned when I gave as good as I got. He trailed his hands down to the hem of my shirt before dipping in.

I knew this was going too fast but I didn't care. I couldn't even remember the last time I had sex and forget who it had been with. Whoever it was didn't light me on fire like Damon did. Everywhere he touched left a trail of heat behind. I knew this man would wreck me eventually, but right now I didn't care.

Chapter Five

Still Two Weeks Ago

I shivered as his roughened hands met the hot skin of my stomach. He trailed his hands up until he came to the bottom of my bra. I moved away from him long enough to pull my shirt up and over my head, tossing it across the room, not caring where it landed. I brought my hands down to the hem of his shirt, ready to drag it over his head so I could get my hands on his hard body without any barriers. I raked my nails across the skin that met the top of his pants. He groaned against my lips, exciting me further. That is until his hand halted my upward motion. I groaned a frustrated sound.

"I want to feel you, let me take your shirt off," I demanded as I looked at his puffy well-kissed lips.

He shook his head before meeting my gaze with a serious expression. "We need to talk before this goes any further, Red," he rumbled.

I didn't know why he wanted to talk, I wanted to fuck. I needed to fuck, hard and fast. I shook my head and leaned forward bringing my mouth to his neck. I kissed, sucked, and licked my way up to his ear.

"How about we talk after you fuck me?" I whispered before bringing my hand down to the front of his pants. I rubbed along the impressive bulge, withdrawing a deep groan from him. I smiled as I nipped his ear and tried to undo his belt with quick fingers.

He stopped my hands once more and leaned further back away from me. I pouted at him.

"Fine," I said. "If you won't let me take your clothes off, I will just take mine off." I reached behind my back to unfasten my bra. He grabbed my wrists and brought them back to my front with those hard eyes again.

"I'm serious, Jill. What I have to say might change your feelings. I won't let you get in over your head with me. I want this to work." He paused long enough to see that I was listening. I looked at him with pursed lips, waiting for him to continue so I could get down to business.

"I have certain … tastes when it comes to sex that we need to discuss," he finally allowed.

"What do you mean? Do you have like a foot fetish or something? That's okay, I've been with plenty of men and you wouldn't believe some of the freaky shit they're into. This one guy, couldn't get off until I p—"

"Stop. Talking," he demanded with a hard voice. I clamped my mouth shut at the sudden change in his demeanor. "I don't want to hear about you being with other men. I know you're not a virgin but I don't want to think about other men touching you," he growled my way.

His tone should have put fear into me but all I could feel was pure arousal coursing through my body as I looked up at him. I was so hot right now and I was afraid if he didn't touch me soon I was going to combust. I sat silently, waiting for him to finish speaking. He took pity on me by bringing his hands back up my torso, coming to rest along my ribs. I sighed and leaned into his touch.

"Like I was saying, I like my sexual experiences to be a certain way. I, also, have controlling tendencies. Mine are different in a way, though. During our everyday lives, I will let you lead me around by my balls, Jill. You tell me to jump and I will ask you how high. I can be the best man you've ever been with, baby. There are only two places where I demand complete and utter obedience. One is if we are ever in a dangerous situation—I expect you to listen to my direction. No hesitation."

He was rubbing small circles under my breasts as he was talking. I was still listening to him but I couldn't keep my mind from wandering about other things as well. I looked into his dark gaze, willing him to finish talking so we could move on to more enticing activities.

He almost seemed hesitant as he continued speaking. "The second is in the bedroom. I want you to submit to me in every way. I want to take your pleasure. If I say I want you on your knees, willing and ready to suck my cock, I expect you to do so happily. If I want to tie you up and fuck you silly, I want you willing to let me. And I will reward you by bringing you the most pleasure you have ever experienced in your life. I want to spank your ass red when you piss me off and then make you come until you can't see straight. I want to dominate you, Red."

He stopped talking to take in my reaction. I'm not sure how I looked on the outside, but on the inside, I was freaking the fuck out. I felt like someone had dumped a bucket of ice-cold water over my naked body.

I pushed his hands down and away from me as I visibly shrank in on myself. He removed his hands from me but when I tried to push at his chest he didn't budge. Panic set in as my breathing picked up and I looked around the room for something I could fight him off with if needed.

"Y-you need to leave," I said in a shaky voice as I tried to stand.

He halted my upward motion with gentle hands on my shoulders. I could feel my chest starting to constrict as I gasped for air. I was still wildly glancing around the room when he spoke in a soothing tone.

"It's okay, Red. Look at me, baby," he crooned.

My heart was beating so quickly that I could hear it in my ears. Images of Jason taking what he wanted from me flashed before my eyes. I could hear his voice in my mind. *"You like what I'm giving you, don't you, you fucking bitch."* I felt pressure on my mouth, halting my breathing. My fingers started to go numb and my lips were tingling all over again. The start of another panic attack was unfolding rapidly. I gripped onto his forearms, digging my nails in.

"Jill, breathe with me. Look at me and take a deep breath, now!" Damon demanded in a deep voice.

He grabbed both of my cheeks with his hands and forced me to look at him. Worry marred his expression as I met his gaze. I gasped again as I felt wetness run down my cheeks.

"That's it, baby. Nice, deep, calming breaths. It's okay, I'm not going to hurt you. That's the complete opposite of what I want to do. I wouldn't ever force you to do anything you didn't want to do. And I would never do anything to you without your permission." His words confused me.

"Y-you said…" I tried to speak around gasping breaths.

"I said I wanted to dominate you, Red. And sure, that means I have some level of control, but you have the final say in what happens. If I want to whip that luscious ass with a riding crop and you say no, then that's it. I will stop. I know a lot of people like you, Jill. They are the bosses of their world and they rule their everyday lives meticulously. Submitting to a partner is a way they can safely let that control go so they can just … feel for once. They don't have to think about what needs to happen to get to an end goal. They trust someone else enough to bring them what they need at that moment. I want to be that for you. I want to be your safe space, Jill," he explained, still holding my face.

I took a deep breath, in through my nose, out through my mouth. And again. Damon sat in front of me the whole time, leading me through my calming breaths. All the while telling myself repeatedly that Damon was not like Jason. I don't know how much time passed like that. Eventually, my chest loosened and I could feel my heart rate go back to normal.

I looked at Damon the whole time and contemplated his words. A million questions ran through my mind. Was he just saying these things to get what he wanted from me? That seemed silly seeing as I was completely willing ten minutes ago. But how would he feel when I said no to something he wanted to do? Would he use his size as an advantage and take it anyway? Something about the way he led me through calming breaths told me he wouldn't. If he wanted to take advantage of me, he had plenty of opportunities to do so.

Every question I asked myself over those few minutes I debunked before they became a full thought. Somehow I knew he would never hurt me physically unless I wanted him to. The only remaining question I had bounced around my head like a ping-pong ball. Would it truly be so bad to let this man control me sexually?

It was odd, but the idea did resonate with me on some level. He had asked when the last time was that I didn't have complete control over my next orgasm. The answer to that question was one I didn't even know how to answer. Never? Certainly not after Jason. Every single sexual encounter I had since that night had been planned out, and I always, *always* controlled the outcome.

Wouldn't it be nice if for once I didn't have to think about how best to please myself? Just hang on for dear life and let someone else take the reins.

I put my hands over Damon's and turned my face into his palm. Before I could talk myself out of it, I kissed my way to the tip of his index finger. I looked into his hooded eyes as I flicked my tongue out and around the tip.

He sucked in a breath and before I could react he pushed me until I was laying on my back. Propping myself up on my elbows I watched as he hastily removed his shirt. I watched him with a lustful gaze, unashamed. He was fucking delicious. His olive skin seemed to glow in the low light of my bedroom. His chest was an image of masculine perfection. He had the perfect amount of hair that spanned the decadent flesh of his chest and then descended to his washboard abs. My fingers inched to trace the V that pointed down, right where I wanted to be. He looked down at me with pure lust in his gaze that made me shiver with anticipation.

He descended on top of me and made room for himself between my legs. He crashed his lips down on mine once more with a long groan. I brought my legs up and hooked them around his hips, grinding myself against his hard length. I moaned my frustration and cursed the fact that we were both wearing jeans. I tried to push my hands down on his belt. Maybe he would get the hint and take his pants off.

He chuckled against my lips and looked down at me with a crooked smile. "So impatient," he murmured. "I'm not going to fuck you tonight, Red."

I glared up at him. "Why not?" I asked, offended at the refusal.

He looked down at me with dominating eyes. "I'm in charge here, Red, and I think you need to think about what I want from you. If we do this, you're mine. I won't share you with anyone else. All your pleasure, present and future, will be mine. This isn't going to be a one-night stand for me, baby. There is no going back after this," he explained.

I huffed below him, a frustrated sound. "Then why did you take your shirt off? Are you just trying to tease me?" I let all my anger come out in my words.

He chuckled again and leaned down to kiss my neck. I melted against him as I felt his tongue flick across my pulse point. "I still want to play with you tonight. If you'll let me, I want to tie you up and make you come against my tongue. I want to shove my fingers in that tight little cunt, Red. I want to feel you soak my hand with your arousal," he said against my throat before he looked back down at me.

I sucked in a sharp breath at his words and felt said arousal flood my panties. As much as being controlled scared me, the thought of him doing exactly what he promised turned me on more.

I squirmed under him and said the words he wanted to hear. "Do your worst, Detective," I remarked with a saucy smile.

He said nothing as he stood up suddenly and I watched as he removed his belt with fast fingers. He stepped around my bed to the opposite side and held his hands out. Without a word, I looked at the upside-down vision he made and held my hands out for him. I giggled as he pulled me toward him in a fast jerk.

Without his belt on, his jeans hung lower than before. I shook one of my hands out of his grasp so I could rub the bulge that hung in front of me like forbidden fruit. Before I could touch him, he gripped my wrists and held them with one big hand. A slight sting of panic shot through my chest for a moment. I had to squint my eyes together and take a deep breath to calm myself.

Damon leaned down and grazed his lips against

mine, still holding me firmly. "You say stop and I'll stop," he whispered against me.

I nodded my head and opened my eyes, making myself look at what he was doing. With practiced fingers, he made makeshift cuffs out of his belt and slipped them over my wrists. He tightened them around me firmly but not too firmly. I was almost amazed when he pushed his fingers between my wrists and the belt, making sure it wasn't too tight. When he was finished, he stood back and looked at his handiwork.

"Normally, I would tie you up with soft silk rope but I have to make due tonight. I want to blindfold you. Are you okay with that?" he asked in a hopeful voice. I nodded my head, unable to speak. I swallowed thickly as I felt my heart beating rapidly. I couldn't decipher if it was from fear or excitement but I was leaning toward the latter.

I lifted my head enough so he could tie his t-shirt around my eyes. My breath was coming out in harsh pants, not with panic but pure need. His scent surrounded me, only adding to my arousal. I listened as he walked to my feet and felt the bed shift as he climbed back on top of me.

"I tied your wrists up but you are still able to move your arms. I want you to keep still for me and not move them. If you move your arms at all, I'll stop what I'm doing," he said.

"Okay." I breathed.

I felt as he urged me to arch my back with his hands. He unclasped my bra and cool air caressed my breasts as he pushed it up over my head and lay it to rest next to his belt.

"Would you look at that…" he purred right before he brought his hands to me, cupping my breasts and dragging his fingers down the hard nubs. "These are the prettiest tits I have ever seen, Red. These tight little pink nipples are just begging to be sucked and licked."

I didn't expect it when he brought his hot mouth down and latched onto me. I moaned loudly and arched into him, begging for more. He nipped and sucked, going back and forth between each hardened peak, working me up into a frenzy. By the time he released me I was trembling with need. Anticipation rose as he unbuttoned my jeans and pulled them down my legs, leaving my thong in place.

"I can see how wet you are through these," he said as he rubbed a finger against my pussy.

I convulsed and whimpered, needing more. "Touch me," I whined.

"*Siempre, Roja,*" he groaned as he slid his thumb up and down a few times before pushing the fabric to the side. He circled my clit slowly, never actually touching where I needed him most. Around and around he rubbed me with soft strokes. I was making all sorts of embarrassing sounds of frustration. I had never been so close to begging for something in my entire life.

When I couldn't take it anymore, I moved my hands to grab him, trying to make him rub me where I needed him. He removed his hand as if I'd burned him.

I yelped as he took hold of my ankles and flipped me onto my stomach, grabbed my hips, and forced me on my knees. Since my hands were tied together, I had to lean on my elbows for support. The position thrust my ass into the air.

I wailed as he brought his hand down on one ass cheek and then the other in hard, sharp slaps.

"What did I say about moving your arms?" he snapped in a harsh questioning tone.

I clenched my teeth at the hot sting on my ass as I shook with adrenaline. Being blindfolded only added to the feeling of excitement. Not knowing what was going to happen next was turning me on in a way I didn't even think was possible. Where he had spanked me hurt, but it was quickly turning to arousal as I felt myself push back for more.

"You said not to move them," I groaned. I was so turned on I couldn't stand it. "Please," I moaned as he rubbed where he had spanked.

"It looks like you have a little pain slut in you. And I call you a slut in the best way possible, Red. Do you like when I spank this juicy ass?" he asked before he brought his hand back down in another harsh smack and then another. It hurt so fucking good.

"Yes!" I whined as the pain turned to heat again.

"One day soon, I will introduce you to my paddle and you will love every minute of it. I'll tie you up and put my clamps on your nipples before I punish you in the most pleasurable way you could imagine. But right now, I want you to hold still so I can play," he commanded roughly. I felt as he pulled my thong down my thighs. The air around the room felt cold against my wet folds and I shivered.

I heard Damon groan behind me as he pushed his fingers around my entrance. My arms were shaking as I moaned, needing more.

"God, you are fucking perfect. And this is a perfect pussy. Already so wet for me, baby," he rasped.

I nearly screamed when he pushed his fingers in my drenched channel before pulling out to rub my wetness around my engorged clitoris. He kept up his circling of my clit and used his other hand to finger-fuck my pussy. I couldn't stop myself from pushing back and grinding myself against his hand.

"Oh, Red, your cunt is a greedy little thing. The way you clench down on my fingers like you're afraid to lose them. You feel so fucking good. You'll feel even better wrapped around my cock. This will have to do for now, though," he said as he picked up speed. He was building me higher and higher with each pump of his skilled fingers.

Before long I was gasping and begging for release.

"Yes, baby. Take what you want. *Ven por mi, Roja*," he demanded with a harsh growl.

There was no language barrier when it was bodies speaking, and my body had no choice but to obey him as I screamed my release.

Before I could come down, Damon unknotted his shirt and flipped me over. I was still trying to get my bearings when he kneeled between my legs and sucked my pussy into his mouth. I screamed again and bucked against him. He held me down with his arms over my hips and devoured me like a starving man. He groaned against me and captured me with his searing glare. He bit down lightly on my clit and I exploded again, this time against his hot tongue.

He pulled away as he pushed his fingers into my needy cunt once more and curled them, pushing me into another earth-shattering orgasm.

"That's right, Red, fucking come for me," he demanded.

I whaled so hard my voice broke in and out. I felt my hot release soak his hand as he kept up his brutal pumping. My vision faded at the edges and my muscles convulsed erratically.

I may have passed out a little because when I came to, Damon was pulling me into his arms and my hands had been released from their binding.

"You did so well, Jill. So fucking perfect," he whispered to me as he rubbed his hands all over my body.

     I felt a lazy smile caress my lips as I sunk into his embrace, allowing his soft praises to flow over me, happier than I had been in months.

Chapter Six

Back to The Present

My heart was racing as my feet pounded on the treadmill. As I crested the last of my five-mile run, I felt like my legs were going to give out on me at any moment. My body was exhausted but my mind still refused to shut down. The music blaring in my ears was barely enough to quiet the thoughts racing through my brain.

After the life-altering orgasms Damon had given me that night, I had happily fallen asleep in his arms. He'd folded us both down under the blanket and sleep came surprisingly easy to me. My body had been utterly exhausted, thanks to his ministrations and soothing words of praise, making me feel secure.

I heated at the memory of him saying, *"Eres perfecta para mi, Roja."* Even though I knew the words he whispered to me were bullshit—I wasn't perfect for anyone—something about him speaking to me in Spanish made my heart race and my insides soft. Part of me wanted to believe his loving words.

I hated to admit it but that night I slept the best I had in months. I liked to tell myself that it was because I was worn out from helping Kate move and then what happened with Damon afterward. I told myself I'd just physically drained my body, but I couldn't ignore the feeling of being safe in his arms. Falling asleep in a cocoon of his warmth had spread an unfamiliar fuzzy feeling in my chest that I tried to ignore. I'd laid in his arms that night and allowed myself to feel something comforting for once. Even if I didn't deserve it, I let myself pretend I did for a little while.

When I awakened the next morning to nothing but cold sheets next to me, I felt my resolve harden again. I kicked myself for allowing anyone to bring my walls down, even for a night. Look what happened the moment I let myself feel solace in someone else's arms—I ended up feeling used and tossed aside.

I'd found his note that he had tucked on my nightstand a little after that. He had written that he hated to leave me but felt like I needed space to think about where we should go from here. He asked that I call him when I was ready to talk. Well, I had news for him. If he wanted to give me space, he was damn sure going to get it.

I knew somewhere deep down that what he did was the right thing. If I had woken the same way I had fallen asleep, I knew I would've put on the fake bravado I so often wore and kicked his ass to the curb. Even if I wanted to do the exact opposite.

Being on the defense was my default setting. If I was the one pushing people away, then there was no way for them to see the true person I was under this false exterior. That person was still very broken, shamed, and didn't want anyone's pity.

Damon had waited three days after that night before he started calling and texting me. They had been innocent at first. Checking in to see if I had any questions for him. I left him on "read" every single time, hoping he would get the hint.

He didn't.

Eventually, his texts turned to just him talking about his day and how much he would love to see me. He said over and over that he was trying to stay away but he didn't know how much more of the cold shoulder he could take from me. I worried that he would try showing up at my house unannounced, but so far he hadn't. The thought of him showing up and taking control of my body again both terrified and excited me.

I could deal with the texts and calls throughout the day, it was the ones that he would text me late at night that were starting to tear down my resolve.

My heart pounded as I kept my breakneck speed on the tread. I knew that the thumping wasn't just from my cardio session, but rather, thoughts of his dirty texts always made my pulse jump.

He had one of the absolute dirtiest minds. The explicit things he texted me were enough to make me think he could write one of the raunchiest smut books anyone had ever seen. What he said he wanted to do to me was almost enough to make *me* blush. Almost.

I had read and re-read his messages over and over again. Playing the words in my head until they had taken on physical form behind my very eyes. Shamefully, I'd found my own release multiple times from the visions he enticed from my imagination.

He was worming his way into my everyday life and I was having a hard time wanting to keep him out. If only he knew that I was doing it for his own good. He may have a filthy mind, but I knew he was too good of a man to have anything to do with me.

I wiped the sweat from my eyes before I felt my legs start to wobble under me. Hitting my palm on the "stop" button, I slowed my aching feet to a halt. Breathing hard, I braced my arms on the handles and leaned forward. Resting my head against the cold panel, I tried to calm my racing heart and thoughts.

I didn't get much sleep at all last night. After my fantasy shower, thoughts of Damon continued to plague me into the early morning. At some point, I had dozed off only to awaken with a violent jerk less than an hour later. The smell of vanilla and musk had plagued my dreams so badly that I swear I still smelled it when I woke. I finally gave up around four o'clock and climbed out of bed. After making my bed and placing pillows and blankets in their assigned spot, I put on my sports bra and leggings.

Lifting weights in my home gym usually was enough to wear me out to the point of exhaustion. Unfortunately, it didn't work lately. So, I had hit the tread hard in hopes I could find some relief. An hour later and I was still in the same space I had started, only now I'd be surprised if I could walk out of here.

Looking at my watch, I groaned in irritation and pushed away from the handles. It was officially time to start my day. Thank God it was Friday. I didn't think I could take much more of this week.

I headed toward the kitchen with heavy limbs. Grabbing the same thing I did every morning, I made fast work of breakfast. Two hard fried egg whites, a toasted whole-wheat English muffin with butter, and a mug of black coffee. Nothing but routine for Jill Brookes.

For some reason when I bought this house I thought I needed a big dining room table. Seeing as I never allowed people to come over, it seemed a little ridiculous now as I sat at my big empty table and ate my meal alone. Normally I found solitude in the quiet, but lately it seemed the silence was deafening.

After finishing, I took my dishes to the sink. I washed, dried, and placed the now clean dishes back into the cupboards. Taking the time to clean up the frying pan I used as well. I cleaned up the rest of the kitchen with repetitive movements. I could do all of this with my eyes closed. As with everything else in my life, all of this was just a constant routine.

I headed to my bathroom to get ready for the day. I turned on the shower to hellishly hot and stepped in.

While scrubbing my body, I mentally went through my schedule for the day. I had multiple meetings, ranging from meeting with the head of the art department, going over cover art of some new authors we were taking in, and talking with the marketing department about some new ads they wanted to release.

I stood in front of the vanity after my shower, curling and styling my already wavy hair with practice strokes. As I brushed my teeth, Fiona rubbed against my legs, purring. "Hey there, girl," I cooed at the feline before bending to scratch her favorite spot behind her ear. I smiled and resumed my readying as she ran off after receiving her attention for the morning.

After applying my makeup, I padded into my walk-in closet to pick out today's armor.

I didn't have a lot of things that brought me pleasure in this world, but shopping was undoubtedly one of those things. Some people would probably say I had a shopping problem if they could see my closet but I would say I had no such issue. I knew what I liked and I had no qualms about indulging in such. I walked through my expansive wardrobe and thumbed through the choices as I went. It wasn't hard to find something I wanted to wear, as all my clothing was sorted by color.

After pulling on my black, lace demi-cup bra and matching thong, I sat on my chaise to pull on my stockings and garter belt. I chose my navy Versace keyhole dress and slipped it on. I smoothed it down my front and turned toward the racks of heels. After contemplating for a moment, I reached for my black Jimmy Choo's and slipped them on. I turned and inspected myself in the full-length mirror.

The blue of the dress really made my eyes pop and the red of my hair look brighter. I smoothed my hands down the rich, formfitting fabric clinging to my curves and inspected myself closely. The woman in the mirror gave the illusion that she was a confident bad bitch. As long as the outside world believed that, then my mission was complete.

I released a long sigh and turned from the mirror, heading back to my bedroom. I turned toward the kitchen to get some coffee to go when something caught my eye on the nightstand. The Krav Maga card still sat where I had placed it last night. I picked it up and ran my fingers over the indented words and considered what Doc had said. I needed to find a new outlet and this might be the thing that helped me.

I palmed the card and decided that I would check the studio out tonight. I couldn't see what it would hurt. I was a little intrigued to at least learn a little more self-defense.

As I left the house for the day with a little pep in my step, I found myself looking forward to something for the first time in weeks.

****

I slid my hands over my face with a frustrated huff as I resisted the urge to slam my head into the keyboard.

"I'm, like, so sorry, Ms. Brookes," my intern Staci said for what felt like the millionth time from the doorway.

I separated my fingers as I glared at the nineteen-year-old with my mantra for the day playing on repeat inside my head. *She's learning, she's learning, she is* fucking *learning!* I took a deep breath and placed my hands on my lap and tried to give a tight smile to the young girl who looked like she was on the verge of tears.

It was literally twenty minutes until we closed for the day and I was trying as hard as I could to restrain myself from telling Staci to leave for the weekend and never look back. If it hadn't been for Ben Hasting, one of my top editors, begging to give his niece an internship as a favor, I would have told Staci, *with an i*, to get the hell out of this business before she was chewed up and spit the fuck out.

"So, let me get this straight. I asked you to get me a copy of Hale's latest chapters for his new book and you can't find the file drive?" I asked behind thin lips.

Staci looked like she was about to burst into tears at any moment. "Y-yes. I swear I put the drive in my purse before I went to lunch and n-now … it's not there." Her voice trembled like she was trying to talk down a wild animal.

She had no fucking clue. I took a deep breath and closed my eyes. Moments ticked by while I tried to calm down before I blew smoke out of my ears. I was officially done with this day. None of my meetings had gone the way they should have. The art department was behind on covers. Five of them to be precise … *five*! The marketing department presented me with multiple different ads they wanted to release and I hated every single one of them. I paid these people because they were supposed to be the best, but I was beginning to question that.

I had spent the better part of my day trying to woo a prospective author who had offers from two other companies. I'd taken him out for a late lunch and he proved to be one of the most pretentious douchebags I had ever met. If he hadn't had such a brilliant mind, I would have told him where to shove his book. And now, right before I was getting ready to shut it down for the weekend, I had to deal with this wanna-be publisher. Lord, just end it now.

It wouldn't be so bad if this happened to be her first offense, but a girl could only wish. This child had fucked up everything she touched. She took being a "dumb blonde" to another level altogether. Within the last month, she'd shredded papers that needed to be copied and distributed because she thought the shredder was the printer. She'd forgotten to write down important changes causing me to miss multiple meetings. And on top of it all, she was always coming in late for reasons like, "Chad had this totally 'bussin' party last night" and she had a massive hangover. This was the last straw.

I still had my eyes closed when Staci finally caved under the loud silence. "Ms. Brookes? Are you, like, okay and stuff?" she asked in a mousy tone.

I couldn't help it, then, I burst into a fit of laughter. I looked up at her, shoved my chair back, and held my stomach as I broke down in a fit of hysterics. Staci just stared at me with wide doe eyes like I had lost my damn mind. She glanced behind from where she was standing in my open doorway like she was trying to find someone to help her. I found that even more hilarious.

I was wiping the tears from my eyes as I looked back up at her. "So, you mean to tell me we had one copy of that file in this entire building and you lost it?" I managed between laughs.

Staci was undoubtedly going to cry now as she nodded her head yes. I laughed even harder now. I could see my assistant, Angie, look up from her computer. She smiled, shook her head at what was happening in my office, and went back to work. I finally got a lid on my giggles as I stood from my desk and grabbed my bag. I threw it over my shoulder and strode toward the incompetent child that stood in my doorway with a smile on my face.

"I suggest you take the weekend to do some self-reflecting, Staci. Really look inward and figure out if this is the path you want to follow. And while you're doing this soul-searching, I suggest you find that fucking drive and have it on my desk by Monday," I told her in a deathly calm voice as I patted her on the shoulder.

Her eyes continued to get wider and wider with each word I spoke.

"And if for some reason you can't find that drive by Monday, I think you had better disappear along with it. Because I can guarantee that if you're frightened by me now, you are not going to like what happens if you show up without it," I said with a sugary sweet smile. I crowded her out of my office and shut the door behind me.

I left her there, looking dumbfounded as I strode over to Angie. "Go head home for the weekend, babe," I said with that same smile on my face. She nodded and started to gather her things as I headed for the door. I had some anger to work out in Krav Maga tonight.

Chapter Seven

I pulled up to what looked like a run-down warehouse and whispered a quiet, "What the fuck" to myself. I checked and rechecked the card Doc had given me to make sure I had the correct place. I glanced around the parking lot at the other cars trying to see if I recognized any. I briefly considered turning around and heading home when I saw a middle- to late-aged man open one of the garage doors that I assumed had been used as a receiving bay at one point. I could then see bodies inside sparring with one another, some slamming their partners to the ground.

The man who opened the bay spotted me sitting in the car and waved me over. Too late to pretend I wasn't here. I grabbed my gym bag and headed toward the man who I assumed must be Hugh.

I took in his rugged good looks as I approached him. For an older guy, he was still very handsome. He had a thick speckling of gray at his temples that matched his well-manicured goatee. He had a fine sheen of sweat gathered across his exposed deep cocoa-colored skin, which I guessed came from teaching a class such as this and lack of AC in the older industrial building. The formfitting tank he wore was darker in spots that had collected the gathering dampness.

I could tell as I got closer that he was a well-defined man. His body was a testament to his physical fitness. Clearly, he was in great shape if he owned and ran this outfit. If he was ten years younger, I would have had a hard time keeping my hands off his hot body. That, and if he wasn't wearing a gold band on his left ring finger. I may be a lot of things, but a home-wrecker was not one of them.

"You must be Jill. Dr. Yorker told me you might be stopping by to check the place out." His smile was warm as he extended his hand in greeting.

I shook the offered hand and smiled back up at him. "I've been told I need an outlet for some of the anger I've been holding in," I said sheepishly.

Hugh laughed as he pulled me close to him, turning me to face the open gym. "Well, this is the place for you, then. And, you came at the right time. I hold beginner classes on Mondays, Wednesdays, and Fridays at six. Right now, we're finishing up one of our advanced classes, as you can see. So, if you want to head over to the locker rooms and get ready, as soon as we're done I'll send one of my co-instructors over. Since this is your first day, I'll have him partner with you to teach you the basics."

He patted me on the shoulder with a firm hand and stepped back into the ring with a couple of sparring men. I winced as one of the men swept out and knocked the other flat on his back with a solid thud. Hugh said this was the advanced class. Maybe the beginner class wouldn't be as rough. Otherwise, I would be sporting some serious bruises come tomorrow.

I pulled my eyes away from the fight happening in front of me and spotted the locker rooms toward the back of the building. I took in my surroundings as I walked around the edges of the matches. It was a simple layout. The building was big enough for bleachers on the far side of the building next to the locker rooms. There were already multiple people watching the matches. I assumed they were waiting for the next class to get started.

There wasn't a place on the floor that wasn't covered with soft mats you would find at a high school wrestling meet. There were exposed steel beams throughout the open space, making the industrial feel of the place even more prominent. The whole building wasn't much to look at but it was still welcoming.

Looking around, there were people of every different race and ethnic background talking, joking, and sparring together. This may be a place to blow off some anger, but I found it refreshing to not feel animosity from anyone.

I pushed through the locker room doors and quickly found an empty locker to stash my bag. I stripped and changed into a clean black sports bra and matching pair of capri leggings that made my ass look fabulous. I exchanged my heels for my Nikes and I was ready to go. I quickly put my hair up into a high pony before I walked back out to the sparring room.

After finding a place on the bleachers, I sat and waited patiently for the next class to start. I was looking over the room at all the matches in progress, when I felt eyes on me. I turned slightly and saw said eyes. And they were some pretty eyes at that.

He was sitting a couple of benches up from me. He wore long black gym shorts and a deep-red tank. My gaze traveled the length of his body starting at his powerful legs and his tan chiseled biceps. He had a square jaw that was clean-shaven, and plump lips. His eyes were a light jade color. His blond hair was cut too short for my liking but still looked good on him. The whole package was nice to look at but I couldn't stop the comparisons as they came rushing in.

I gave him a tight smile and turned back around, facing the match in front of me. I sucked in a breath and braced myself to be hit on when I felt him move from his seat and sit next to me. Almost too close for comfort.

"I haven't ever seen you here before. My name's Vince." His deep voice rumbled as he extended his hand to me. I gave him another tight smile as I took his hand in mine.

"Jill," was all I offered.

He revealed straight teeth as he smiled down at me. I'm sure that smile got him all kinds of attention with the ladies, but I couldn't stop thinking about the fact that he didn't have that sexy crooked smile that haunted my thoughts.

"Nice to meet you, Jill. Have you ever done this before?" he asked, gesturing to the match in front of us. I shook my head and he smiled even brighter at me. I had to resist the urge to roll my eyes at him. "I could help you out if you want. I've been doing this for a couple of months now and I don't want to brag, but I am kind of a natural at it," he said with an arrogant shrug. "I could be your partner if you wanted?" He gave me a sly grin.

Oh, I'm sure he could *help me out.* I was confident that even a deaf person could have heard the innuendo in his voice. I wasn't really in a place to entertain him at this point and my patience was already hanging on by a thread. I really didn't have the energy to put up with half-cocked come-ons today.

I turned my full attention to him so he couldn't misunderstand my next words. "Look, I appreciate the offer, bu—"

"She already has a partner," a familiar deep voice cut me off.

I stilled with my words caught in my throat. I knew that voice, that tone. I remembered when that voice whispered to me in that Spanish I loved so much. I closed my mouth and swallowed hard. Slowly, I turned to see the man I had been trying to avoid.

Damon stood in front of me in all his hot Latino glory. I felt shell-shocked as I took in his imposing form. His shoulder-length curls were held back in a queue at the base of his neck. He stood with his arms crossed over his delicious chest, making his arm muscles bulge even more than normal. I nearly drooled when I noticed he wasn't wearing a shirt. His exposed olive skin was covered in a layer of sweat that I suddenly wanted to feel against me.

My eyes traveled to his tapered waist and that incredibly sexy V that I wanted to trace my fingers down. When I looked up at his face he was staring between me and Vince with a menacing glare that made all of my lady parts perk up and take notice. I sucked in a sharp breath and clenched my thighs together. The movement didn't go unnoticed by him as he looked down at me with his crooked smirk.

"How're you doing, Red?" he asked in a deep rumble that seemed to rake over my nerves.

I cleared my throat. "I, ah … I'm fine." I frowned up at him. "What the hell are you doing here?"

I hadn't meant for so much animosity to come out with my words, but I couldn't help the flustered feeling he incited in me as I looked up at him.

Damon smiled again and my heart fluttered. "Well, I just so happen to be in the advanced class that's just finishing up. I have to say, I'm surprised to see you, what with you ignoring my texts and all." I didn't miss the dark look he gave me at the mention of his texts. I felt my face heat as I looked away from his piercing gaze.

The rest of the sparring matches were wrapping up when I looked around the floor. I swallowed the lump in my throat as I watched Hugh make his way over to us on the bleachers. I stamped down a thrill of excitement at the prospect of leaving this conversation.

"It looks like my class is getting ready to start. Would you mind moving out of the way so I can pay attention?" I tried not to look too long at Damon's searing gaze as I dismissed him. He smiled when he backed up from me but didn't leave.

"All right, who's ready to get started?" Hugh asked as he clapped his hands together with a ready expression. "We have a couple of new people here today so I wanted to take this time to introduce you to my assistant from our advanced class," Hugh continued, and I felt my heart sink into my butt. "This is Damon," Hugh said as he clapped Damon on the chest. "He's been with me here for five years and he's at the top of his class. Feel free to ask him any questions you may have."

I looked back over to Damon who hadn't taken his hot eyes off me. I squirmed as he glared at me and tried to ignore the wetness gathering between my legs. What was wrong with me?

"All right." Hugh clapped his hands together again. "Everyone, partner up and we will get started."

Before I could take in the gravity of the situation, Damon made a beeline straight for me. I stood and glanced around the room as everyone was finding a partner.

"You're the newest person here today, and you need to partner with me so I can catch you up on some basic moves," Damon said as he crowded me.

I sucked in a sharp breath as his scent hit my nose, bringing back memories of his body on mine. I started to panic as I looked for a way out of what was sure to be the most frustrating two hours of my life. I saw a flash of red out of the corner of my eyes and felt a thrill run through me.

"Actually," I said as I slapped my hand on Vince's bicep and pulled him to me. "Vince has already offered to catch me up on what I've missed," I finished in a much too breathy voice.

I nearly rolled my eyes as Vince put his arm around my waist and puffed his chest out as he looked at Damon. I winced when I saw the deep scowl Damon gave him in return. I had to give credit when credit was due. That look Vince was receiving would surely make another man back down. I don't know if it was bravery or stupidity that made Vince pull me in tighter to his side. I tried not to gag as his too-thick-smelling Axe body spray assaulted me.

Damon said nothing more as he watched us walk to an unoccupied mat. I tried not to look back at him as class started.

Chapter Eight

My breath left me in a *whoosh* as I was slammed down on my back for what felt like the hundredth time. I could feel my body forming bruises in places I didn't even know could bruise. At this rate, I would need to take an ice bath. Even through all the padding I had on my body, I could still feel every hit Vince landed on me.

He bounced up and down waiting for me to get back up. I think he was able to move a little faster than me because he didn't have all the padding Hugh had insisted we wear. Since I liked my face the way it was, I opted to wear everything given to me. According to Vince, he had no need for it, since I was a complete novice.

When I finally managed to get to my feet, he rushed me again and I barely avoided his grasp. I swear, between his hits, he took every chance he got to touch some part of my body that I was sure wasn't part of the exercise. Somehow I didn't think grabbing someone's ass repeatedly was part of the curriculum. I scolded myself once again for not letting Damon teach me. At least I knew he wouldn't try to cop a feel when I was trying to learn something. Doc thought this would help my anger issues, but all sparring with Vince was doing was adding to my raising frustration.

The day hadn't been a complete loss, though. While listening to and watching Hugh and Damon explain some basic moves, I learned a few things that could be useful. The only downfall was that Vince acted like he wanted to just get his hands on me more than to help me learn. I held my hands up for him to stop so I could get a quick drink. All I got in return was a cocky smile as he rushed me again. He spun me until my back was to his front. He held me tight around my upper arms, trapping them to my sides. I swear I heard him inhale deeply, smelling my hair.

"Okay, you got me. But I need to take a minute." I panted.

He still held me tight to him while he murmured in my ear, "I will give you a break if you can get out of this hold." I could hear the smirk in his voice that just served to piss me off more.

I tried to bring my arms up to break his hold but all it did was enable him to hold me tighter. He chuckled behind me.

"You're gonna have to do better than that, honey."

I cringed at his nickname. It was getting hard to breathe as tight as he held me. I tapped his forearm like we had been shown but he still didn't let go. "Seriously, I'm done. You need to let me go." I panted shallowly.

I felt him shake his head before he spoke. "Tell you what, you go out with me for a few drinks and I'll let you go. What do you say? I could give you some private lessons," he taunted as I felt the start of his excitement pressed against my backside.

I felt panic slice through my chest as I tried to get a deeper breath but couldn't. I looked up and saw Damon watching us from across the room. We stared at each other as I spoke again. "That's not going to happen, let me go," I demanded.

Vince locked his meaty hand around my wrist and held still. "Not gonna happen," he said. The feeling of his hot breath across my neck was making me nauseous.

I continued to look at Damon and he must have seen the desperation in my eyes at that moment. He started to stalk toward us but I was already seeing red. I tried to bring my arms up one more time to break his hold but it didn't work.

I started to feel panic slither up my spine as visions of Tom holding me hostage crept into my mind. He had held me almost exactly like this, only he had a pistol to my head at the time. I remembered the way I'd gotten out of his hold. I tried to dismiss it because of the sheer violence, but right now I was pissed off enough that I didn't care. I needed to get out before the panic dug its cold claws in and refused to release me. I widened my stance and used all the remaining strength to bring my right forearm up as high as I could. With everything I had in me I brought my closed fist down as hard as I could right on Vince's crotch.

He released my arms with a loud howl and I took the advantage. As he doubled over in pain, I grabbed the back of his neck and brought my knee up to meet his nose. I heard a sickening crunch and smiled to myself. *Should I be concerned at the joy that sound brought me?*

Vince fell to the floor in a heap, one hand on his bloody nose and the other on his mangled manhood.

"You fucking bitch!" he shouted up at me.

"I tapped out, you pompous little cum stain. Next time you try to strong-arm your way into a woman's panties, you probably want to think twice about doing it in a self-defense class. Or maybe at least put on some fucking padding before you do!" I yelled back at him. I took my headgear off and threw it at his curled body before I turned around.

I almost fell back on my ass when I ran straight into Damon's naked chest. He grabbed my biceps and held me to him, looking down at me with hard eyes. I opened my mouth to say something spiteful to him but stopped when I realized how quiet it had gotten. I looked around the room and noticed that everyone had stopped their matches and was looking at the scene I had just created.

I squeezed my eyes shut for a moment and reinforced my *fuck off* walls. When I opened them again I looked up at Damon as I shrugged off his hold and pushed away from him. I walked as fast as I could to the locker room and slammed through the door. I wanted to scream and cry just to let the frustration out of my body. I didn't ever let anyone know when I was overwhelmed. Preferring to keep it all bottled in until it just exploded in private. Unfortunately, this time it spewed out in front of a room full of people I'd just met. I felt like such an idiot.

I let my head fall to the front of my locker a little too hard and winced at the dull ache it created. I exhaled a shaky breath. "Good job, Brookes," I said to myself.

The door of the locker room creaked open and I straightened. Opening my locker, I ignored whoever came in until I felt a body press against my back. I immediately knew who it was when his spicy smell surrounded me.

I turned and craned my neck back to look into those brown eyes. "You know this is the ladies' locker room, right? What, did you come to escort me from the building?" I asked Damon with a condescending tone.

He looked down at me with a soft look and shook his head. "No, I came to see if you were all right," he answered, ignoring half of my question. The pity in his eyes was enough to light another kernel of anger on fire still inside of me.

I squinted my eyes up at him. "I am just *peachy*, thanks. It's something I've sadly had to get used to. Men just take what they want from me. All they see is a pretty face and fuckable body and they just take, take, take. Don't worry, I don't need someone to save me. I've been saving myself for a long time now. So, you can take your good guy act and fuck right off with it," I snarled as I started to turn back around.

He grabbed me by my shoulders and forced me to stay put. "I didn't deserve that, Jill," he said angrily as he towered over me.

I gave a loud humorless laugh as I glared at him. "Right, you didn't deserve that. In fact, you don't deserve any of this," I snarked as I gestured to myself. "And you can save your pity for someone who needs it. What the fuck do you want from me, Santos?"

He scowled at me, giving as good as he got. "Well, to start, I want you to let me help you. I don't pity you, Jill. You are the strongest bitch I've ever met in my life. The way you handled yourself out there just now turned me on so much I can't stand it. Why would I pity that?" he said as he looked down at me with lust in his eyes. I swallowed hard as I tried to ignore the warm feeling expanding in my chest. "Next, I want you to answer my goddamn calls and texts. I've tried to give you space, but it's obvious that's not what you need. Apparently, the best way to get your attention is to force our interactions." He crowded me further. My back was almost touching the locker.

I glared up at him with a cruel smile. "If you think a couple of mediocre orgasms was enough to make me follow you around like a lost puppy, you're sorely mistaken." I turned around sharply, making sure to flick my hair into his face. I knew I was full of shit. He had played my body like a finely tuned guitar and we both knew it.

I started to grab my gym bag but didn't get too far. Damon grabbed the bag from me, pushed it back into the locker, and slammed the door shut. Before I could turn around and lay into him, he pushed me forward and trapped me between the cold door and his hot body. He grabbed a fistful of my ponytail and held me still. I could feel his hard length against my lower back as he pressed his body to me. My pulse jumped and my breath caught as he nipped on the shell of my ear.

"Mediocre, huh? It didn't taste like a mediocre orgasm when you creamed all over my tongue, *Roja*," he said as he pushed his fingers under my waistband. His fingers were rough as he squeezed the naked flesh he found there. "When I felt that tight little cunt clamp down on my fingers and the wetness from your orgasm soak my hand while I pumped into you." I moaned and arched into him, unabashedly.

He slid his hand further down and I nearly convulsed when he drug his fingers over my swollen clit. I felt his rough facial hair drag across the sensitive skin of my neck as he trailed hot kisses down to my shoulder.

"Even if you weren't begging for more, this…" He swirled his skilled fingers around my clitoris before sinking two thick fingers into my drenched pussy. "This was." I cried out as he thrust his fingers into me, hitting that button that made me go crazy.

"Leaving you enough room to think this over was a mistake. I should've never left you that night because you can't get out of your head long enough to realize that this is something you want. This is something you need," he promised as he kept up his slow torture.

"This is how it's going to go from now on," he rasped against me. The lust in his voice was almost as thick as my need for him. "You're going to let me take you to dinner. We're going to talk about where we go from here. You are going to stop ignoring me and act like the mature woman I know you are."

He was talking to me like he owned me and it was rubbing me the wrong way. "How about you stop telling me what I am going to do before I rip your balls off your bo—" I nearly screamed as he pinched my clit, cutting my words off.

He chuckled against my ear. "I wasn't finished talking, Red." I felt heat flush over my body as he lightly twisted my clit before pushing his fingers back into my aching pussy. I groaned deep in my chest as he continued talking. "As I was saying, we are going to sit down and figure out where to go from here. And only after I'm satisfied will I give you what you truly need."

I pushed my ass back at him so I could feel that hard part of him close to where I craved him. The need to come clouded out my better judgment as I begged. "Please..." I whimpered.

He groaned and ground his hardness against me as he pulled my hair, forcing me to meet his scorching gaze. "That's right, baby. *Te daré esta polla dura*," he growled before he took my mouth with a dominating kiss.

He pulled me back toward his hard body as he plunged his tongue in. He fucked my mouth at the same slow rhythm he fingered my pussy. I moaned around him as I rolled my hips against his palm. I was so close to the release I craved, I almost cried when he ripped his mouth from mine.

He held my stare with his. "You want to come?" he asked in a rough tone while he kept up his smooth slow plunges.

"Yes!" I nearly screamed.

"You come when I tell you that you can." He smiled at me before he pulled his fingers from me, leaving me on the edge.

"What the fuck, Damon!" I screeched as he spun me back around to face him. I wanted to punch the smug look off his stupid face. Before I could say anything further, he brought his drenched fingers up to his mouth and sucked them in with a long groan. His eyes flared when he looked back down at me.

"You taste so fucking sweet, *Roja*. Here, taste." He didn't give me a chance to think about his words before he pushed the still wet fingers past my lips.

An erotic flood of fresh arousal coursed through my body. Nothing like this had ever happened to me before and I found it incredibly hot. I kept his heated gaze as I grabbed his hand and pushed his fingers deeper into my mouth. I sucked and swirled my tongue around his fingers, tasting the unique essence of myself mixed with his own hot flavor.

He sucked in a sharp breath before pulling his fingers away from me. He grabbed the back of my head and crashed his lips back down on mine for another dizzying kiss. I was left reeling when he pulled up for air.

"Get dressed, Red. We have dinner plans."

I nearly melted into a puddle when he pulled away from me. I watched as he left the room just as all the other women from the class started piling in. Some glanced from him to me with curious looks. Others just smiled at me before going on their way. I shrugged and turned back to my locker. I smiled to myself as I pulled out a t-shirt and hastily put it on. I didn't have time to think about what others thought of me, I had dinner to catch.

Chapter Nine

We pulled into the public parking lot that overlooked the bay. I looked over at Damon with a cautious expression. "I thought we were going for dinner?" I asked, confusion evident in my tone.

Damon just gave me a crooked smile before he opened his door and walked to my side of the vehicle. When he opened the door and extended his hand to me, I looked at it as if it were a snake. I reluctantly gave him my palm and he gently pulled me from the vehicle, humor written in his crooked grin.

"You didn't bring me all the way out here to kill me, did you?" I asked as we started walking toward what looked like a park. It was already late evening so it was pretty much empty, with the exception of a few people out enjoying the cool night air.

Damon threaded his fingers through mine as we walked along the dimly lit path. I looked down at our joined hands dumbly for a beat. When was the last time someone held my hand like this? Probably not since high school.

The last boyfriend I had was Bobbi Fletchall. He played for the basketball team and he was also crowned Homecoming King our senior year. He convinced me to have sex with him after the dance. Said he wanted something to remember me by before he left for college. He was a typical teenage boy who got what he wanted and went away the following fall. I never heard from him again. He hadn't been my first but that didn't make it hurt any less. I didn't hold it against him anymore. Life had shown me that there were worse things boys could do than break your heart.

Damon's low chuckle brought me back to the

present. "If I was going to kill you, I could think of a thousand better places to do it than a public park. Remember, I'm in law enforcement, Jill. I could get pretty creative if I wanted to." He grinned down at me and my stomach somersaulted. *Stupid stomach.*

"Okay, smart-ass. Since you aren't currently plotting my untimely demise, may I ask where you're taking me? You mentioned food?" I asked.

I felt off-kilter, not knowing what was happening from one moment to the next. Some people liked surprises. I was not "some people."

Damon stopped walking and turned to face me, never dropping my hand. He stepped forward until our chests were almost touching. He brought his other hand up and cradled the side of my head. It took everything in my power not to lean into him. His touch was so warm when he ran his thumb over my furrowed eyebrows.

"You're cute when you're frustrated," he murmured with that stupid grin of his.

I jerked my head back and deepened my scowl. "If you think I'm cute now, just wait. I'm about to be fucking adorable," I argued.

I briefly thought about kicking him in the shin as he threw his head back and belly-laughed. I almost did just that until I realized I was smiling too. I couldn't help it. His genuine glee was infectious.

When he calmed his snickering, he glanced down at me with moisture in his eyes. He was still softly smiling when he rubbed his thumb across my lower lip, his eyes following the motion. My breath hitched and I wondered if he was going to kiss me. God, I wanted him to kiss me again. The world always fell away from me when he brought his lips to mine.

Before I could lean into him, he pulled away from me. He brought our joined hands to his lips instead and held my gaze as he kissed the back of my hand before starting our forward motion again.

Still glancing down at me, he finally gave me the answer I was looking for. "There's an amazing food truck that comes here around this time most nights. I figured we could eat and enjoy this nice night for a bit," he said.

I looked up at him with a bewildered expression. Not that I had much experience in this whole relationship thing, but didn't most men want to impress women with how much money they could spend?

"You're looking at me like I have two heads right now," Damon said, bringing me from my thoughts.

"I just figured you would take me to a fancy restaurant or something. I don't know, try to get into my panties by stuffing me with decadent food," I voiced.

He chuckled at me again as we neared the delicious smells coming from the nearby truck.

"Well, I'm not exactly a fancy restaurant type of guy, for one thing. Not to say I wouldn't spoil you with good food, but I would honestly prefer to cook it myself. And I don't need any help getting into your panties, *Roja*," he said in a low heated voice.

I should be offended that he insinuated I was easy, but I couldn't get past the look he gave me. It was like he had a direct line straight to my naughty bits.

We walked in silence the remaining distance to the food truck. When we got to the window, Damon held his free hand out to a man named Julio. The two embraced each other in a manly hand slap/shake and spoke to each other like two good friends. I watched how he interacted with the other man and was amazed by his easy friendship. He introduced me then ordered for both of us.

Before I knew it we were seated on a park bench

overlooking the bay, eating the best street tacos I'd ever had in my life. I was the furthest thing from ladylike as I scarfed down my first taco and was already halfway through my second one. I caught Damon staring at me while he was still on his first. I felt an unfamiliar flush creep up my neck as I looked at him after swallowing a huge bite. He was the only man to ever make me blush. I laid my mostly devoured food back into its wrapper and whipped my mouth with a napkin before looking at him again.

"What?" I asked.

He shook his head at me and grinned.

"I was just about to ask if you wanted to eat mine too." He laughed.

The heat in my cheeks deepened and I punched him in the shoulder. "Oh, shut up!" I couldn't keep the embarrassed laughter out of my voice. "I haven't eaten since noon and even then it wasn't much. Plus, if you didn't see earlier, I used a large amount of energy getting the shit knocked out of me. I don't think Krav Maga is for me," I said before I took a sip of my drink.

"Hey, I like a woman who isn't afraid to eat. I just don't know where you put it. And about class, I hope you don't let that asshole ruin it for you. From what I saw, you're a natural at it. You won't have to worry about Vince anymore, though. Hugh kicked him out and told him not to come back."

His words shook me. I figured if anyone was going to get kicked out it would have been me. I didn't feel guilty that the fucker got kicked to the curb, but I definitely wasn't expecting it. After all, I was the new one in class, they could have easily placed the blame on me.

Damon must have seen the shock on my face when he said, "There had been a couple of complaints from the other women in your class about Vince. Hugh gave him a verbal warning once already and he obviously didn't take it seriously. He's probably wishing he had listened. I bet he's icing his balls tonight, if he can find them. I have never seen anyone act so savagely in class before. He should have known not to fuck with a redhead with anger issues. I wouldn't have expected anything different from you, though." He shook his head before returning to his food.

I looked down at the last of my taco and felt what I had eaten turn to lead in my gut. Was that my identifier now? Just another hotheaded bitch. I knew most people thought I was an icy shrew, but knowing Damon saw me that way too made something ache inside of me.

There were very few people in this world that got to see the real me. I preferred it that way. The fewer people who saw my vulnerability meant there wasn't as big a chance for them to fuck me over in the end.

I've never cared much about what people thought of me. The people I loved most in this world knew what kind of person I truly was. Sure, I was a bitch any way you sliced it, but I was a loyal bitch. If you hurt someone I loved, then you had better hope I didn't find out about it. I protected what was mine fiercely and I took shit from no one. If that made it hard for people to like me, then so be it. But I couldn't help the hurt that bloomed in me at the thought of Damon thinking of me as just another hateful jerk.

I shut down the emotion I felt rising before I let it fully sink in. This is why I didn't do relationships. It took too much of my energy to worry about what the other person thought of me. I didn't need more people in my life to make happy. I had a hard enough time making sure *I* was happy. If he thought poorly of me now, I didn't want to know what he would think if he ever learned about my past. He would probably be disgusted by me then.

I put my food to the side and started to stand. Damon put his hand on my thigh, stopping my upward motion. "Hey, what's wrong? You look like you went somewhere in your head," he asked, concern lacing his voice.

I shook my head and gave him my best fake sunshiny smile. "Nothing's wrong. It's just getting late and I need to be heading home. Thank you for dinner," I said before I stood.

I got exactly one step before Damon tugged me back down. This time I landed in a huff, right along his lap.

"Seriously!" I practically yelled. He circled his arms around me and scowled down at me. I tried to push his hands off but he held firm. "Did your brain spontaneously stop working or did you just forget what I did to the last guy that tried to hold me against my will?" I seethed.

My before-mentioned anger problem was rapidly making another appearance and the fact that Damon just kept scowling at me was only making it worse.

"I don't understand where this animosity is coming from all of a sudden. Why are you trying to leave? I thought we were having a good time," he questioned. I rolled my eyes and glared right back at him.

"I was, until I figured out that all you see me as is some delusional, angry, psycho-bitch. If I had known that you find me so distasteful, I never would have agreed to come out with you tonight. I think it's better if you just cut your losses now and let me leave."

I gripped his wrists and pulled them away from me. Standing, I tried my best not to let the hurt I felt take over. I turned and started back toward the parking lot.

My breath left me in a whoosh as strong arms spun me and pulled me back down again.

I don't know how he managed it, but Damon had pulled me back down onto his lap, and this time I was forced to straddle his hips. My heart sped up as he gripped my ass and brought his lips onto mine for a scorching kiss. I put my hands on his chest to push him away but couldn't make myself do it. I melted into his embrace with a soft sigh. When he pulled away from me, the look he sent my way set me on fire.

"There isn't a single part of you that I find distasteful, Red. I don't think you're delusional or psycho. I do think you're a bitch, but only in the best way possible," he murmured against my lips. "I can see you, Jill. I know you're passionate and have strong feelings for the things you believe are right. You stand up for those lucky enough to be loved by you. And I know without a shadow of a doubt that you would never allow anyone to treat you badly. All these things make me that much more interested in you."

I could feel the swell of emotion clog the back of my throat. For not knowing this man very long, he sure did have a way to tame the beast that always lurked inside. I didn't know what to say to him at that moment. It wasn't every day that I was rendered speechless by someone.

"And I have to confess something," he continued. I watched as a smart-ass smile appeared on his plump lips. "It turns me on when you get that fire in your eyes. Watching you kick Vince's ass tonight got me so hard that I had to follow you into the locker room before I embarrassed myself."

I slapped him on the chest before I busted up laughing. I couldn't remember the last time I'd laughed like that. Howling so hard that my side cramped. Damon chuckled under me, bouncing me up and down. I leaned my forehead against his chest and continued to chuckle.

When our laughter finally subsided we just sat like that for the longest time. I listened to his calm breaths and he rubbed his hands up and down my back. I nearly sighed when he kissed the top of my head. I was content to just sit like that.

Damon had done the impossible at that moment. What he'd given me that night was something I would've never been able to create for myself no matter how hard I tried. He had given me my first moment of peace in the last sixteen years. Uncontrolled, unplanned, unrestrained peace.

Chapter Ten

"Hey, I have an idea. Come with me." Damon's low rumbled words broke the fog my mind had slipped into. He nudged me until I slipped from his lap and settled on my feet in front of him. I stepped back as he stood, and he looked down at me with a jaunty grin before taking my hand in his again, leading me away from the park.

"Where are we going?" A rush of nervous energy shivered down my spine as I let him guide me. We made it past the dimly lit park and were now traveling down what looked like a residential jogging path. Every so often we passed the low glow of a light post. I couldn't imagine why anyone would want to jog out here at night. With all these trees, anyone could jump out and grab you. I shook off the unpleasant thought.

"You'll find out soon enough," he replied, glancing back at me with that same carefree look in his eyes. What I wouldn't give to have that same look.

A thought struck me as we walked. "So, how long have you been a detective?" I asked, genuinely curious.

He looked down at me and answered, "For about eight years now. I've worked for the police station since I was twenty-three and worked my way up over the years. I put in my time as a beat cop for almost five years before I was promoted." He grinned at me like he found my question humorous.

I frowned despite myself. "You have seen people at their worst, their absolute lowest. You've probably seen some true evil in this world, right? How do you still feel secure enough to wander down dark paths when you know bad shit happens to people who do?" I asked.

He squeezed my hand as we came to a dip in the

path, slowing to make sure I didn't tumble down the short hill. Houses on my left were becoming fewer and far between. In some recess of my mind alarms were going off. We were on a secluded part of the path. Out here it wouldn't be hard for someone to attack. I doubted anyone would hear me scream.

My breath was coming in deeper pants the longer I thought about it. I was looking all around us, the intrusive thoughts of someone watching me running wild. I could almost feel them waiting. I didn't realize Damon had stopped walking until I bumped into his chest with a huff. He brought one arm around my lower back and then lower still. I looked up at him as he squeezed and kneaded my ass with his big hand. He brushed his lips against mine in a sensual dance that had the rest of the world falling away.

"I'd never let anything happen to you, Red," he muttered over my parted lips. It was like he read my mind. He knew I was starting to freak myself out and stopped the panic from truly setting in.

"How—"

"You're squeezing my hand so hard I'm not sure I'll be able to feel my fingers later." He chuckled.

I sucked in a startled breath and tried to shake his hand out of mine.

"Don't," he commanded as he brought our joined hands to his mouth. He kissed each finger before sucking my pointer finger in and giving the tip a sharp nip. I hissed as the sting turned to heat, making my nipples hard.

"I like it," he rumbled while still keeping my stare.

He'd taken his hair out of its restraint earlier in the evening so it hung like a curtain, secluding us both in our own world. He let go of my ass after one last knead and stepped away from me, taking his heat with him. He didn't release his hold on my hand as we continued down the path.

"We're almost there, just around this corner," he reassured.

And then I saw it. It wasn't huge by any means but it was still impressive. The rustic cabin was something one would see in a dream or on the cover of a magazine. It sat in a clearing amongst the trees, surrounded by well-manicured grass. The front of the home sat facing the bay with its huge floor-to-ceiling windows showcasing a beautifully lofted ceiling. I couldn't help but think it would be an amazing place to watch the sun rise and set. It was situated uphill from a large boathouse that sported a big floating dock perfect for fishing and swimming. A few chairs surrounded a firepit that beckoned for one to come and waste the night away with friends and family.

With the seclusion in the area, it wasn't surprising that we couldn't see any other houses from this little carved-out cove. I watched the moonlight shimmering off the gentle waves of the bay and one word came to my mind.

Paradise.

"Wow," I muttered.

Damon released my hand and started walking toward the dock. "Follow me," he whispered.

Alarm bells rang again. "Why are you whispering?" My hushed voice sounded harsh in the quiet night.

"I don't want to wake up the guy that lives here and get in trouble." He waved for me to follow him with that stupid grin again.

"What!" I screeched before slapping my hand over my mouth. I looked back at the house before I jogged to catch up with Damon, who was currently laughing quietly.

"What do you mean? If we aren't allowed to be here, then let's leave. I'm not some teenager who enjoys breaking and entering," I whispered harshly at his back.

He just continued walking onto the floating dock. I was still on the grass in front of the dock when he faced me again with a mischievous glint in his eyes.

"Come on, Jill. Old man Boone sleeps so heavily, he'll never know we were here," he teased before he grabbed his shirt and brought it over his head.

My mouth dried as I watched him strip. He held my stare as he hooked his fingers into his shorts. He smiled at me before turning from my view and lowered the garment. He stood with his back to me in all his glory. My eyes ate up the sight of his strong thick legs, up to his deliciously toned ass I'd love to sink my teeth into. His tapered waist led up his muscular back to his broad shoulders. The shine from the moon left a luminescent glow against his olive skin. He was absolutely stunning.

Without saying a word, that dumbass ran straight to the end of the dock and plunged into the bay. I was left there with my mouth hanging wide open as he resurfaced with a splash.

"Come on, *Roja*. The water is so cool this time of night," he coaxed.

I half-ran to the end of the dock to look down at him. "What the fuck do you think you're doing?" I chided him like he was a small child. Even though there was nothing small about him.

I shook my head to clear the lusty thoughts that filled my mind. Looking back at the house, half expecting lights to come on at any moment.

Damon laughed as he looked up at me. One of

those deep belly laughs that made my stomach twist into knots.

"Are you afraid we'll get caught? Come swim with me." He seemed to be amused with himself.

"Unlike you, if I get arrested for trespassing, I won't be able to get that off my record by asking a few friends for some favors. Get out now! I'm not going to swim with you," I scolded. Wasn't this man older than me? Why was I having to be the grown-up in this situation?

"What's wrong? Scared to get your hair a little wet?" he teased as I glared at him. "Chicken Shit."

As much as I would've liked to show him that I was not a chicken, I wasn't going to play his game. "No, I'm not. I just don't want to swim with you. Now let's go before you get caught."

He laughed. "I think I'll stay right here. When you decide to not be a fun sponge, let me know," he baited. I rolled my eyes. Fine, I wasn't going to stick around to see him get caught.

I turned to march off the dock when I heard a loud splash right before I felt a huge amount of water hit my back. When I turned around to face Damon, he was looking everywhere else except at me. The mischievous look in his eyes had me stifling a smile.

Fuck it, I thought to myself as I brought my shirt over my head and stared him down. "You're in for it now, fucker," I said as I stripped.

Never taking my eyes off him, I brought my sports bra up and over my head, exposing my breasts to the chilled night air. I watched as his gaze went from humor to hooded as I hooked my thumbs in my leggings and pulled them down, removing my shoes with them. Soon, I stood in front of him naked as the day. He stayed where he was, treading water and scorching me with his gaze.

Before I could talk myself out of it, I took off at a run and jumped into the water right next to him. The water was cool and refreshing against my hot, too-tight skin. When I resurfaced, Damon was wiping water from his face with a smile.

"There, happy now?" I asked. The look he gave me could have thawed the polar ice cap.

"Extremely," was all he said before he lunged for me.

I squealed an extremely girly sound as I tried to swim away from him. I didn't get too far before he gripped his hand around my ankle and pulled me toward him. I giggled unabashedly and tried to wiggle out of his clutch. He released his hold on me in favor of grabbing my hips, bringing me to his front.

I sucked in a breath and heated as I felt his hard length against my belly. I lost all sense of self-preservation then. I gripped his shoulders and tangled my legs around his strong hips. I could feel his thick cock prodding at my entrance, begging for entry. I moaned as I ground against him, dragging the head against my clitoris.

He kept us afloat with his unyielding leg strength as he devoured my lips. My eyes were closed but I could feel us moving. Soon I felt the rungs of the ladder at my back as he pressed firmly against me. He ate at my lips with firm presses. He licked, sucked, and nibbled at me. Every second made me hotter until I thought the water around us would start boiling.

He pulled away and I gasped as he thrust against me, sending another jolt of pleasure through me as he raked against my swollen bundle of nerves.

"Reach up and grab the ladder. Don't move," he

ordered roughly.

I surprised myself by obeying as I gripped the top rung and held myself up.

Damon wasted no time as he brought his hands down my arms. Raking over my ticklish spots making me squirm. He gave me a hard look before he twisted my right nipple with firm fingers. I squealed and jerked against him as the pain turned to something hotter.

"I said don't move," he said roughly.

I furrowed my brows as I looked down at him. "Then don't tickle me," I gritted behind my clenched teeth.

He chuckled before giving my other nipple the same treatment. Again, I yelped before the pain turned to that delicious heat that nearly ripped a moan from me.

"And no back talking. Unless you want me to gag you," he threatened with a dark look.

Taking a gag didn't seem like much fun so I clamped my mouth shut but kept my scowl in place. He chuckled before he looked back down at his task. I didn't move again as he brought both of his hands up my torso, lifting me from the water slightly. He sat me down so I was straddling his thick upper thigh.

I nearly groaned as he rubbed against me. The coarse hair of his leg caused the most wicked friction. He ran his hand up further until he was caressing my breasts, bringing them up to his hot mouth.

"I've dreamed about these tits for two weeks now. Look how perfect they fit in my hands," he rasped before he sucked a tightened bud into his skilled mouth.

I shouted and arched toward him. He used his thigh to rub against me in firm passes. He sucked on me hard and I swear my eyes rolled to the back of my head.

He went back and forth between my sensitive peaks, sucking and biting. All the while his thigh was driving me higher and higher. I was still wound tight from earlier in the locker room. I needed to come, desperately.

"Please, Damon," I whimpered.

He groaned against me as if my words gave him pleasure. He pulled away from my breasts and lowered his right hand into the water. Before I could protest the loss, his fingers replaced his thigh. He rubbed my clit in tight circles and I nearly came out of my skin.

"Since you asked so nicely I'm going to give you what you want, but you have to be quiet. If you can't be quiet, I'm going to punish you in the sweetest way," he threatened.

Then he was pulling me to him, away from the ladder. I wrapped myself around him and kissed his neck. I felt us moving and coming out of the water but it didn't register what was going on around me. Before I knew it, we were on the dock and Damon was laying me on my back.

I shivered as a cool breeze blew over my wet body. I waited for him to come over me and settle between my thighs but he never did. I felt his big hands spread my thighs open further and further until he was satisfied. I looked down at him and my breath caught in my throat.

He was dripping wet and leaning over my most intimate area. His hair hung in front of his face in loose wet waves. Water droplets bounced off my heated flesh. His breath fluttered across my pussy. His dark brown gaze leisurely ate up my body. He took his fingers and spread me apart so he could take it all in. I moaned and arched my back as he blew softly on my most tender parts.

"Remember, no sounds," he reminded me with a devious smile.

Bastard. He knew I would never be able to be quiet.

Before I could say anything he lowered his mouth to my pussy. I nearly screamed as he sucked and licked at me. When he added two big fingers to the mix I nearly lost it. He was pumping into me with one hand and keeping me spread wide open with his other as he flicked that wicked tongue against me. He licked me like a popsicle on a hot summer day. I was writhing against the wet wood at my back as he ate at me. I bit my lower lip to stop my moans of pleasure before they came to the surface. The only sounds you could hear were my labored breathing and the waves from the bay softly lapping the shore.

I was so close. Damon told me I had to be quiet, but he didn't say anything about not moving my arms. I thrust my hands into his wet hair and pulled him closer to my center. He groaned deep against me as I moved my hips up to meet his eager mouth. I knew I was being rough but I couldn't help it.

I exploded against his tongue, arching my back and breathing heavily. How I managed to stay quiet was beyond me. Before I could come down, Damon pulled his mouth from me and replaced it with his fingers. He pumped those big fingers into me with one hand and rubbed my clit in tight movements with the other.

"Your cream tastes as good as I remember it, Red. I want to watch you come again. *Ven por mí*," he ordered as his movements quickened.

I couldn't help it this time, I screamed my release as I came in a rush. I swirled my hips against his hands and whimpered loudly. He stared down at my writhing body with lust in his eyes before he pulled his hands from me and smiled.

Shit.

A.E. NALLE

"Oh, Red." He tsked

Chapter Eleven

I didn't fully register what was happening as Damon picked me up from the dock floor. I was still in a post-orgasmic haze when he walked us over to the seating area by the firepit. When he stood me on my feet again he leaned down for another drugging kiss. He pulled away enough to murmur against my lips.

"Since you couldn't follow directions to be quiet, I'm going to put something in your mouth to make you quiet. I'm going to sit in this chair and you're going to sit between my legs and suck my cock with that loud mouth of yours. And when I come, you are going to swallow every last drop. Do you understand?"

His words had a fresh flood of arousal coating my inner thighs. I squeezed them together as I glared at him around the lust coursing through my body.

"I don't know how you expect anyone to be quiet when you make them come like that." I frowned.

I saw a glint of humor in his eyes before he brought his hand down for a sharp smack against my ass. I yelped from the sting left behind. My skin was still wet, making the sting all the worse.

"That's the point, Red," he mused.

I took a step away from him and watched as his powerful body sunk into the lounge chair. My heart picked up its pace as I looked at the huge appendage I'd felt against me in the water. His cock was rock hard. The veins that ran along the bottom bulged like they were about to burst. He was so long, his head nearly hit his navel. I squeezed my legs together again and fought the urge to melt into a puddle. He chuckled and brought my attention back to that crooked smile.

"See something you like, *Roja*?" he asked in a

husky voice before he grabbed the monster between his legs.

I bit my lip as he leaned his head back and stroked himself. He groaned and his abs flexed as his hand met the base of his cock.

"I've only ever been this hard when I think of you. You would call me a pervert if you knew how many times I've yanked my own cock to the memory of you on my tongue," he rasped as he continued to pleasure himself in front of me.

I could see the pearly liquid seeping from the tip as he cradled his balls with one hand and stroked himself with the other.

I would be surprised at this point if I wasn't dripping with need for him. Out of all the men I had been with, none had ever turned me on the way Damon did. The thought of giving a man head had never wrung my bell. But thinking of tasting him had me drooling.

"I thought you were going to teach me how to be quiet," I taunted as I stepped to stand between his spread legs. I looked down at him, my gaze flicking between his heavy-lidded eyes and his working fist. I gracefully sank to my knees and came face to face with his thick erection.

The bay couldn't wash away his intoxicating scent I found myself wanting to be surrounded by. I licked my lips while watching his movements slow with heavily hooded eyes. I ran my hands up his inner thighs until they met in the middle, a breath away from his manhood.

He sucked in a shuddered breath as he watched me, removing his hands from that glorious length. I grinned at him as I brought my hands further up, starting at his heavy balls. I cradled him like he had himself earlier and reveled in the shiver that traveled up his body.

My other hand gripped him firmly at the base. My fingers were barely able to touch each other, he was so thick. It would be a fight to take all of him in my mouth, but it was a fight I wanted to win.

He groaned and thrust his hips as I pumped my loosened fist to his bulbous head, before making the slow descent back down to the base. I worked him a few more times before I leaned forward, flicking the tip of my tongue over the pre-cum I found there. He jerked in my grasp and I chuckled against him.

I started to lick him again when his big hand worked its way into my hair. He gripped hard and pulled my head back. My scalp lit on fire and I shivered, making my nipples tighten further. His dark gaze held mine.

"Stop fucking around and suck my cock with that smart mouth of yours. If you don't, I'll tie your arms behind your back and fuck your mouth. I will take you roughly and you won't have any choice but to take all of me as I tunnel down your throat," he threatened deliciously and I shivered again.

If another man said that to me, I would have twisted his balls right off his body. But, this was Damon. And Damon turned me on with his harsh words.

His grip on my hair didn't loosen as he brought my mouth to him. I gripped him hard at the base and sucked him past my lips, rolling my tongue along the V on the underside of his cock. He groaned deep in his chest and relaxed his hold on me slightly. I looked up at him through my lowered lashes. His mouth was open in a gasp as he watched me with dark eyes. I sucked him in deeper with each pass, using my hand and saliva to stroke what I couldn't reach with my mouth.

"Yes," he hissed between clenched teeth as he urged me on. "*Chupas mi polla tan bien*, don't stop."

His words made me bob my head faster. Before I knew it, he was moving my head with his hand still clenched in my hair. I pushed to get him deeper and deeper. He was going wild now. Thrusting up into my mouth while pushing my head down at the same time. I gagged and choked around his cock. I was so fucking turned on I couldn't take it any longer as I shoved my hand off his shaft and lowered it to my throbbing clit. I moaned as my fingers brushed over the sensitive nub.

"That's right, baby. Rub that little cunt while I fuck your mouth. You get that pussy ready to take this cock," he grunted.

My fingers moved faster and faster. I was going to come soon and I wanted him right there with me. I moaned around him and pushed my head down as far as I could. He held me there and fucked my mouth from below in short passes. I shoved my fingers in my drenched pussy as his cock reached the soft spot at the back of my throat. I swallowed around him and he jerked violently as he came. I gulped at his release heavily, not wanting to spare a single drop of him. His orgasm shoved me over the edge. I screamed around him with my release as he grunted long and hard.

"Fuck!" he growled viciously.

He stood suddenly, dragging my mouth from him with a *pop*. He picked me up and I straddled his hips once again. His softened cock started to stir as he took my mouth in a heated kiss. He didn't care that I just had his dick in my mouth as he pushed his tongue past my lips.

I didn't even realize we were walking until cold glass pressed against my back. I paid no mind to the sound of a door closing as he continued to devour my mouth.

I wiggled against his now hard length, trying to

get it where I wanted it. I shuddered when his head slipped past my entrance. He pulled his mouth away long enough to murmur against me.

"*Oh Dios*, you're going to strangle my cock with that tight cunt, *Roja*." He groaned as he pushed in a little further as he took my mouth once more.

I could feel the cool air from the AC against my heated skin, but it still didn't register with me. My need for him was too great. Damon pushed through another door and before I knew it he was leaning down and I could feel a soft bed at my back. I groaned in frustration as he pulled away from me, what little I had of his cock inside of me, going with him.

The room was dark around me, except for the soft glow of the moon coming through the windows. I was so fired up that none of this clicked in my lust-infested brain.

Damon stood in front of me, looking down at me like a savage barbarian. He was all hard lines and divots. I couldn't take it anymore. I pushed to sit up in front of him, moving to grab his cock and put it where I wanted it. He chuckled and pushed my shoulder until I was laying back down.

"So impatient," he muttered before he reached into the nightstand and pulled a foil wrapper out. I watched as he ripped the package open and pushed the condom onto himself. He slowly descended back onto me and I welcomed him with hungry kisses.

"I need you," I whimpered against him.

He groaned as he edged himself into me. "*Ya me tienes, Roja*," he muttered. I shivered as a warm feeling filled my chest. *You already have me, Red.*

"I want your hands on me and I want all of your little noises now, Red. I want to feel and hear everything," he whispered as he looked in my eyes.

He pulled back and plunged into me with a fast, hard thrust. I gasped and dug my nails into his back. He was so big and I was impossibly stretched. If I hadn't been so wet, the invasion would've hurt.

Damon made a choking sound as he held still. Both of our harsh breaths filled the room. Adjusting to one another. Moments passed like that and eventually I needed him to move. After letting out a sound of frustration, I churned my hips. Begging without words for him to fuck me. His chest rumbled as he pushed a hand down onto my hip, halting my movements.

"This will be over before it starts if you don't hold still, Red. I have wanted this for so long and you are so perfect, you're going to unman me," he rasped as he pulled himself from me and slowly sank back in.

I moaned and writhed. "I've wanted this too, but if you don't go faster I'm going to die. Fuck me, please!" I blurted a bit dramatically.

"*Siempre, Roja.*" He chuckled above me before picking his pace up.

He grabbed one of my breasts and brought the tightened peak to his waiting lips. I arched into him as he sucked it into his mouth, hard. He pumped into me in sync with his sucks. Each time, he pulled out of me almost all the way before he slammed back into me with a fleshy smack, grinding down on my clit before starting it all over. Winding me tighter and tighter.

He released my breast with a *pop* and sat up, wrapping my legs around his thighs as he sat back. He spread me wide and continued to pump into me deeply. I screamed as he rubbed his thumb around my clit.

"Fuck, you're so beautiful wrapped around my cock," he grunted.

He tilted further back, the position rubbing my G-spot with each pass. He slowed his thrusts and fucked me in short little passes.

"Oh, God!" I screamed as the pressure intensified. He pushed hard on my clit and kept up his sweet torture.

"I can feel you squeezing me, baby. I'm not going to last much longer. But first I need you to come on my cock. Come for me!" he demanded roughly before he pinched my clit and I went flying.

I screamed my release and he went wild. Grabbing my legs, he put them on his shoulders. He leaned heavily on me and fucked me hard. The vulgar sounds of his cock pumping in and out of me spurred us on.

I could feel him grow even thicker inside of me as his thrusts became erratic. He groaned deep in his chest as he spilled his seed inside of me. His length jerked almost violently, throwing me into another harsh orgasm. Letting my legs fall from him, he brought our bodies flush together as he rubbed the rest of his release out before giving me his full weight. With my past, I normally wouldn't be able to handle a man's weight on top of me. But with Damon, it was comforting.

I sighed when he took my mouth again before he pulled away. I watched with heavy eyes as he removed the condom, discarding it into a nearby trash can. When he was done, he climbed back into the bed and pulled me into his arms. Tucking us in under the blanket, he held me to his chest and pushed my still wet hair away from my face.

I fell asleep in his arms, to his tender kisses and sweet nothings murmured against my skin.

Chapter Twelve

The smell of bacon frying roused me. I'd slept so well the night before, I found myself not wanting to open my eyes. Stretching my arms above my head, I arched my back and yawned. I smiled to myself sleepily as I felt a delicious ache between my legs, evidence of what had occurred here last night. I relaxed back down under the warm blanket and let the events of the evening flow over me.

Everything that had happened seemed to pass in such a heated blur of ecstasy. I remembered the way Damon had taunted me until I'd gotten in the water with him. After I felt the press of his naked body against mine, all hope of self-preservation had washed down the bay with the soft current. He had been dominating and compelling and I for some reason had eaten up every minute of it.

When he'd first told me that he wanted to control me in bed, I thought he was crazy. I couldn't have ever imagined that I would have submitted to him so easily, so willingly. But, I couldn't pretend that doing just that hadn't led to the best sex of my entire life.

The way he had demanded his pleasure last night, turned me on more than words could properly explain. Before Damon, I never would have sucked a guy's cock if he demanded it. But last night, not only had I done as he ordered but I'd shockingly enjoyed every single moment of it. I wasn't even ashamed that the thought of doing it again made me hot.

I knew that I hadn't unlocked some new sort of oral pleasure kink. No, I didn't have a fetish for that, it had everything to do with Damon. I couldn't put my finger on what it was about him that made me act so out of my perfectly placed persona.

It wasn't even just my sex life he had rattled. Whatever he was doing to me was slowly breaking down my walls. When I was around him, it was like I was a completely different person.

Normally, I never showed vulnerability around anyone. I always showed confidence in all aspects of my life and I was guarded at all times. The way I'd opened up to Damon in the park last night, never would have happened with anyone else. If someone had implied that I was a cold bitch, I would have smiled while telling them to fuck off. No further explanation needed.

Instead, he had forced me to talk to him about what I was feeling and I reluctantly had. Now, the morning after, I was feeling very off balance and anxious about everything that occurred last night.

Eyes still closed, I wiggled my feet restlessly. I'd had my one night with Damon and now I needed to end it. Even if last night had been the best night of my life, I couldn't continue down this path with him. I knew in my heart that he would ruin me if I let him. He would tear through every wall I had carefully built around myself and leave me with a pile of rubble when he was done with me. And, I had no doubt he would be done with me eventually.

People like him didn't end up with people like me. He was too good for me. I would just taint him by staying because ultimately my stain would rub off on him.

I finally opened my eyes and glanced around the bright room. I sucked in a startled breath as I took in my surroundings. I hadn't let myself contemplate where I was last night while Damon and I were otherwise involved. For some reason, I figured we were in the boathouse by the dock. I don't know why that made sense in my head but it did. I didn't even stop to think that he may have taken me inside the beautiful cabin we'd snuck around. But, as I looked around the room, I realized that is exactly where I was.

I sat up slightly and stared out the huge windows in front of me. This time of day the sun gleamed off the bay, making it look like a million diamonds shimmered on the surface. I could clearly see the dock from this vantage point. Looking out over the large expanse of water, it became obvious why the house had been built on top of the hill—it offered a stunning view.

I tore my gaze from the floor-to-ceiling windows and looked around the room. It was extremely cozy, to say the least. The floor was covered in a plush dark carpet that complemented the lighter gray color of the walls. The four-poster king-sized bed I sat in was covered in satiny white sheets with big puffy pillows. The thick white blanket I hugged to my chest was soft against my skin and begged for me to crawl under.

Looking closer at the black metal bed frame, I could see where rings were welded onto them on all four corners. I furrowed my brows, wondering what they were for. They kind of looked like a place to put long-stem flowers, but that seemed odd.

Dragging my gaze away, I looked around the room once more.

The room itself was quite large. Besides the bed, it hosted matching black nightstands and a large dresser. There was also a desk that sat in the corner, kitty-cornered so the user could take advantage of the view. There was a large glass door that was meant to fold like an accordion that led to the patio right outside. From here, I could see a couple of lounge chairs. I briefly imagined myself having coffee out there while enjoying the view on a lazy Sunday.

To my left was a door that was slightly ajar, showcasing a large master bath. I could spy a large tub from where I sat.

The whole room was neat and well organized. Even the effects on top of the dresser looked like they had their place. I spied a clock amongst those things and gasped at the time. It was almost noon. I hadn't slept in that late since I was a teenager. I shook my head at myself. That had to be wrong.

"I would have woken you, but you looked so peaceful."

I yelped and clasped the blanket to my chest before turning to the deep voice in the doorway. And then I promptly drooled at the sight Damon made. I felt my arms relax as I stared at him. He stood there in nothing but low-hung gray sweatpants. I could see from here that he wasn't wearing anything under those pants. The delicious outline of that impressive cock was visible under the fabric.

I clenched my thighs together before I tore my gaze from that area of his anatomy. His hair was mused and hanging free around his face. He was holding onto the doorway as if to stop himself from entering the room. His dark eyes drank in the sight of me with lingering passes. I would've been self-conscious if I hadn't been doing the same exact thing.

I cleared my throat and attempted to speak. "I shouldn't have slept that long," I said with a frown. Then a thought occurred to me. "Old man Boone?" I asked.

I saw a flash of perfect teeth as he smiled at me, a genuine look of amusement in his eyes.

"Boone!" he yelled and I panicked. There was no way he would let a stranger come in here while I was naked in his bed. Would he?

Then I heard the sound of four paws running

across the hardwood. I braced myself as a large golden retriever came barreling into the room at breakneck speed.

I giggled as he jumped onto the bed and promptly started to lick my face. I put my hands into his fur and pushed him until he backed up a bit so I could pet him. He had a thick speckling of white fur around his eyes and mouth, a testament to his years. He laid down on my legs and rolled onto his back so I could give him a proper belly rub.

"I see we didn't wake you last night, Old man Boone." I smiled down at the dog while I pet him.

I was still smiling as I looked back toward Damon who had finally made his way to the bed.

"Asshole. I can't believe you made me think we had to sneak around or we'd get caught. I'm going to assume this is your home," I said before Boone jumped from my lap and happily trotted out of the room.

"Yes, this is my house. Sorry I tricked you, but I couldn't resist. Seeing the shock on your face when I jumped into the water was enough to make the fib worth it," Damon said as he stared down at me. Heat was growing in his eyes.

I lost my smile as I looked at him again. He was towering over me now. I swallowed hard as I caught a glimpse of him hardening under his sweats. My nipples tightened as I realized I'd let the blanket go while I was petting Boone. The fabric had slipped to my waist where it lay in a heap, exposing me to Damon's fiery stare. I kept eye contact while I grabbed it to cover myself.

Damon moved fast and was on top of me in the blink of an eye. He was above the blanket but between my legs nonetheless. He had my wrists above my head and held them firmly while he grinned down at me.

I sucked in a sharp breath at the sensation that

clawed at my chest. I was having a hard time deciding if it was panic or excitement that I felt.

"The last thing I want you to do is to cover these pretty pink buds," he mumbled before he leaned down and swiped that wicked tongue across the peaked flesh. I sighed and arched into him, giving him greater access.

He took his time lavishing attention on my breasts. I was squirming and on the cusp of begging when he finally pulled away. He kissed me then. Not the dominating, devouring kiss that I had come to crave, but a slow sweet kiss. He swiped at my lower lip with his tongue before dipping inside briefly. He kissed my lips so softly that it had me trembling for more when he let me up for air.

"I hadn't planned on doing this when I came in here," he murmured against me. "I was going to gently wake you and ask you to come eat breakfast with me. I couldn't resist once I saw you sitting here like this. You looked so soft with your ruffled hair and your sleepy eyes. Seeing you like this in my bed makes me want to keep you here like this forever." He spoke softly, as if he spoke too loudly I would run away.

The only problem was that it was the soft words, not the loud ones, that made me want to run. I felt a warm feeling bloom inside my belly before harsh dismay took its place. I needed to get out of here sooner rather than later.

I wiggled under him as I avoided eye contact. "Let me up," I said.

To my surprise, he didn't even hesitate. He released my wrists and sat back on the bed. If I hadn't been so distracted with my need to run, I would have noticed that he had honored my request to stop immediately. While some men would try to talk their way out of halting their actions, Damon had respected my boundaries and backed off accordingly.

I sat rigidly and brought the blanket with me, covering myself. This would be a lot easier if I was fully clothed. "Damon, we need to t—"

"I know what you're going to say and I wish you would stop before you ruin what was the best night of my life," he said, his lips in a flat line.

I winced and shut my mouth. It's not every day I'm rendered speechless.

"Can we just pretend, for now, that you woke up with no regrets about last night? I sure as hell don't have any. I wouldn't take back a single moment with you, Jill." I swallowed hard as I let his words wash over me.

"Let's pretend you don't have any hang-ups about this"—he gestured between the two of us—"and that you're happy to be with me." He paused and laughed to himself but it held no humor. I felt the back of my eyes burn as I looked at him.

"Sometime soon, we will get through your doubts or fears, or whatever it is you think will cause us to fail, and you will see that I can make you happy if you let me. But, right now I just want to have breakfast with you and try to enjoy the day. Can we do that?" he asked.

I was stunned into silence as he stood from the bed and walked out of the room. I didn't even have a chance to say anything to him as he left. Was I truly so transparent? He had known I was going to stop this from going any further before I'd even said anything.

I shouldn't entertain this anymore, I thought to myself. *I should go find my clothes and phone, wherever I left them last night, and call an Uber.* It would be cruel to both of us if I were to go along with his pretending. Because when this ended—and it would end—it would crush me even more. I couldn't allow these fake illusions to have one single breath. I needed to stop it before it even started.

So, tell me why I got out of that bed and walked to his dresser. Tell me why I put on one of his shirts and padded out of that room with nothing else covering my body. Call it stupidity or blind intuition, but I walked into that kitchen with full intentions of playing pretend. I may have signed up for my own cursed fate but I wanted so badly to be someone else. To pretend not to be me, even for just a day.

Chapter Thirteen

The smells permeating from the kitchen were enough to make me salivate. If I was a stronger person, I would have walked past all those decadent smells. I would have strolled right past the man with his shoulders hunched, leaning heavily against the counter with his back toward me.

How hard was it to want someone who wanted to constantly run from you? I felt terrible as I looked at him. Couldn't he see that I was trying to save him before he got in over his head? I had been resigned to the fact that I would spend my life alone. I knew nobody would want me after they learned about Jason, and I couldn't even blame them. In the end, I wasn't worth it. Damon had yet to learn that.

I couldn't ever tell him what happened to me. Even though he deserved to know so he could make his own judgments, I was a coward. I didn't want him to know of my defilement for fear of his reaction. I didn't want to see the way he looked at me vanish from his eyes.

I wanted so badly to be someone else. Someone that would take everything Damon gave me with open arms. I wished I could be someone who deserved it. Sadly, I just wasn't. But, I could pretend to be.

I walked forward until I was standing right behind Damon. I didn't doubt he knew I was standing there. I wrung my hands and released a shaky breath before I brought my arms around him. He stiffened against me and I thought for a moment that he would shrug off my touch. To my surprise he grabbed my hands and raised them to his chest, letting me hug him from behind. I pressed my ear against his back and listened to his steady heartbeat for a moment before speaking.

"I'm sorry for pushing you away. If it's any consolation, I'm not doing it for fun. I thi—" I swallowed thickly as my heart rate picked up. I was not the person to open up to anyone, so this was extremely hard for me. "I think you're better off letting me leave before this gets any more serious." I exhaled in a rush.

Damon started to turn to face me but I held him firm. "Don't," I begged and to my surprise, he stopped. "If I don't get this out now, I never will." I breathed against him, placing my forehead between his shoulder blades and closing my eyes before I continued.

"I know that what you want is for me to be with you and not fight when you try to show me affection. But the truth is, that's not who I am. I know you're a good man and anyone would be lucky to have you want them as much as you seem to want me. But, that's the problem."

I fought the burn in my eyes as I continued. "I know this will end badly for both of us. There are things in my past that you won't like, and you'll end whatever this is between us just as quickly as it began. I'm not good enough for you. And telling you now is a lot easier than you figuring it out later." I blew out another shaky breath. "I feel so weak even admitting this, but I'm terrified of the way you will look at me when you finally see how tainted I really am."

I sucked in a breath and lifted my head from his back. Blinking back the tears, I tried to compose myself. His head was turned to the side as if he was trying to look at me. He was so calm it was almost maddening.

I sniffled before I finished. "But," I shook my head and let him turn in my arms. He faced me and I focused on the hollow of his throat. I couldn't even look the man in his eyes. I didn't know what I would do if I found pity there. "I want to pretend with you. Just for this weekend, I want to be the person you think I am. I don't want to be the person that has to have everything in my life planned and controlled to death. I don't want to be Jill. I want to be Red. I want to be who you need me to be," I admitted as I finally looked into those dark eyes.

I was amazed when I didn't find pity lurking there, although I couldn't name the soft look he gave me. Damon gazed down at me as he pushed my hair away from my eyes, tucking it behind my ear. He left his hand at the base of my neck, his thumb making tiny circles at my pulse point.

"I want you to be you, Jill. I don't need to pretend you're someone else or that you're any different than you are right now." He paused. "But, if that's what you need then I will give it to you. I'll take this weekend and prove to you that this can work. And if you want to be Red, then that's who you can be," he finished as he pulled my lips to his.

His lips locked with mine and I sighed as I leaned into him. I brought my arms around his neck and all but climbed up his body. He squatted to pick me up. Turning, he placed me on the counter, making a place for himself between my legs. I pulled him closer to me and locked my ankles around his ass. Thrusting my hands into his hair, I was the one doing the devouring this time. His hands gripped my ribs, so close to my breasts.

I moaned against his mouth as I felt his hardness press against my naked sex. The only barrier was those damn sweats he wore. Before I could think better, I pushed my hands down to his waistband and started to lower the fabric. Damon shocked me by pulling away.

"I need you inside of me," I mumbled before I pulled him back down to my lips. He groaned as I rubbed myself against him.

He ripped his lips away from me again and pinned me with his stare. "I wasn't going to fuck you until after breakfast, but you seem to be very impatient," he growled before he bit my bottom lip. I swiped my tongue across the swollen appendage to calm the sting left behind. He watched me with hooded eyes.

"Fuck," he rasped before he backed away further from me.

I almost whimpered as he lounged against the opposite counter. "I think I have a new favorite shirt now," he said as he looked at me.

I looked down at the front of his sweats and nearly melted at the sight of his cock poking out of his waistband.

"You're completely naked underneath, aren't you?" he asked, drawing my attention back to his eyes. I nodded. He smiled at me. "Show me."

Never one to back down from a challenge, I spread my legs. Just enough to tease him with the slightest view of my pussy.

"Wider," he crooned as he rubbed his hand down his hard length.

My breath hitched as I watched him and did as he asked. I placed my heels on either side of me on the countertop, exposing my whole self to his view. I shivered as he devoured the sight with scorching eyes.

"That is a pretty little pussy, *Roja*," he said nastily. "Show me how wet it is," he commanded.

My heart skipped a beat before I did as he asked. Bringing my hand down to my sex, I used my fingers to spread my labia for him to see. He groaned and grabbed onto the edge of the counter with white-knuckle force as if to restrain himself.

"Put those little fingers in that cunt. I want to watch how you play with yourself, baby."

I did as he ordered and pushed my middle finger into myself, keeping my palm against my clitoris. I was so drenched that when I pulled back out the wet noise filled the otherwise quiet kitchen. I added my ring finger this time and fucked myself in slow passes. Keeping my eyes on him as I did. I watched as his cock jumped like it was trying to get to me. Shoving my fingers deep, I curled them just as I liked and rubbed that bundle of nerves inside of me, eliciting a shudder and moan from my parted lips.

"Don't you dare make yourself come," Damon barked at me. "I want all your pleasure for myself. I'm selfish like that." He grinned at me. "Fuck yourself, Red. I want to hear all your noises. I want to watch you go wild."

I did just that. I fucked myself fast. Pushing my palm down on my swollen clit with each pass of my fingers. Using my other hand to pinch my nipples under my shirt. I moaned and writhed as he watched me. The fact that he was watching me only excited me further, getting me closer and closer to that edge I desperately wanted to fall off.

The sounds my pussy and fingers were making would be enough to make a porn star blush. I churned my hips against myself as I slipped my fingers out of my soaked channel. I rubbed the wetness around my sensitive nub until I was shaking with the need to release. I was so close now. I closed my eyes and tossed my head back as the wave of ecstasy creased and started to crash down over me.

Suddenly my hand was jerked away from my body and a hard cock was taking its place against my clitoris. My eyes sprung open to find Damon standing in front of me with his pants just low enough to let his monster cock free. He grabbed the hem of his shirt and ripped it over my head roughly. A shiver ran down my spine as cold air caressed my blazing skin.

Grabbing my other hand, he pushed one against the cabinet above my head while he looked at the fingers I'd used to play with myself. His hungry eyes soaked up the sight of my glistening appendages before he sucked them into his mouth with a long groan. When he was done he brought that hand up to meet my other, holding both with one big hand.

"You were going to come, weren't you?" He glared down at me. I was too hot to speak so I shook my head, denying the accusation I knew to be true. His glare deepened before he picked up a rubber spatula from the utensil jar. I gave him a curious look right before he brought the spatula down onto my nipple. I squealed and panted loudly.

"Fuck! That hurt!" I yelled at him but already the sting was sinking into my bones, making me hotter than before.

Damon smiled down at me before he kissed the offended nipple. "Don't lie to me. I know what you look like right before you're about to come, *Roja*. Your legs start shaking and you curl your pretty little toes." As if to accentuate his point, he put the spatula down before he grabbed my ankle and brought said toes right to his waiting mouth. I gasped and felt a fresh flow of arousal flood my pussy as he bit down on them with a wicked grin before he sucked at the digits. I panted as my eyes rolled back in pleasure. I didn't know that was an erogenous zone until that moment.

He released me, letting my leg fall back open before he grabbed his cock. I arched into him as he dragged the head down my center, gathered the moisture he found there, and traveled back up.

"You only come when I tell you to," he taunted

while he rubbed me.

He was applying the right amount of pressure, that if he kept going like this I was going to explode and I wouldn't have a choice in the matter.

"Ah, fuck. I want to sink into your heat, but I need to get a condom," he rasped before he started to pull away from me.

"I have an IUD and I get tested once a month," I blurted quickly in an attempt to keep him from stopping.

I'd never let anyone fuck me without protection before so this would be a first for me, but for some reason unbeknownst to me, I wanted just that more than ever right now. I had a primal need to feel him with no barriers between us.

Damon held himself still against me while his hot gaze seemed to sear me where I sat. He searched my eyes like he was looking for an answer.

"I'm clean too. I've never taken a woman without a condom before," he rasped and paused as if asking for permission.

I simply nodded my head. "I trust you," I mumbled as I tried not to let myself get hung up on my words.

I sucked in a hard breath when he started to move again. He dipped his big cock inside just barely and then rubbed my clit.

"Oh, yes! Please!" I begged.

He pushed himself inside of me in an achingly slow manner as he picked his torture spatula back up. He watched where we were connected before he shuddered.

"You feel so good, Red," he groaned as he continued his slow plunging.

Before I could beg him to move faster, he pushed himself into the hilt as he flicked the spatula down on my other nipple. The noise I made was somewhere between a scream and a moan. I arched into him as he pulled out slowly and tunneled his way back in.

"Does my little fuck toy like it when I punish these perfect tits?" he asked as he whacked me again. I felt myself lean into the hit that time. The sting traveled all the way to my pussy.

"Yes!" I hissed, wanting more.

He fucked me slow and steady all while alternating his hits. He was good, never hitting the same spot twice. Each time he pushed back into me, he would ground down on my clit. He kept telling me to hold off, not to come, but that was becoming impossible. Soon the pressure built too high. I was going to come and I didn't think I'd be able to stop it.

I was a writhing mess when I started to beg. "Oh, God! I need to come!" I screamed as my legs started to shake uncontrollably.

Damon grinned down at me, the bastard. "I'm not ready for you to come yet, Red. You take this cock like a good girl and hold off just a little longer," he growled.

Then he picked up his pace. He put the spatula down and let his hand travel up my body, coming to rest at my throat. I moaned as he closed his big hand around my neck and squeezed, not enough to cut my air off but enough to make the blood flow slow. He fucked fast and hard now. Every one of those thrusts pushed my body further up the countertop. The sound of his balls hitting my ass in wet slaps drove me higher and higher.

"I can't hold it!" I screamed.

And I couldn't. I exploded around him in a heated rush. I felt a rush of my arousal soak us both as he groaned above me, his gaze on where we connected. I screamed as he held me still and fucked into me faster than before, his rapid strokes prolonging my orgasm.

Before I was ready, he pulled out of me and

stepped back. I almost blushed as I saw the front of his sweatpants was soaked with my release. I'd never done that before. He looked at them and then at me as he grabbed his still-glistening cock and gave it a long stroke.

"You made a mess, Red, and now I have a new favorite pair of sweatpants." He grinned at me wickedly. "Now, I believe I told you not to come. You didn't listen." He tsked as he looked down at me and I trembled with anticipation. "Off the counter, turn around, and show me your ass," he demanded in a hard voice.

The need to fuck took over and I didn't even try to argue with him as I rushed to do his bidding. Standing on shaky legs, I turned. Placing my hands on the counter, I bent forward so he could get a full view of my backside. I felt, rather than saw, him come up behind me. I jumped as he ran his fingers against my soaked pussy, gathering my juices. I moaned when he brought his fingers up to my puckered asshole and rubbed them around. I pushed against him when he started to breach me there.

"Oh, Red. Do you like having this tight hole fucked?" he asked in a hushed voice. I stumbled for words as he pushed into me with his big finger.

"I ha—I've done it a couple of times. It was different, it didn't hurt but also didn't really feel pleasurable," I managed.

As if he wanted to prove me wrong at that moment, he pulled his finger out and pushed another one in, lighting up nerves I didn't even know I had. He was stretching me from the inside. My breath left me in a rush as he kept fucking into me with his big fingers. Soon, I was pushing back into him as he withdrew, trying to keep him in. I was building to something earth-shattering.

"Because you came without permission, I'm going to fuck this asshole, Red. But first I need to get you some proper lubrication. Stay right there," he said before he removed his fingers.

I watched as he left the room, but it wasn't long before he was back, lube in hand and gloriously naked. I sucked in another shuddered breath as I looked at his cock. A shiver of nerves had me almost ready to run. Almost.

As if he was reading my mind, he stopped so he could look at my face. "You were built to take me, Red. But if it becomes too much, you tell me to stop and I will," he assured me.

I nodded my head in acceptance and he disappeared behind me. Soon I felt a drop of cold lube against my puckered hole. I shivered as he rubbed it around with his fingers before slipping back inside. This time he used his other hand to rub my pussy while he fingered my ass. I brought my hand back and wrapped it around his cock. He pushed into my hand with a deep groan. I jacked him as he played my body like an instrument.

Soon, it became too much and I found myself teetering toward the edge again. Damon knew it and spoke the words I was looking for. "*Ven por mí, Roja.*"

I hurtled over the edge and was lost to oblivion. If it hadn't been for his hold on me, I would have crashed to the ground.

Before I was fully back down to earth, I felt him start to push his way into me. I breathed deep and pushed against him as he gripped my hips. He fucked me in short passes, getting further and further each time. My breath left me in short pants as he stretched me further than I thought possible.

"Fuck, I don't know how long this is going to

last. You're squeezing me so tight, Red," Damon gritted out behind me.

His fingers dug into my hips so hard I thought I might bruise. The thought brought a weird surge of pride to me. I pushed my hands back to his and held his wrists. I cried out loudly, a mixture of pleasure and discomfort. Just when I thought I couldn't take any more, he sank in all the way. We both stayed like that for long moments, both of us breathing heavily while he let me adjust to his size.

"I'm going to start moving now, *Roja*," he spoke. I braced myself for the worst as he started to pull away from me.

I expected pain and was shocked when all I felt was pleasure. A deep groan ripped from my chest as he raked across every nerve inside of me, setting me on fire. He pulled out until his head was the only thing left inside before he started to tunnel back in. He kept up that same slow pace for a few pumps until I couldn't take it any longer. I pushed back against him, wanting more.

"Fuck!" he growled right before he slammed into me.

The force from his thrust pushed my hips into the countertop. I had no choice but to bring my back to his front as he dragged me to him by my throat. He held me tight as he fucked my ass, his mouth against my cheek as he held me.

"I was going slow just in case you were uncomfortable," he admitted against me before he brought his other hand down to my swollen clit and started to rub. "But, I can see you're enjoying this as much as I am. This tight asshole feels so fucking good wrapped around me. It's going to feel even better when you come for me. You're going to milk my cock with how hard you squeeze me." His rough words drove me higher as he fucked me hard. The sounds of our flesh slapping together filled the kitchen.

I screamed as he pinched his fingers around my clit and I exploded. I pushed back against him, fucking him as much as he was fucking me.

"Oh, God, yes!" I screamed as I rolled into another orgasm. I felt myself squeeze around him again as I convulsed. Fresh arousal leaked down my thighs. I was too hot, too sensitive, too full, too … everything. When I heard Damon roar, I knew he would finish right behind me.

"It's too fucking good!" he rasped right before he slammed in one last time. I felt his cock jerk inside of me as he came in hot jets with a long groan on his lips.

I collapsed against his chest in exhaustion. He pulled out of me gently and tugged me to him, gently setting us down on the cold wood floor. We sat together, neither of us saying anything, just catching our breath. I leaned into his embrace as he kissed my neck in slow, tantalizing movements. I was utterly content, sated.

I almost believed him when he whispered in my ear, "*Podría perderse en ti, Roja.*"

Chapter Fourteen

I don't remember the last time I allowed myself the freedom to do something completely out of the norm. To just laze about and not worry about all the things on my ever-growing to-do list. There was always something that needed my attention. And even if something didn't need to be done, I never let myself just do nothing. I guess it was probably a fear that if I sat still for too long the intrusive thoughts would eventually burrow into my mind again.

Needless to say, I was kicking this weekend off on the right foot. I was doing something completely out of character by just allowing what happened—and was still happening—to occur in this kitchen. The differences between Jill and Red were vast.

Jill would never think to lay naked on a floor with a man she just had mind-blowing sex with. She would have never had mind-blowing sex in the kitchen at all. She preferred to have all of her sexual relations in an environment that she controlled.

Jill would never be caught dead relaxing on her belly, propped up on her elbows eating bacon and eggs straight out of the pan with a fork. She would have said something rude to deflect the feelings she was having. Choosing to push away the one person that made her feel wanted. She most definitely wouldn't allow that warm feeling to bloom in her lower belly or to let herself smile around a mouthful of food at the devastatingly handsome man lying next to her.

But *Red* would.

Red enjoyed every second of what happened here today. She loved the way it felt when Damon ran his fingers delicately up and down her spine. She craved his crooked smile more than she wanted her next breath. Red never wanted this moment to end.

I wished I could be Red all the time.

"Maybe I should have made more bacon," Damon said around a shit-eating grin.

I suppressed the moan of pleasure I felt rising while savoring the salty flavor of bacon coating my tongue. I playfully slapped his bicep as I swallowed the last of my breakfast, trying to hide my grin as I spoke.

"If you only knew when the last time I had bacon was, you wouldn't tease me so much," I defended myself, suppressing a giggle.

I pushed the now-empty pan away from me before I rolled onto my back. "It's not my fault you don't eat faster," I snarked. "You should probably make more if you're still hungry."

Stretching my arms above my head, I groaned as my sore muscles protested the action. Placing my hands behind my head, I relaxed back and peaked at my lover next to me with a sly grin. I watched as his stare took a lazy stroll over my body. He wasn't touching me but I could feel the heat he left behind with his dark gaze.

He started at my toes and I felt him rake over my legs, taking his time. His eyes blazed a heated trail as they made their way up my torso, lingering on my breasts. When he finally made it to my eyes, I couldn't help but stare back for a moment.

God, he was so gorgeous.

He tucked a stray strand of hair behind his ear before prowling closer to me. I risked a look down his body to watch his hard cock bobbing between his legs. Swallowing hard, I met his intense stare again. He rose above me before bringing his sinful mouth down to mine. I closed my eyes and prepared myself for the all-encompassing kiss that never came.

"I *am* still hungry. Starving, actually, just not for food," he whispered against my lips. My eyes fluttered open and I took in his smile before he lowered himself down my body.

He took his time, lavishing my every nook and cranny with his unique affection. By the time he reached my sex, I was trembling with the need to feel his hot mouth on me. I looked down to see him watching me with lust plain in his eyes. He held my stare as he swiped my center with a long lap of his tongue. My back arched and I thrust my fingers into his hair, pulling him closer to me. He groaned against me and something akin to a growl rumbled out of his chest.

If I had been in the right state of mind, I would have taken note that he didn't try to dominate me this time. He allowed me to hold him close while he devoured me.

It was a long time before we left the kitchen.

****

Hours later, I found myself on the very dock that started this whole endeavor, watching the sunset. Damon and I had lazed away the day and I had soaked in every moment of it greedily.

After our breakfast on the kitchen floor, and Damon's second helping, we had reluctantly gotten up and dressed. Of course, all I had from last night was the workout clothes I had come here wearing and my work clothes shoved in my gym bag, so I opted to just wear Damon's shirt all day.

We stood side by side at the sink and washed the dishes he had used to cook with. I washed and he dried and put them away. I'd kept feeling an unfamiliar tug at my lips as we chored. The feeling of normalcy washed over me relentlessly. When that familiar feeling of dread started to creep in around the edges, I'd been quick to shut it down. I was not about to let Jill's hang-ups ruin what could be one of the best weekends of my life.

After we cleaned up, Damon had taken me on a small tour of his stunning home and property. His home was a loner's dream come true. The whole property was excluded from his neighbors and left no chance for prying eyes. Big thick pine trees surrounded us to make sure of that.

If I'd thought that the best view of the bay had been from his bedroom, then I ate my own words after seeing the rest of the house. His kitchen and living room offered an open floor plan and it was where the big floor-to-ceiling windows came to their peak up to the top of the loft. The crystal-clear glass showcased the best view in the whole neighborhood, I was sure of it.

I'd watched from the living room sofa, with a big mug of coffee cooling in my hands and a soft throw over my legs, as Damon played fetch with Boone right outside the windows. He had put on a pair of athletic shorts, forgoing the shoes and shirt entirely.

Watching him with his carefree smile and hearing his booming laugh as he played with his dog was enough to make me melt. The sight he made with the dramatic backdrop of the bay behind him was stunning, to say the least. What a girl wouldn't give to be able to see this every day.

When he caught me staring at him, his eyes had darkened and his smile turned wicked. I felt heat flush up my body as he stalked back inside and over to the couch I lounged on. He was glistening with sweat from his earlier exertion as he took the mug from me and placed it to the side. Saying no words as he ripped the blanket from my lap. He grabbed my ankles before pulling me down the sofa causing my shirt to ride up, exposing me to him. A squeal of surprise parted my lips before it turned into a delighted giggle.

He smiled down at me, his eyes glittering with amusement. "You don't do that nearly enough," he'd said as he lowered onto me, making a place for himself between my legs.

"Do what?" I asked, feeling myself getting ready as I squirmed beneath him.

He kissed me softly as he rubbed himself against my naked sex. "Laugh," he murmured against my lips.

His statement had almost brought me out of my lust fog until he pulled away long enough to pull his hard length from his shorts.

When he descended onto me again, all thoughts of laughing vanished. He slid inside of me with ease. Pinning me down with his hips as he pumped into me with long slow strokes that had me begging for him to fuck me harder. Eventually, he had worked me into such a frenzy that I dug my nails into his back hoping to spur him on. He'd growled and pinned my hands to my sides before he sat up and gave me what I needed. The sounds of skin slapping together and harsh breathing filled the room.

I still marveled at how he played my body better than any man before him. When Damon fucked me, he showed me ecstasy I had only ever read about. Sure, I'd experienced orgasms before, but nothing like the total body and mind release he offered me. When we came together, it was like nothing else in this world existed.

After we were completely sated, we lay together nude on the sofa. I was curled up against his side, my head on his chest as I drew tiny circles along his belly with my finger.

His voice rumbled along my cheek. He had spoken in soft words as he shared bits about himself with me. He told me story after story about growing up in a big Latino family. Apparently, he had three siblings, two of them brothers, and his sister, Sofee, was the baby of the family.

I couldn't help but feel bad for the girl, growing up surrounded by men. But, it didn't take long for that thought to completely vanish as he told me his fondest memories of his childhood. From the sound of it, she was very well protected and loved by all of her brothers.

I didn't understand the pang of jealousy I felt for the female I'd never met. Maybe it was because I never had anyone to protect me. Maybe if I had, I wouldn't be the person I was today.

I shook off the thought as I listened to him talk more about his family. "You remind me a lot of *mi madre*," he said.

I jerked my head up and pinned him with a flabbergasted look. "Hasn't anyone ever told you that you're not supposed to say shit like that to the naked woman laying on top of you?" I questioned, arching my eyebrow.

He looked down at me with humor glittering in his eyes before he pinched my ass, eliciting a yelp from me. I couldn't help but laugh at him. He smiled down at me, showcasing that crooked grin again. I felt my breath catch in my chest, stopping my laughter.

"*Daría lo que fuera por escuchar esa risa*," he muttered as he swiped his thumb across my lower lip.

I shuddered before I turned away from the warm touch. *I would give anything to hear that laugh.* Why did he have to say things like that? Things that made me want more. I closed my eyes to ward off the burn I felt building there.

Damon placed his hand on my back and rubbed in firm strokes as if to soothe me. He cleared his throat before he spoke again. "I mean that my mom was the strongest woman I know. My dad left us shortly after Sofee was born, so my mom was forced to be a single mother for most of my life. That woman could make *El Diablo* bow down to her." I could hear the smile in his voice as he spoke fondly of her. "She doesn't take shit from anyone."

He threaded his fingers into my hair and gently tugged until I was forced to look up into his piercing gaze. "She's tough as nails but deep down she has a heart of gold. She makes people earn her love and affection and I always admired that."

As he spoke the words, I couldn't help but feel he was no longer speaking about his mother.

Before I could take a breath, his lips descended onto mine again for another all-encompassing kiss. He ate at my lips gently and I felt myself soften right along with my resolve. I don't know what was scarier—that he could break through all my barriers or that I was letting him.

I thought he would take me again but he had surprised me by coming up for air and laying my head back down on his chest. We both laid quiet after that and his deep breaths eventually lulled me to sleep.

When I had awoken, the sun was setting and I was alone. My body had been covered in a plush blanket and Boone lay on the floor next to me snoring softly.

I had sat up, in search of Damon, only to find a note folded neatly on the coffee table. It said that he didn't want to wake me but needed to get his car and go to the station to check up on some cases. That he would be back as soon as he could.

Not really knowing how long he had already been gone, I contemplated what I was to do by myself. I stood, wrapping the blanket tightly around my naked body before striding to the glass door that led to the front yard. Walking outside into the crisp evening air, I let the sounds of nature consume me. Everything was so clear out here, peaceful. The crickets had just started to chirp and the birds were quieting down for the night. Soon, stars would fill the sky and it would get so quiet you could hear the waves of the bay gently lap at the shore.

I padded on bare feet down to the dock. The feeling of cool grass between my toes was something I hadn't experienced since I was a child. A soft smile spread across my lips at the memory it brought forth of Kate and me running around her backyard, playing some imaginative children's game. I remembered the secrets we shared in the tree house her dad had built. Oh, if only I could go back to that time in our lives. That was something everyone would wish for, I'm sure. Back before this world ruined fragile hearts.

Boone trotted happily behind me with his tail wagging and tongue dangling from his jowl. I wasn't sure why the dog felt the need to stay close to me but it was comforting nonetheless.

I stood at the railing overlooking the water for long moments, contemplating jumping. I found myself becoming jealous of Damon at that moment, knowing it wasn't fair to be that way. He got to go to bed and wake up to this stunning view every day. This fresh oasis was all his and he didn't have to share it with anyone. So why did he choose to share it with someone like me?

He seemed so carefree all the time. How did someone grow up in the same world I did and come out on the other end so clean? Even worse, he saw humanity's dark side daily in his field of work. I couldn't understand how someone could see the underbelly of society so often and still be the same great person he was.

I tried to steer my thoughts away from the darkness that lurked inside of me. Maybe it was because I was by myself in this place or because it was so damn quiet, but I was having a hard time keeping my intrusive thoughts in check. I shook my head and dropped the blanket to my waist, hoping the chill air would wash away my haunted memories.

I knew Damon approached me the moment he stepped onto the dock. His solid footfall stalked me with determination. Soon his smell surrounded me, clearing my mind.

I sighed and leaned into him as he wrapped his arms around my middle. "*Hermosa*," he whispered along the crook of my neck.

I released a harsh breath and turned in his arms. I locked my lips with his and pushed my fingers into his hair, dropping the blanket to the ground. I moaned as he pushed his tongue in and plundered my eager mouth. His hands gripped my hips and lifted me up his body. I don't know if it was my attempt to ward off my treacherous memories or if my need for him was that great, but I wanted him at that moment enough to beg for it.

He saved me the embarrassment of just that when he placed my rear on the railing and spoke, "You looked lost in thought, *Roja*." His hushed tone raked across my kiss-swollen lips. "Let me help you get out of your head. I want you to experience what it genuinely means to submit to me. To fully trust me to take care of you and stop thinking for once. Will you let me do that for you?" he murmured.

Jill was already telling him to fuck himself, but Red nodded before sealing her lips to his once more.

Chapter Fifteen

Damon carried me back up to the house without pulling his lips from mine once. I still didn't know how he managed to not fall along the way.

When we made it back to his bedroom, he allowed me to slide down his length. I had to squash my moan of frustration as he released my lips and stepped out of my reach. I stood naked as I watched his hot gaze eat up the vision I created in front of him. He had a sultry grin on his lips as he fixed me with his stare at last. I felt my need for him spike as I waited for him to make his move.

He took a black hair tie off his wrist and handed it to me. "This is all you'll be wearing tonight. Normally, I like to see that wild red hair of yours splayed under you. But, I'm going to be using rope tonight and I don't want any of it to get tangled," he said with a wicked grin.

I took the outstretched band and quickly put my hair in a high pony. I don't know when I became so compliant, and if I stopped to think about it for too long I might not like the answer so I brushed off the thought.

I watched as he pulled his shirt up and over his head with hooded eyes. The vision he made standing with the low light streaming in the windows was what you would expect to see in a romantic movie. He was stunning.

He unbuttoned his jeans but left them on. The low-slung denim exposing the top of his thick cock was enough to make me wanton. It felt as if we stood like that for hours, just looking at one another before he finally spoke.

"Sit," was all he said.

I arched my eyebrow at him and promptly gave

him a view of my backside as I strode to the bed. I sat down and looked up at him as he approached me.

I watched as he opened the top drawer of his nightstand. Craning my neck, I tried to see what was inside before he closed it. He saved me the trouble of guessing when he pulled out a long length of red rope, a vibrator still in its package, a bottle of what looked like oil of some sort, and two shiny metal things, I wasn't quite sure what they were.

I frowned when I looked over the contents in his hands. Were those things in there for other women this whole time? An unfamiliar feeling of jealousy clouded my thoughts as I stared at him. My face must have said everything I was thinking because Damon grinned at me before speaking.

"I made a little pit stop at a certain adult store when I went to town," he murmured before placing all his effects on the nightstand, except for the rope.

My pulse jumped and my breathing picked up as I watched him unwind the rope with practiced hands. Was I actually going to allow this?

"I'm going to tie this around your torso. I'm also going to tie your hands and your feet to this bed. Then I'm going to put my jewelry on those pretty little tits before I use this vibrator on your sweet pussy and torment you for a while," he explained as he grabbed one of my hands.

I felt a jolt of panic run through my body before I tried to stand up. What the fuck was I doing? My chest heaved rapidly as my adrenaline spiked. I didn't know if I could go through with this.

Before I could stand completely up, Damon stopped me. "Talk to me," he said as he brushed my hair back. He settled his big hand on my lower back, helping me sit back on the side of the bed. He knelt between my legs and regarded me seriously.

"I don't know if I can do this. What if I want to get out?" I asked. "I feel like I can hardly breathe right now. Let alone when you tie me up so I can't get away." I exhaled in a rush. I felt like my heart was going to beat out of my chest.

Damon reached into his pocket and took out a pocket knife, placing it on the nightstand with the other items before he spoke.

"You say stop, and this all stops immediately. I'll cut you out and we'll talk." He regarded me seriously. "I would never hurt you, Red. I want to tie you up so you can focus solely on what I'm doing to you. My ropes make it feel like I am touching everything at once. It's for your pleasure," he promised.

I took a shaky breath and tried to calm my nervousness. I didn't know if it was my earlier dark thoughts that had me stopping to think or if Jill was popping back to the surface all of a sudden, but I was having a hard time with this. It was one thing when Damon held me down with his hands, it was completely different thinking about him tying me up. I couldn't easily get out of restraints if I didn't have the use of my hands.

I shook my head to clear my thoughts. I wasn't going to let Jill's past ruin what could be the best weekend of my life. Before I could talk myself further out of it, I leaned forward and slammed my lips onto Damon's. He groaned and grabbed the back of my head before leaning into me.

I reached my hand down into his unbuttoned jeans. Wrapping my hand around his hardness, I squeezed. He pulled his mouth from mine and looked down at what I was doing to him with a gasp on his lips. He pumped himself into my hand a few times before standing, taking my fun with him.

"If that's a yes, then I need you to sit still, Red," he said with a crooked grin.

I furrowed my brows and did as he asked, straightening my spine as he unfolded the rope. Then he went to work.

I watched him as he wound the rope around my body. He wove the long cords together with each pass. The design he made along my skin was simple, yet intricate. I would never be able to replicate it so easily.

He threaded the ropes between and around my breasts, thrusting them up in the air. Then wound around my torso in a corded fashion. It was stunning to look at. I found myself with an easy smile on my lips as I sat and watched him work. I had a sense of euphoria come over me as I felt the tug and pull of his bindings squeeze my body almost as if I was being hugged.

When he helped me stand I teetered the slightest bit before he pushed his body flush to mine. I looked up into his chocolate eyes lazily before he kissed me softly. I felt his hands slide the rope lower.

"Spread your legs for me," he rasped in a husky tone. It was almost as if he was getting the same sated feeling I was experiencing.

I did as he asked, spreading my legs as he took the ends of the rope and threaded them on either side of my sex. I gasped as the side of his hand rubbed across the throbbing flesh there.

When he pulled away to secure the rope, I nearly whimpered at the loss. I hadn't realized in my euphoric state that I'd become so deeply aroused.

He tied a knot, leaving a long tail on the rope before instructing me to lay on the bed with my feet where my head would normally go. My head nearly dangled off the foot of the bed. When I relaxed back I presented him with my wrists.

I watched him as he wrapped the silky rope around the offered limbs in practiced motions. He made sure the bindings weren't too tight before he looped the opposite end through the rings welded on the bedpost.

I nearly giggled to myself at my earlier thought. *Long-stem flowers ... I was an idiot.*

In no time, he had both my hands hoisted above my head and secured firmly. I squirmed under his gaze as he leisurely ate up the sight I made. I could feel myself becoming wetter with each passing moment that I watched him from my place on the bed.

He walked over to the bedside table and picked up the two shiny metal items. The bed dipped as he climbed between my spread legs. He lowered his head and flicked his tongue over my sensitive nipple, causing me to jerk. He continued to work me into a frenzy, going between each tightened peak with his strong sucking and nipping. I was growing needier and needier with each passing moment.

I closed my eyes and arched my back into him, needing more. Just when I thought he would latch onto me one more time, I felt something cold close over my right nipple. I looked down in time to see him close the clamp down over the tightened peak with a wicked grin.

I nearly screamed at the sensation of the clamp tightening against me. Just when I thought I couldn't take anymore, he slipped the other one on as well. This time I did scream as it clenched me.

"Oh!" I gasped heavily.

Satisfied with his work, Damon leaned back. "My jewelry and ropes look so good on you, baby," he murmured before he used his index finger to flick one of the clamps.

I jerked at the pain it created but then felt a flood

of arousal coat my inner thighs as it turned to heat.

Damon kissed each peak before he blazed a trail down my body. He alternated kisses and bites on his way down. Stopping at my belly button to dip his tongue in, making me clench at the sensation. I nearly came off the bed when he bit down onto my hip bone. The sting quickly turned to that hot pleasure I craved.

When he made it to the apex of my thighs, he spread me wide with his hands. I watched him as he stared down at my most intimate area. With a deep groan, he swiped his fingers down my clit and sank into my heat.

"This cunt is so fucking wet for me," he growled before he curled his fingers inside of me and latched onto my clit with his scorching mouth.

I screamed as he sucked hard. I dug my heels into the mattress on either side of him so I could grind up into his waiting mouth. Without the use of my arms to help, I could only rely on my trembling legs to get me where I wanted to be.

Damon slid lower and speared me with his tongue but it still wasn't enough. I whimpered and moaned as he made his way back up to my nub with lazy licks.

Before I wanted him to, he sat up. He continued to slowly fuck his fingers inside of me, adding another digit to my drenched channel. He reached up and flicked the other nipple clamp and curled his finger at the same time. I screamed and convulsed around him. A fresh flood of arousal coated his fingers.

"Fuck," he groaned as he continued his slow torture.

I was pulling on my restraints hard as I felt sweat break out along my brow. The need to come took over my body as I swirled my hips.

I nearly cried when he removed his fingers

altogether. I watched him as he slipped more rope around both of my ankles and secured them to the posts. He left the ropes a little looser between myself and the bed, and before I knew it I was spread wide and rendered completely immobile.

"If you don't fuck me soon, I'm going to combust," I gritted between clenched teeth. It was true. I could feel the deep throbbing in my pussy as he looked down at his handiwork.

Damon chuckled as he raised from the bed. He stood just out of arm's reach from me as he slowly shoved his jeans down the rest of the way. His long cock sprang free and I had to bite my lip to keep from whimpering. *When did I start begging to be fucked?*

He stared down at me before he grabbed the packaged vibrator and left the room. I watched his naked ass as he walked into the bathroom, removed it from its package, and thoroughly washed it. When he came back to me he stood at my head. His cock was so close to my mouth that I could almost taste it.

I heard the soft click of the vibe turning on before he leaned forward and placed it right on my sensitive clit. I pulled against my bindings as I had no choice but to feel all the high-powered vibrations coursing through me.

"If we're playing that game where I'm not allowed to come until you say, you better give your permission now. I'm not going to last long!" I moaned.

He chuckled again as he grabbed for the oil and rubbed it in his palm before grabbing his thick erection. He pumped himself from head to root a few times before coming back up to my head. I licked my lips as I watched him work himself.

"No, *Roja*. You're free to come anytime you want." He smiled down at me with a knowing grin.

I wasn't sure what he was playing at but I was

sure this was another game. But, before I could contemplate further, he grabbed me under my arms and pulled me closer to him. Now my head was hanging off the bed in the perfect position to suck his cock.

I waited eagerly for him to step a little closer. I wanted to taste him again so bad.

Just when I thought he was going to tease me all night, he finally came forward and held his cock out like a tasty treat. The sweet-tasting oil he rubbed on himself made it easy for him to push past my lips. He pushed in and pulled out in tiny passes as I sucked hard, trying to keep him in.

"That's my good girl," he growled as he looked down at me.

He leaned forward and ramped up the speed on the vibe and I moaned around his thickness. He moved the vibe up and down against me in slow passes. My orgasm was building inside of me tighter and tighter with each pass. My legs started to tremble as I felt the wave start to crash down on me. But before it could, Damon removed the vibe quickly. I cursed him around a mouthful of cock as he chuckled above me.

"Did you genuinely think it would be that easy, *Roja*?" He grinned down at me and I briefly thought about biting his dick.

He picked up the long excess of rope he left from my handmade corset and flicked it right on my clit with a solid thump. I screamed around him and he burrowed in further, touching the soft spot at the back of my throat.

He fucked my mouth in long passes as he flicked the rope against me harder and faster and tweaked my nipple clamps at the same time. He alternated flicking his rope against my thighs and my achy sex. The suspense of waiting to find out where the rope hit next made all the sensations that much more intense. I felt like he was everywhere at once. The noises coming from him, as I sucked as if my life depended on it, were almost enough to throw me over the edge.

He turned the vibe up another notch and placed it back on me again. Immediately I was on the cusp of orgasm. I whimpered and moaned around him as he picked his pace up further. He fucked my throat with punishing thrusts as he slid the vibe through my wetness wildly.

Each time I came close to the edge, he would remove the vibe and slow his thrusts. I felt like I was an exposed nerve. Like my body had been shoved into an inferno. I would make frustrated noises and he would start all over with his torture.

Eventually, he pulled out of my mouth and I panted wildly. He stepped back and I watched his chest heave heavily before he grabbed his thick cock and stroked himself all over again.

"I thought you wanted to come, baby?" He panted while grinning down at me.

I scowled at him. "Yeah, me too."

He smirked again before he came around the bed. He climbed up my body, settling himself against my entrance. He sat back and used his bulbous head to slap me right on the clit before he slammed into me.

"Then come for me," he demanded harshly before he pushed his thumb down onto my clit and swirled.

The wave that had been hanging over my head for so long now finally crashed down and my body convulsed under him. I screamed my release as he pounded into my body with brutal thrusts. The euphoria seemed to last forever as multiple orgasms washed over me in unyielding succession.

He groaned deep in his chest as he leaned forward to take my swollen lips. His pumping never stopped as he thrust his tongue into my eager mouth. He sucked my tongue and bit my lower lip before he grabbed hold of one of the nipple clamps. He ripped away from my lips to look down at me as he released the clamp. I felt the blood rush back to the sensitive nub all at once.

I howled at the liquid fire that seemed to lash my nipple before Damon lowered his mouth to the achy peak and sucked on it hard, easing the pain. Warmth flooded my body again as I climbed up that cliff once more. My legs trembled as he moved to the next nipple and released it from the clamp. Same as before, my body blazed until he soothed me with his hot mouth.

"Damon, please," I begged.

He groaned before grabbing the knife and cutting my limbs free.

"Touch me," he ordered harshly as he gave me his full weight.

I wrapped my arms and legs around him as he pumped into me fiercely. He ground down on my clitoris hard.

"*Ven ahora!*" he demanded harshly, and I did.

I gripped him roughly as my release washed over me in wave after wave of ecstasy. Damon slammed his mouth to mine and swallowed down my wails of pleasure. He fucked me fast and hard with fleshy smacks before he groaned long and deeply against me. His pumps slowed and became languid as he rubbed his release out inside of me. I could feel every hot jet flood my pussy.

He released my mouth and put his forehead against mine as shudders wracked our sweaty bodies. He didn't fully stop thrusting into me for long moments, letting me feel each aftershock leave his body.

Before I was ready, his weight lifted from me. He walked to the bathroom where I heard the water running shortly after. When he returned to me, he pulled me to him and picked me up from the bed as if I weighed nothing.

Once in the bathroom, he placed me in front of him, next to the running bath. He made quick work of releasing me from my bindings and before I knew it he was helping me into the hot water. He slid in behind me and cradled me to his body. I sighed as I relaxed my sore muscles with a lazy smile on my lips. He released my hair from its constraint and took his time washing it.

"That feels so good," I moaned as he massaged my scalp. I felt him harden again against my back before he spoke.

"Those little noises you make are going to get you fucked again, Red," he teased. I couldn't help the giggle that escaped me.

He continued to wash my body with soft strokes of his hands, spending extra time on my intimate areas. I moaned as he rubbed the knots out of my shoulders. By the time he was done, my eyes were heavy and I was completely relaxed. I had never felt so pampered in my life.

When the water was cold, we reluctantly raised from the tub. Damon dried me with a soft towel before drying himself. My chest felt heavy after the way he took care of me.

He carried me into the bedroom and laid me down under the blankets. I was having a hard time keeping my eyes open as he pressed his naked body against mine. He pulled me tightly to him and kissed my neck. I grinned as I closed my eyes and dozed off.

Chapter Sixteen

"Come with me, you fucking bitch." Tom's harsh tone hisses against my ear as I feel the cold metallic press of his gun against my temple.

Panic slithers down my spine as I look at my best friend. Needing her help but wanting her to get away at the same time. Terror grips my throat as the gun is pointed her way. Hot tears leak from my eyes as Tom squeezes me too tightly.

Now, I'm running for my life. Kate's hand grips mine as we make our mad dash for escape.

Almost there.

Pain rips through my body as a bullet burns through my shoulder. Dark-red blood blooms across my chest before I collapse. Tom stands over me. His hateful gray eyes turn blue within a blink.

Musty sheets cling to my sweat-soaked skin. My panicked eyes fly all around me as I try to move. Nothing works. I'm a prisoner in my own body. Pain courses between my legs as my air is cut off. His hand covers my mouth and nose. "I can't breathe!" *I scream internally.*

"You asked for this." Jason's harsh words rake across my skin like a million fire ants.

No! No! No!

He pushes harder on my mouth and holds my wrists so tight I think I'm going to break soon. I can taste hot tears clogging my throat as I whimper. He pushes into me, ripping and tearing as he takes his pleasure.

"You're going to be okay!" Damon roars over me, trying to stop the blood from coming out of my chest.

White-hot pain lashes my body as he pushes against the wound.

"I've wanted you for so long, beautiful," Jason grits above me as he slams into me over and over again.

"Don't do this to me, Jill. Stay awake!" Damon shouts as I close my eyes again.

"I finally fucked Jill Brookes." Jason leers down at my abused form.

"You deserve all of it. You deserve every minute of this!" my own reflection yells at me from the mirror I glare at.

Surrounded by my vomit and tears, I scream.
My own hateful gaze scowls back at me, I scream.
A bullet rips through my shoulder, I scream.
Chocolate eyes begging me to stay, I scream.

****

"Jill!" Damon yelled down at me as he shook me from my nightmare.

My throat was raw as I whimpered and came to. My arms held firm in Damon's clasped hands like he was stopping me from hitting him. I kicked wildly and tried to get away from him.

"Let me go!" I screamed, tears streaming down my face, clogging my throat.

Damon released me with worry in his eyes. I scrambled away from him and fell off the bed, landing on my hip with a hard thud. I cried out at the pain that radiated through me before I scooted away from the bed. I watched as Damon lunged out of bed in his rush to get to me.

"Stay away from me!" I wailed as I scrambled into the bathroom before slamming the door and locking it. I crawled to the toilet before I emptied the contents of my stomach. I heaved and sobbed, breathing hard.

"Jill!" Damon pounded at the door. "Baby, let me in so I can help you," he begged.

I sobbed louder as I tried to catch my breath. I

sucked in deep, sharp breaths as my lips quivered. I shook violently as the last of my dream started to release its death grip on me.

I pushed away from the toilet and hugged my knees as I leaned against the cool tub. Rocking back and forth, I tried to calm my racing heart.

"Jill, please," Damon begged from the door again.

Guilt panged through me as I realized what I'd done. I hit the back of my head against the tub over and over as I tried to clear the thoughts racing through my mind.

"You're not there. You're not there. You're not there," I whispered to myself.

I pushed the hair out of my eyes as I stared at the door. Squeezing my eyes shut at the embarrassment that flooded me.

"Good job, Jill," I murmured to myself.

"I'm about to knock down the door, Jill. I'm not good at being shut out," Damon's desperate voice sounded from the other side of the door.

I couldn't leave him out there much longer. I stood on shaky legs before I made my way to the door. I fortified myself by leaning my head against the cool wood for a moment, listening to him on the other side. Taking a deep shaky breath, I unlocked the door.

I barely got out of the way in time before Damon thrust the door open and rushed me. His hands were everywhere at once as he looked me over. He rubbed my arms, my back, and my sore hip before he cupped the back of my head, drawing my gaze to his.

"Are you okay?" he asked in a hushed tone.

I nodded my head and tried to smile. He searched my eyes and shook his head before pulling me to him. He hugged me tightly against him and kissed the top of my head. I clinched my arms around him as I sighed.

"Tell me about it," he said softly into my hair.

The last thing I wanted to do was talk about it. Just thinking about it made me feel like the cold fingers of the dream were starting to latch back onto me. I clenched my eyes shut and willed it away. I wanted to erase it from my mind. What I needed was a distraction.

I pressed myself further into him and ran my hands down to his ass. I rubbed him up and down his naked back and behind. Feeling him harden against my belly, I pulled away and sank to my knees. I grabbed him firmly and pulled him past my lips in a hurried movement.

Damon groaned before pulling away from me. I pushed back forward as he slid from my lips, desperate to get him back in my mouth. I had no choice but to stop as he threaded his fingers in my hair and gently tugged me away from him.

"Jill, I need you to talk to me," he grumbled above me.

I shook my head. I couldn't relive that dream again.

"Please," I begged and watched as his eyes softened but he didn't release my hair. I rubbed my hands up his thighs and grabbed him firmly. I pumped him as I held eye contact.

"Please," I begged again.

He seemed to realize that I needed a distraction as he closed his eyes and straightened, releasing my hair as permission. I leaned back in eagerly and sucked him past my lips again. I flicked my tongue against the underside of his cock, eliciting a long, tortured groan from him.

He pushed my hair out of my face and held it at the back of my head, using his fist as a ponytail holder as I bobbed my head up and down his shaft. I licked and sucked my way down his hard length, pulling him deeper and deeper with each pass.

"Fuck," he groaned above me as his fist tightened on my hair, lighting up my scalp.

I could taste his release rising rapidly and I wanted nothing more than to swallow him down along with my emotions. I pushed him past my threshold and gagged as he touched the back of my throat. I held him there and looked up at him. His hooded eyes, ajar mouth, and heaving chest were enough to spur me on.

I pulled my mouth off to his head only to tunnel him back down as far as I could. When he touched the back of my throat that time, I swallowed around him. He jerked in my mouth before he ripped himself away from me. Before I could protest, he pulled me up and into his arms. He slid into me easily as he held me to his front. He used the globes of my ass to move me up and down his length in powerful movements.

I threw my head back as he sucked at my neck. Each suck and lick from his hot mouth sent rapid shivers down my spine. Moaning loudly as each movement he made rubbed against my swollen clit with his pelvis.

He walked us back into the bedroom and sat on the bed, never pulling out of me. I straddled his hips as he laid back and moved us further up the bed, until he was leaning against the pillows, propping himself up to face me.

"Ride me," he ordered gruffly. He didn't have to tell me twice.

I rose up his shaft to where he almost slipped out before I descended onto him again. This position made him go deeper and I felt every long, thick inch of his cock. He grabbed hold of my thighs right where they met my pussy and squeezed me.

"Take what you need from me now, but you will

tell me what haunts that beautiful mind, Jill," he rasped before he thrust up into me.

I realized in that moment that he wasn't dominating me like he usually did. He knew how much I needed to have some semblance of control and he gave it to me willingly. I was just too damn stubborn to let myself feel the full reality of his offering. I ignored that he was basically telling me, begging me to take all of him, body and soul, and not just sexually.

I shook off the emotion I felt flooding my throat as I rode him. My pace picked up as he helped me move atop him. His breathing grew heavy before he thickened inside of me. He was close. He sat up fully and brought my breasts to his scorching mouth, nipping at me. We moved together as I felt myself tighten around him.

"Come with me," I panted as I held him to my breast. "Bite me, please!" I wailed, begging for more.

He groaned against me before he bit down on my tightened peak, pinching the other one with the same pressure. That was all it took as I went careening off the cliff and he followed after me. We both shook with aftershocks as he pulled me to him and laid down with me still on top.

I could no longer hold off my emotions that made a surge to the top at that moment. My body trembled as I was wracked with silent sobs. My throat burned and I squeezed my eyes shut to stop the tears that were already escaping.

Damon rubbed my back in firm strokes and let me cry. I should have been able to shove everything down after spending my body as I did, but I couldn't. I cried for the old Jill I used to be before Jason. I cried for the Jill right after it happened, broken and ruined. I cried for yesterday's Jill that wouldn't be able to go back to her old ways.

I was stupid to think I could pretend for a weekend and then go back to reality as if nothing had happened. Damon had proved that in just one day he could break down all those walls I built for my own protection.

My dream had proved that I would never be able to escape my past no matter how much I wanted to be someone else. The reality was that Red didn't exist, Jill was all I was. That thought shouldn't have hurt like it did.

I sobbed for what felt like an hour as Damon rubbed my back, letting me release what I needed to. When I finally dried up, I was sure my face was a puffy red mess. I tried to roll off him but he held me firm.

"Talk to me, *Roja*," he begged in a soothing voice. I kept my head to the side so he couldn't see my face as I finally spoke.

"It was just a bad dream," I answered, hoping he would take that and drop the subject. I should've known he wouldn't.

He rolled us so he was on top of me. He stared down at me with intense eyes.

"Bullshit," he said in a harsh tone. "I've seen bad dreams before and this was something entirely different. You kept saying 'No!' and you were hitting anything you could get your hands on. Jill, you were screaming bloody murder," he finished.

I flushed with new irrational anger from underneath him. Why couldn't he just leave it alone?

"I don't want to talk about it. Why do you feel the need to push me? If I didn't offer up the information willingly, then obviously I didn't feel the need to fucking discuss it. You're not my goddamn boyfriend so why do you even care? Get off me!" I yelled up at him.

I knew I was being cruel but I didn't give a shit.

After the emotion that was pulled from me because of the dream, I was feeling way too raw and I needed to lash out.

Hurt flashed in his eyes before he quickly snuffed out the emotion. He scowled down at me before he lifted himself. I felt a pang of regret as he took his heat with him.

"You're right, I'm not your boyfriend, but that doesn't stop me from caring. You might not be in tune with your feelings, Jill, but if you haven't noticed I have very strong inclinations toward you. But you're too goddamn stubborn to let anyone love you the way you deserve," he admitted, and I flinched as if he struck me.

He laughed but it held no humor. "For fuck's sake, I've never even brought another woman to my home before, let alone stayed the night with one. You may not have meant to, but you've dug your claws in so deep that I can't get them out. You're all I think about every fucking day and here you are ready to run every time this gets a little too real. I just want you to be real with me!" he finished as he towered above me.

My anger rose swiftly and I was out of the bed and in his face before he could blink. Both of us were unwilling to back down from one another.

"You want real?" I gritted between clenched teeth.

"That's what I said," he seethed

"Fine!" I exclaimed. "You want to know what I dream about? Why I don't let anyone in? You want to know why I fuck so many different men?" His jaw clenched as I mentioned my other sexual conquests. My chest heaved as my adrenaline spiked. "I dream about my past. I dream about getting shot by some crazy motherfucker and waking to you pressing on my chest! But then that morphs into something much, much worse." I couldn't stop myself now. "One minute, Tom's standing above me and the next there's someone on top of me, holding me down while I fight to breathe. I have no choice but to lay there as he fucks me against my will!" My voice shook as I finally came clean.

Damon flinched as if I struck him before he visibly paled. I swallowed hard before I continued. I took another step toward him as I held his gaze.

"You want me to talk about how he drugged me and forced me to take everything he had to give. How he bruised and ripped me wide open. He took it all," I admitted as I held my arms out wide with a cruel smile on my lips. "He didn't ask and he wasn't gentle. He called me his dirty little whore and said I loved what he gave me. Said that I asked for it." My voice broke.

Damon took a step back and I followed. Crowding him.

"Is that what you wanted to hear? Is that real enough for you? You want to know why I don't do relationships? It's because I don't deserve them. Don't you get that yet? You don't want me! I'm dirty, used up, ruined, stained, tainted!" I screamed at him, chest heaving.

Damon stared at me like he had seen a ghost. He ran a shaking hand through his hair in a frustrated motion before his eyes hardened.

"Who?" he asked with a hard voice.

I laughed but it was a cruel sound. "As if it matters. What's done is done, Damon. You can't change the past."

"A name, Jill," he demanded, his voice deadly calm.

"Why?" I asked, deflated. I sat back down on the bed, completely spent.

He smiled at me but it was a menacing look. "So

I can kill him," he gritted out and I flinched at his answer. He sounded so serious.

I sighed as I looked out the window at the rising sun. My anger was gone and I was left feeling numb. I didn't want to do this anymore. I wanted to go home so I could forget that I ever tried being someone else in the first place.

Damon knelt before me and cupped my chin, forcing me to look at him. New tears burned my eyes as I met his gaze. His eyes held no pity but empathy instead. He kissed me softly before bringing me to him and hugging me.

"I would never call you tainted, Jill. Just because that fucker did something so foul doesn't mean you're the dirty one. He is, baby." He pulled away so he could look at me once again. "What he did to you would never make me not want you." He paused. "There's nothing in the world that would make me not want you," he whispered before he took my mouth again.

This time he laid me back and ascended on top of me. He made a place for himself between my legs and I sighed against him as I wrapped my arms around him.

"Let me love you," he begged against my lips as his hardness prodded my entrance. I moaned and nodded my head as tears fell down my face.

I let Damon make love to me for the first time that morning. He loved me softly and whispered how brave I was and how proud he was of me to share my past with him. After we both found our bliss, he cradled me to his body as he spoke sweet nothings in Spanish.

I let him comfort me for himself more than for me. He needed the assurance that I was with him more now than ever. I laid there and accepted what he gave me but I could feel all the walls he ripped down slowly repairing themselves.

I knew I would need to get out as soon as I could. I was a fool for ever thinking I could just enjoy myself and be someone else for even a weekend. I was born Jill Brookes and I would always be Jill Brookes, no matter how much it hurt to be just that.

Damon might think he had strong feelings for me but it would only be proven later down the line that he didn't truly want me. I wasn't what he needed at all and that fact would eventually come to light.

But, I laid there while he spoke those sweet nothings to me. I let myself close my eyes and enjoy my last moments with Damon Santos. I could let myself pretend for just a little while longer that this was right and I was where I was supposed to be.

I think it was a perverted trick of my mind when I thought I heard him say the words most women would kill to hear whispered to them. Thinking that he truly said, *"Eres mi amor,"* was a cruel way my psyche chose to punish me at that moment.

Chapter Seventeen

I stared down at my phone from the back seat as the car bounced slightly from a pothole in the road. I checked my email as I tried not to think about the man I left in bed as I fled his house like my ass was on fire.

I'd laid there in his arms while the early dawn light trickled in the large windows. I'd let myself feel his comfort for long moments until I felt his breathing become even as sleep took him once more. I hadn't shed any more tears as I crawled out of his embrace and gathered my things in silence. I padded to the living room where I had gotten dressed in Friday's clothing, grabbed my gym bag, and patted Boone on the head before I quietly slipped out the front door.

I ignored the heart-wrenching feeling of wrongness as I jogged down the very walking path Damon had taken me on that first night. I neglected the feeling of guilt that pressed down on me as I ordered an Uber to pick me up from the same park I'd felt so peaceful at only two nights ago. I hadn't spared another last glance toward the home where I first got to be someone else as I climbed in the back of that car and gave the driver my address.

I tried not to giggle hysterically at the ridiculousness of it all. The great Jill Brookes, reduced to sneaking out of a man's house like some dirty little secret. The irony of the whole situation was not lost on me.

I tried to calm my racing thoughts as I scrolled through the mass amounts of unread emails. I read and reread the same damn email five times before I finally gave up and threw my phone into the seat next to me with a frustrated huff. No matter how many times I tried,

I couldn't get my mind off Damon.

Was he awake yet? How long would it take him to realize that I'd left him? I wondered if he would be furious enough to say the hell with me. Honestly, it would be best. So why did the thought make my chest hurt?

I wasn't so oblivious to the fact that Damon had incited feelings in me I had never felt before. He had awoken something deep inside of me. It was almost sad how fast it had happened. It felt as though he'd burrowed his way under my skin and it would take a miracle to remove him.

I huffed loudly and raked my hand down my face in irritation. Trying to ignore the look of confusion from my driver as I was brought closer and closer to my house. I was being entirely ridiculous. I'd only known Damon for a couple of months. It shouldn't be this hard to forget about him and move on with life as if I'd never met him.

My driver turned on my street as soon as I heard a ding from my phone. My heart lurched in my chest at the sound. I grabbed the device quickly and then scolded myself internally as I placed it on my lap. Stilling my rapidly beating heart, I tried to calm myself.

I covered my mouth to smother the erratic giggle that escaped. I caught the eye of my driver in the rearview mirror and almost giggled again at the look she shot me. She must bet that I was an absolute loon.

She pulled up to the curb outside my house and I thanked her quickly before exiting the vehicle. I pulled my keys from my bag and unlocked the front door. Closing it behind me, I slid to the ground and sat with my back to it. Finally, I gathered the courage to look at my phone and released a breath I hadn't known I was holding.

My heart finally calmed when I saw a text waiting from Kate.

I didn't understand the flare of disappointment that coursed through my body. I had wanted this. I'd left this morning to cut all ties before things got any more serious. And now I felt disappointed because the man I walked out on hadn't texted me? I was a different kind of crazy.

Rather than text her back and tell her what I was up to, I decided to call her instead. She picked up on the second ring.

"Heath, stop it!" Kate's delighted laughter rang out across the line. "It's Jill, I'll be right back..." Kate's muffled voice came over the line and I hid my smile for my bestie behind my hand.

I could almost hear Heath's response in the background as Kate walked out of arm's reach.

"Please tell me I wasn't interrupting something? I hope you still have clothes on." I giggled.

Kate's laugh was genuine. I could almost see her smile over the line. "Nothing I can't finish in a few minutes! How's your weekend going?" she asked, completely ignoring my inquiry about her state of dress.

My smile wavered as I stalled for an answer. What was I supposed to say? *"My weekend was full of the hottest sex of my life and I'm dying to tell you about it!"*

"It's going." I paused. "Are you busy today? I need to get out of this house and do some shopping," I said. I needed a distraction before I got too far lost in my own thoughts.

"That sounds like a blast to me! Lindsey's going to a party later tonight so she was wanting to get a new outfit anyway. Mind if she tags along? Maybe I can give Em a call too?" Kate asked.

I stood and placed my bag on the entry table, not caring to place it on its hook. I glanced around my entryway. *Where was Fiona? She always ran to greet me when I came home.*

"Sounds like a plan to me. Let's meet for brunch first, I need a drink." I kicked my shoes off and left them where they lay before heading to my bedroom. Maybe the cat didn't hear me as I came in and was hiding. "What time do you want to mee–"

Then the thought struck me. "Shit, would you mind picking me up? I left my rental at the Krav Maga studio I went to on Friday." Why didn't I have the Uber take me to the damn car instead of my house?

Kate paused on the line. "Sure, but you're gonna need to tell me why you left your car behind in the first place," she said suspiciously.

I stood at the foot of my bed with a pause. That was weird. I could have sworn I made my bed before I left the house on Friday. But, as I looked at the rumpled blankets and thrown-about pillows, I wondered if my sleep-deprived brain had been playing tricks on me again.

I stared down at the bed in confusion. Not once in the last thirty-something years had I forgotten to make my bed. I liked the way it looked when it was neatly assembled. Even if I was just going to get in it again that night and mess it up, I always, always made it every morning.

"Jill? Are you there?" Kate's worried tone came across the line again, jarring me back to the conversation.

"Yea–yeah, sorry. I must have fazed out for a second. What did you say?" I mumbled.

"I said, how about I pick you up in an hour?" Kate paused again. "Are you okay? You seem ... off."

I shook my head and started to head to the

bathroom with a backward glance at my bed. I guess I must have forgotten to make it.

I started the hot water in my shower as I spoke. "Yeah, I'm fine. I'm going to shower and get ready. I'll see you in an hour."

We hung up and I went about showering and getting ready for brunch. I scrubbed my body, all while trying not to think about the way Damon had washed me last night. Right when I felt myself start to get hot and needy, I flipped the water to cold and nearly screamed. I finished my shower quickly and tried to squash the rest of my thoughts of crooked grins and olive skin.

I dressed in a white cotton thong and matching mesh bra. I chose a short white ruffle wrap dress with flowy sleeves, pairing it with a pair of brown open-toed booties and the matching purse. I pulled my hair up in a stylish messy bun and applied a light gloss to my lips, forgoing all other makeup.

For the first time in a long time, when I looked in the mirror I didn't see someone who hated me staring back. The woman in the mirror looked like she was well-rested and flush with youthful energy. She almost looked happy. Which was ridiculous given I had just left the only man that had ever made me feel that way only hours before.

I didn't have time to dwell on the fact that I didn't recognize the woman in front of me, as I heard a horn beep from the driveway. I grabbed my phone and purse before I rushed out the door to meet my best friend.

After climbing into the front seat of Kate's car, I rushed to give her a quick hug. When she pulled away from me, she gave me a questioning look.

"What?" I asked, no longer able to stand the silence.

She shook her head before putting the car in

"reverse" and backing out of my driveway. She glanced at me again. "You just look … different. What happened this weekend?" she asked.

I offered her a small smile, took a deep breath, and spilled my guts.

****

"So let me get this straight," Kate said as she put her mimosa back onto the white-clothed table we were sitting at. We had chosen one of those upscale restaurants that specialized in brunch. Bottomless mimosas being one of their finer attributes.

"Damon turns up at your new Krav Maga class, takes you back to his gorgeous home, fucks your brains out for almost two days straight, and then you sneak out of his house after rehashing your past?" she finished with a long whistle. "Damn, girl, you work fast," she said with a knowing smile.

I was glad when Kate and I were the first to show up to brunch, so I had plenty of time to relive every dirty detail of my weekend with Damon. Lindsey knew a little about my past, but not enough that I felt comfortable openly talking about it around her. And, it's not that I didn't like or trust Emily, but our friendship was still new and I didn't want to drop that bombshell on something so fresh.

I'd sat with Kate and downed my first mimosa before she had even taken a sip of hers. I told her everything from jumping into the bay with Damon, to telling him about Jason after my nightmare. I knew Kate would be honest with me no matter what, and that's what I needed right now more than anything. I put my elbows on the table and let my head fall into my hands.

"For the first time in my life, I have no idea what I'm going to do, Kate." I swallowed hard as I looked back up at my friend. "You know as well as I do that I've never wanted more than just a good time. But now all of a sudden, Mr. Big Cock Detective wedges his way into my life and I can't help but want more," I admitted a little too loudly. "I swear the guy whips out that monster and I lose all brain function," I mumbled.

Kate snorted as the older lady at the table next to us gasped at my crude words. I rolled my eyes as I grabbed my drink. Looking over at the pearl-grasping woman, I saluted her with my champagne flute.

"Men, am I right?" I said before I tilted my glass to my lips. I downed half the contents of my second glass before Kate pushed the drink down away from my lips with a gleeful laugh.

"All right, slow down there, Mötley Crüe. You haven't had anything to eat yet and I don't want you to get all drunky on me before noon on a Sunday," she said with a humorous grin.

I gasped as I handed her the glass. "You see! I never drink excessively, but I was totally going to drink excessively!" I exclaimed. "Clearly, that man has made me lose my mind. This morning I didn't even bother to put my purse on its hook. I didn't put my shoes up where they belong either, Kate! My shoes!" I screeched.

Kate's face flushed bright red as she bit her bottom lip to keep from laughing at me. I looked around to see that I had drawn the attention of not only the pearl-grasper, but also two other tables were now openly gawking at me.

I scowled over at all of them. "What? Haven't you ever seen a mental breakdown at brunch before?" I nearly shouted.

Kate grabbed my hand, bringing my attention back to her. "I know this is going to be hard for you to hear, but maybe this is good for you, Jill," she offered with a small smile.

I frowned at her in confusion. "How could this be good for me? You know better than anyone else that I need control in my life so I don't fly off the fucking rails," I admitted.

"Yeah? And how's that going for you so far?" I flinched as Kate surprised me with the question.

I sat back in my seat, completely defeated. I covered my eyes with my hand and pinched the bridge of my nose where a sharp ache was forming. How did I get here? Just four months ago I had my shit together. My career was thriving, I was happy to have my best friend living so close, my sex life was sporadic at best but I was fine with it. I had complete control over everything in my life. And now? Now, everything felt like it was unraveling. I shook my head as I took a deep breath and held it.

I heard Kate get up from her chair and take the one next to me. I didn't fight her as she brought her arms around me and rubbed my back in reassuring strokes. I leaned into her, accepting her comfort.

"I know it doesn't feel like it right now, but this is good for you, babe. You might have thought your life was perfect before Damon came into it, but I can tell you from an outsider's standpoint, it wasn't." Kate's hushed tone raked over me as she pulled away in favor of holding my hands. I looked down at our hands before releasing my breath in a harsh puff. Kate continued.

"I could tell you've been unhappy for quite some time now, Jill. You don't think I notice the look in your eyes when you watch Heath, Reid, and me together? I see you, Jill. I know you crave more and you're just too damn stubborn to take it for yourself." She paused to catch my eyes. I stared back at her. "What worked for you all those years ago served its purpose when you needed it most. But, maybe as you've grown and healed little by little, so have your needs. Maybe you don't need to clutch onto your sense of control so tightly anymore. Maybe it's time to hand the reins over to someone else for a change. To let *him* take care of you instead of you doing it on your own."

I felt the all too familiar burn at the back of my eyes as she finished. "What if…" I started, sucking in a shaky breath. "What if I'm too scared to let him in?" I sniffled, refusing to cry.

Kate smiled at me before she squeezed my hands reassuringly. "Being scared just means that you're going after something worth losing. Being afraid doesn't mean you're weak, babe. It means you're strong enough to fight for yourself, for your happiness."

I thought about fighting for Damon to be in my life. The thought of letting him love me the way he wanted, unleashed that new warm feeling in my stomach. For once in my life, I needed to let myself feel something more than my own strong will to have everything perfect. I wanted to know what it felt like to be adored, to be taken care of. And I knew without a shadow of a doubt, Damon would do all of those things for me. That is, if I hadn't fucked it up by leaving him this morning.

I choked around a hiccup as I hugged my best friend fiercely. She was right. I needed to fight for my own happiness for once in my life. Instead of trying to control an inevitable outcome, I needed to steer my life in another direction. To loosen my grip on my control and let someone else in for a change. Even if it scared the hell out of me.

"When did you get so smart?" I mumbled into Kate's shoulder before we broke apart.

She chuckled before responding. "Becoming sexually liberated will unlock parts of your mind you didn't even know existed." She smiled as I laughed.

"But, don't tell Reid I said that. He would never let me live it down. I can hear him now. *'You get smarter each time we fuck because I fill you up with my intelligence.'* " Her impression of one of her husbands was spot on.

The pearl-grasper from the next table gasped again and we both dissolved into a fit of laughter.

I was wiping the tears from my eyes when I spotted Lyns and Emily walking to our table with big grins.

"Looks like we missed quite the conversation," Emily remarked as she took her seat next to Kate. Lyns embraced her mom and then me before sitting.

"Care to tell us what's with the smiles?" She grinned at me as she picked up her glass of OJ.

"Oh, we were just talking about a guy I've been seeing," I offered. Her eyes went wide before I gave Kate a knowing wink. I turned to both the newcomers and told them all about my detective.

Chapter Eighteen

After brunch and shopping, Kate drove me downtown to pick up my rental. When we hugged goodbye I promised to text her with any updates on the Damon front. I decided I would give it a few days before I went to him. I think we both needed time to cool off after the things that were disclosed this weekend.

Even though I decided I'd give this whole relationship thing a shot, that didn't mean Damon would still want me. After all, my original thinking of him not wanting me due to my past still held firm in my mind. No matter what Kate and I had talked about, it would still be hard to convince myself that I was good enough for him. Years of self-doubt didn't just vanish in one day, unfortunately.

It was late afternoon as I drove home. We four girls had walked from shop to shop, spending indecent amounts of money as we went. I bought a few new outfits at a couple of designer stores and of course the shoes to match. Emily had shopped at a few of the designer stores as well. That girl could keep up with my shopping addiction.

I found myself half jealous that she looked glamorous in almost everything she tried on. She was painstakingly gorgeous, with her long, curly, strawberry-blonde hair that framed her heart-shaped face and the cutest freckles that spanned under her hazel eyes. She was taller than all of us but she held it with a confidence that most would kill for. Her tall frame was evened out with a thick hourglass figure, ample breasts, and an ass I'd seen many try to replicate with surgery. It was a surprise to learn she was still single, but if I had to guess, that was a conscious choice on her part.

She had kept up with me at every designer store. When some people would balk at the sticker price, Emily just laid down a shiny black credit card. At one point, Lindsey had nearly fainted when the sales associate had given her the price. Emily had just smiled at Lindsey and handed over her card without even blinking.

She admitted later that her family was uber-rich and it was her life's mission to blow through that money as fast as possible.

"When I divorced Chris, most of my family took his side. He was from another prominent family in upstate New York," she had offered. "My mother had told me over and over that I would never be able to do better than Chris." She laughed but it held no humor. "In the end, most of them just saw the dollar sign that marriage brought. They didn't give a shit how he treated me."

She had gotten a dim look in her eyes at the mention of her ex but said nothing further about him or her marriage. She shook her head as if to shake off her thoughts before smiling brightly back at me. "So, fuck 'um. I'm going to blow as much of their dirty money as I can before they stop paying the bill." She beamed.

I lifted my complimentary glass of champagne those stores offer you in hopes that you spend lots of money. "I'll drink to that!" I laughed with her as we clinked glasses.

I got the impression she didn't like to talk about her past so we dropped the subject after that. Maybe one day we could both share our stories with one another and help each other heal a little further.

When we were done at the designer stores, we moved on to the smaller posh boutiques that lined the busy street we walked along. Lindsey and Kate took turns trying things on while Emily and I sat and chatted.

All that was missing from our shopping excursion was one of those cheesy 80s songs for a musical montage.

Kate had picked out some new dresses that she was guaranteeing the boys would absolutely "eat up." I felt myself flush at the thought. *Oh, to be a fly on that wall just once.* What could I say? I was a pervert most of the time.

Lindsey picked out a short little black dress that fit her like a glove for her party tonight. I tried not to cringe when she said she would wear her red Converse sneakers to complete the outfit. She was definitely her mother's daughter.

If her obvious choice for comfort over fashion wasn't enough to tell you who spawned her, she was built just like her mother too, meaning she had curves for days. Most people would say the two were on the thicker side but they carried it so well.

"So, where is this party of yours tonight, Lyns?" I'd asked her.

She'd rolled her eyes before she looked at me in the mirror. "Some stupid frat house. Alpha Sigma something-or-other. I don't know the name. My roommate has been begging me to go with her almost every weekend since school started back up this fall and I keep saying no. I figured I needed to try and be a good friend for once," she remarked as she returned to inspecting her dress.

I gave her a tight smile as I tried to squash the turmoil rolling around in my gut. I always knew that when Lindsey went to college there would be parties with stupid boys and even stupider decisions. I just had to hope that Lyns was smart enough not to put herself in a bad situation.

"So…" I cleared my throat. "You know to keep your phone on at all times, right? Call me or your mom if you need anything." I stared at her with a serious gaze in the mirror.

Lindsey looked up and met me with a playful grin. "Well, obviously, Aunt Jill." She winked at me before continuing to look at herself in the mirror. "I also know not to drink and drive and to call you guys if I need a ride," she added.

If only that was all I worried about.

"Always get your own drink, and never take your eyes off of it," I blurted

Lyns turned around to face me then. "I know," was all she said with confusion laced in her voice.

I'd glanced at Kate and she offered me a reassuring smile. I needed to calm down. Lindsey wasn't me. She was way smarter than me. She wouldn't put herself in the same situation I had put myself in all those years ago.

Our conversation still lingered on my mind as I pulled onto my road. I tried to shake it off and move my mind to other things, like what I was going to say to Damon. That was, if he even wanted to see me again. I'm sure it was a big ego hit to have the woman you've been fucking sneak out of your house before the sun had risen.

I pulled into my driveway as I contemplated sending him a text. Was that too impersonal? Maybe I should drive out to his cabin and see if he was home. What would I even say? *"Sorry I fucked you and then dipped out. Shit got real and I couldn't deal because I have trust issues."*

Honestly, that wasn't half bad.

I shut the car off and started to open the door when I heard screeching tires as they barreled my way. Looking in the rearview mirror I watched as a familiar black car pulled into my driveway and slammed into "park" inches away from my bumper. Well, there went my plan to take my time to figure out what to say. Damon was here and he looked pissed off.

I exited the car and stood by as I watched my bull of a man quickly walk toward me. His hair was free of any constraint and flowed easily behind him as he rushed me. His eyes held all the anger that I knew was directed at me. A lesser female would have flinched away from that look, but I stood my ground. Crossing my arms over my chest and widening my stance, I readied myself to take on that hot Latino anger.

"Look, I know you're upset right now, but—" I started before Damon cut me off.

"Shut up, Jill," he gritted out before he crashed into me and sealed his lips to mine.

My breath left me in a rush and ended in a moan as he shoved me against the car. He thrust his tongue past my lips as he picked me up. I wrapped my legs around his lean waist as he ground his thick erection against my sex. He pressed me tightly between his body and the car so his hands were free to roam as my dress rode up around my hips.

He sucked and nipped at my lips as he feasted from my mouth. I pushed my hands into his velvety locks and tugged him harder against me. He groaned deep in his chest as he released my mouth to travel further south. He kissed his way roughly down my jaw, coming to my neck where he nipped me hard enough to elect a hiss from between my teeth.

He pushed me harder against the side of the car before he searched for the sash of my dress. Once he found it he tugged hard, releasing the knot and exposing me to his hungry mouth. He blazed a trail down my neck to my shoulder before biting me once more. This time I moaned at the pain before he eased the ache with his tongue.

His fingers played with the band of my thong before dipping in. I shuddered as he breached my entrance and thrust inside of me. My arousal made it easy for him to slip in and out. He groaned against me before pulling his mouth off me. He grabbed my throat with his other hand and squeezed, forcing me to look at him.

"Do you know how fucking crazy you make me?" he growled before he kissed me again. Drinking down my moans of pleasure as he swirled his wet fingers around my clit. My legs started to tremble as his movements picked up speed.

He released my mouth again to travel lower. Letting go of my throat to grasp my breast. His scorching mouth closed over my puckered nipple trapped by the thin see-through material of my bra. I whimpered as he bit down.

"Oh, God!" I exclaimed as I felt the wave of my orgasm quickly approaching.

"No, *amor*, not God," he corrected harshly. "You say my name when you come," he demanded. He pinched my clit and raked his mouth over mine, staring at me with his intense will.

The wave crashed down, nearly drowning me.

"Damon!" I wailed as he prolonged my orgasm with skilled fingers.

"That's right, baby. Cream all over my fucking fingers. Remember what you left behind this morning," he gritted between clenched teeth before he crashed his lips against mine again, swallowing my wails of passion.

When he finally let go of me, I was shaking with the force of my release.

"*Nunca me dejes de nuevo*," he whispered against me.

My heart squeezed at his words. *Never leave me again.* I licked my dry lips and searched his eyes for the right words to say. He almost seemed broken and it chipped away at my already crumbled walls the longer I looked at him. I opened my mouth to speak when someone cleared their throat.

"Uh, Jill, you okay?" a deep voice came from the end of my driveway.

I squealed and tried to push Damon away from me but he wouldn't budge. He was still pressed hard against me as he removed his fingers from my panties. I panted as he held eye contact with me before pulling those fingers into his sinful mouth for a taste. He groaned and closed his eyes as if he was tasting something decadent.

"Mmm…" he hummed. "*Deliciosa*," he mumbled as he opened his eyes again.

A shiver ran up my spine as I watched him. I felt a fresh rush of arousal flood my already soaked panties. His crude behavior was almost enough to make me forget we had a visitor. Almost.

I turned my head in a sharp jerk to the end of my driveway where my twenty-something neighbor, Glenn, stood holding a pair of trimming shears. From his vantage point, he wasn't able to clearly see what Damon had been doing to me. It just looked like he was holding me against the car.

He pointed the shears at Damon with a hard look. "Is this guy bothering you?" he asked with dark eyes.

I used to think Glenn was handsome, with his almost black eyes and thick dark beard covering his strong jaw. But, compared to the savage beauty that held me now, he paled in comparison.

"Glenn, it's okay…" I started before Damon whipped his head in my neighbor's direction.

"I'm not doing anything she hasn't begged me to do multiple times, fuck off," he snarled menacingly.

"Damon!" I yelled as I slapped his chest, pushing him away from me. This time when I pushed, he backed up and released me.

Glenn was glaring at him now. Damon flexed his jaw before grinning in his direction, silently challenging him. I rolled my eyes as I wrapped my dress back around me and hastily tied the knot.

"Glenn, truthfully, I'm fine. Just ignore this asshole, that's what I do," I gritted out before I turned and marched toward my front door.

Once inside, I tried to slam the door but a booted foot stopped the forward movement with a thud. I grunted my frustration as I turned on my heel and walked away from the arrogant man following me. I made it to my dining room before Damon grabbed my wrist and whirled me around.

I didn't stop to think about my actions until it was too late. I raised my hand and smacked Damon across the face. His head jerked to the side from my strike. I cringed after I pulled my stinging hand away. He slowly faced me with a fresh red mark across his cheek before he smiled down at me.

"Urgh! What the fuck is wrong with you?" I screeched at him.

He chuckled as he released my wrist so he could grab my hips before he spoke. "Well, you see, a few months ago I met this fiery little redhead and she's been driving me insane ever since. It's a real problem, I think I've gone mad," he admitted before he brushed his lips against mine.

I sucked in a sharp breath before I pulled out of his grasp, taking a few steps back. "You can't blame your devious antics on me. What the fuck were you thinking doing that to me in my driveway? I have neighbors, you know," I clamored.

Damon raked his fingers through his hair before answering me. "You mean neighbors like *Glenn*?" He said his name like it left a bad taste in his mouth.

"What's wrong with Glenn?" I scrutinized, putting my hands on my hips, confusion marring my brow.

Damon barked a humorless laugh. "You mean, besides the fact that he wants to fuck you?"

I don't know what made me do it. Maybe I wanted to get even with him for embarrassing me, or I still wanted to punish him for getting under my skin so quickly. Whatever the reason, I didn't stop myself as I gave Damon a sultry grin before I swayed my hips and walked toward him. He watched me with heated eyes as I trailed my finger down his chest. I went up on my tiptoes and teased his lips with the tip of my tongue before I whispered, "How do you know I haven't already fucked him, baby?" I challenged before I twirled around and strode away from him.

He was quick as he caught me around my hips and dragged me to him. I gasped as he pushed his hard cock against my ass before rasping against my ear.

"Careful, Red." He was deadly calm as he spoke. "You have no idea how close I am to bending you over this table and showing you just who you belong to. I will mark you as mine so no one will ever think to touch you ever again. I'll make you forget every other man that came before me and you'll never want another after me. You won't be able to walk away from me ever again without knowing that You. Are. Mine." He growled a primal sound.

I shivered against him as he finished his threat. I must've had a death wish as I pushed my ass back against him before I turned my face over my shoulder to look at him.

"Promise?" I asked and watched a feral smile spread across those sensual lips.

Chapter Nineteen

Damon was absolutely ferocious as he ripped my dress from my body. He didn't even untie the knot at my waist before he pulled the fabric from my shoulders. The seams of my dress popped as he tore at them. If I hadn't been so insanely turned on, I would've cared more that he ruined a $400 dress.

The tattered remains puddled at my feet as he kissed and nipped at my neck. I leaned into him as his hasty fingers trailed down my torso to my soaked panties. Just when I thought he would push his hand past the fabric again, he stopped and spun me to face him. I wobbled on my feet as he sank to his knees in front of me. Before I could register what was happening, I felt a tug and heard a snap as Damon ripped my thong, exposing me to his lusty gaze.

This guy was hell on a girl's wardrobe.

Damon released a long groan as he looked at my drenched sex before he leaned forward and buried his face in my pussy. I gasped as he lapped at me like I was his favorite flavor of ice cream. He hummed against me and the vibrations nearly had me undone.

I grabbed the top of his head and held on for dear life as he jerked my leg up and over his shoulder. He pushed his fingers into me as he licked me fiercely. My legs started to quiver as the start of my orgasm wound tight.

I looked down at him as he pulled his mouth away from me. He stared up at me while he continued to fuck me with his thick fingers. His mouth glistening with my arousal turned me on more than words could describe.

"I could eat you all day, baby. You are my

favorite meal. You're going to cream on my tongue, Jill. I want to hear you scream my name when you come. Do you understand?" he asked before he brought his flattened palm down on my ass cheek.

"Yes!" I wailed from the sharp pain he inflicted on my behind.

"That's my good fucking girl." Heat flushed through my body at his praise before he brought his mouth back down on me.

I gripped his hair hard as he sucked my swollen clitoris into his mouth. I was so close I could taste it. Right when I thought I couldn't take anymore, Damon curled his fingers inside of me, spanked me again, and bit down on my clit gently.

I screamed his name as I went flying. He groaned against me, enhancing my release.

Never once taking his wicked mouth off me, he picked me up and walked me to the dining table. I held on for dear life as he laid me on my back as he continued to suck and lap at me.

"It's too much!" I screamed as he thrust his fingers into me faster now, dragging across my G-spot each time. I was building to something far too explosive.

He finally pulled his mouth from me only to replace it with his hand. He continued to finger me with vigor as he pressed down on my pelvis with his other hand.

"This is exactly how you make me feel, *Roja*. It's all too fucking much. But I can't just stop, I can't walk away. Not from you," he confessed as he stared down at me.

I was moaning wildly as the sounds of my arousal filled the room. I could feel myself getting wetter and hotter with each passing second. Just a little more and I would go careening off that cliff he dangled me from.

Damon continued his erotic torture as he added his thumb to the mix. He never slowed as he pressed down on my clit with his harsh order.

"Come," he snarled.

I didn't have a choice as my body listened to his command and I exploded around him. I screamed as I looked up at him. He watched what he was doing to my body with searing eyes.

"Fuck, yes!" Damon groaned harshly. "Soak my fucking hand, Jill," he ordered.

I let my head fall to the table as my back arched, allowing every pleasure-induced convulsion to course through my body. My vision blurred as I fought to stay conscious from the intense waves of ecstasy rolling over me.

Damon removed his fingers from me and flipped me over so my belly was on the table. I should have been disgusted by the mess I'd made, but I wasn't. I was so hot that I burned with need.

I felt as Damon ripped what remained of my thong from my body. He grabbed both of my hands and quickly tied them behind my back with the tattered remains. I was completely at his mercy and I basked in the sensation. I heard the rustle of clothing being shed and felt anticipation rush through me at the thought of him taking me. I braced myself to be filled with his big cock, but it never came.

Instead, I felt his hands rub up my sides and down my back in loving caresses.

"*Tan hermosa*," Damon murmured as he kissed my lower back.

I wiggled my ass and lifted my cheek from the table to glance at him. He stood gloriously naked behind me. Dark eyes drinking in everything I offered. His unruly hair hanging free around his handsome face. That thick cock bobbed heavily between his legs. Powerful muscles, primed and ready. He was beautifully wild.

"I could say the same thing," I whispered quietly.

His lips twitched on a smile before he hid his reaction. I grinned before laying my head back down.

He rubbed his hands down my back before laying one to rest on my lower back as the other disappeared. We stayed like that for so long that I thought maybe he forgot what he was supposed to be doing. I started to raise my head again to ask if he needed any help when I felt the sharp smack he doled out to my ass.

I yelped and jerked forward, going on my tiptoes. "What the fuck!" I shrieked as white-hot pain lanced my ass.

Damon struck again, this time in a different area. I bit back my squeal that time as he left his hand on the offending area, letting his warmth seep in. The pain morphed into something much darker as I felt fresh arousal coat my inner thighs.

"I'm going to punish this juicy ass before I fuck you, Red. You're going to lay there and take every spank I offer you because you tried to leave me today. You left without trying to talk to me first. I didn't appreciate that, Jill," he growled angrily behind me. Before he thrashed me again.

This time I had to bite my lip to stop the moan that rose up. This was a punishment?

"I thought leaving was the easiest way to end this before it got even more serious. I told you some dark shit about my past and I was giving you an out," I explained.

"Bullshit," he said as he peppered my ass and thighs with fleshy smacks. "I don't want an out, Jill." *Smack.* "I want you." *Smack.* "I don't give a fuck about your past." *Smack.* "All that matters now is our future." *Smack. Smack. Smack.*

I sank into his punishment with open arms. It became less punishment and more cathartic at some point and I found myself silently begging for more. It no longer hurt, all I felt was intense heat as it traveled to my core and something deep inside of me released.

I don't know how long it lasted but I almost whimpered when he stopped. That is, until he reached between my legs and found evidence of how much I was enjoying this little session of ours. I tightened and moaned loudly as he raked his finger across my engorged clitoris.

"You're so wet, baby," he groaned before he withdrew his fingers from me. I nearly cried and begged him to touch me until I felt the head of his cock push into me. My fingers clenched around my binding as he held himself still.

"You want this cock?" He panted as he thrust just the bare minimum into me. Not enough. I wiggled my ass against him and tried to push back but he held my hips too firmly.

"You know I do," I whined.

Damon pulled me up to his chest by my throat and forced me to look at him over my shoulder. "Ask nicely," he demanded as his soft thrusts continued.

I panted wildly as I looked at him. "Please fuck me, Damon," I begged.

That was all it took. Damon groaned as he pushed me back to the table before slamming into me. I cried out, not from pain but pure elation, as the force of his thrust slammed my hips into the table.

Damon thrust into me hard and fast as he fucked me from behind. He held onto my tied hands as he pulled me back to him with each forward motion. His hard cock slid against the bundle of nerves inside of me with each pull. The sounds of slapping skin and both of our harsh breathing filled the room.

He rammed into me over and over again, driving me higher with each twist of his hips. I was so close I just needed one more push. It was as if he could read my mind as he thrust into and smacked my ass one more time. I screamed as I came in a rush.

"Fuck!" he roared from behind me before he untied my hands. He pulled out of me just to roll me over and thrust back into me. He pulled my hips up to meet his every thrust, lifting my lower half off the table each time.

He looked like a barbaric warrior towering over me, glistening with sweat as he pumped into me fiercely.

He pulled my breasts free from my bra and gripped them roughly. I moaned deep in my chest as he tweaked and played with the sensitive tips. My pussy clenched down on his thick cock as I came again with a long, tortured cry.

"I'm gonna come," he panted as his thrusts became sporadic. "Lay there like a good girl while I mark you as mine," he growled.

I felt him pulse inside as his thrusts slowed and he pulled himself out of me. I watched as he gripped himself tightly and continued to rub himself. I couldn't help but be extremely turned on as his orgasm contorted his face almost painfully and he shot hot jets of cum all over my pussy and lower stomach, his thick cock twitching with each stream. He groaned as he watched himself mark me as his.

He collapsed on top of me, not caring about the mess he had just made. Our chests heaved with the effort it took to catch our breath. I rubbed my hands up and down his muscular back in long soothing strokes as he kissed my neck and jaw.

His tenderness after being so rough with me,

made my stomach do somersaults. I felt unhashed tears burn my eyes for what felt like the hundredth time that day as emotion swamped me. My breathing shuddered as Damon lifted his head, concern written on his face. He brushed the hair that escaped my bun back from my sweat-soaked temples.

"Did I hurt you?" he asked timidly.

I shook my head as I looked up at him. I gasped around a sob as I opened my mouth to speak.

"I-I'm sorry," I managed in a broken voice.

His eyes softened before he kissed me tenderly. "Oh, baby, it's okay. Don't cry. I can't take it when you cry. It kills me," he begged as he brushed my tears away.

I broke then. I cried softly as he coddled me. I let him pick me up and take me to my bedroom. I didn't fight him as he laid us both down on my unmade bed. I didn't argue as he soothed me softly until my tears ran dry. I trusted him enough to allow myself to find comfort in his arms.

Chapter Twenty

We'd spent long hours worshiping each other, finding our bliss in one another's bodies. I'm not a religious person, but I think I could see the divine when Damon looked at me.

When we were sated, he leaned against my plush headboard and dragged me to his chest. We lay like that in peaceful silence for a long time. My front pressed to his side with his arm around my back, dragging his fingers up and down my exposed skin in long motions. The sheet slung low on our hips, leaving our torsos naked to the other's view. My thigh settled on his lower stomach, above his manhood, and my cheek rested soundly against his big chest. The steady beat of his heart lulled me into a soothing trance.

My fingers played in the soft speckling of hair that scattered across his chest and abdomen. I relished in my lazy motions, trailing all the peaks and divots of his defined muscles. I traced my fingers around his nipples just to watch them tighten. I couldn't keep the grin from my lips when he would flex against me and tighten his grip on my hip, silently letting me know I was tickling him. I reveled in the way he had thickened under the sheet from my ministrations.

I realized that having Damon show up at my house was probably the best way this could have happened. I knew myself well enough to know that I would have never gone to him. Sure, I had told Kate that I would try again with him, but I wasn't fooling anyone. I would've chosen the path of least resistance.

The way he asserted himself may have been abrasive, but it was effective. Maybe all this time, all I'd needed was a man who wasn't afraid to piss me off.

Someone who didn't scare easily.

I smiled to myself thinking of going toe-to-toe with someone with an equally dominating personality. It was almost perverted how much I secretly enjoyed it when he didn't back down from me.

The longer I lay with my head on his chest the more I thought about this morning after my dream. I winced at the memory. The whole situation could have been handled better on my part.

I wasn't used to letting people in, but that was no excuse not to talk about my past with someone that cared about me. And it was obvious that Damon cared about me, otherwise, why would he stick around and put up with my shit? Kate was right, what worked for me in the past wasn't working any longer. My methods of coping needed to change. *I* needed to change.

So, I took a deep breath, held it for a moment, and released it in a rush before I relived my worst nightmare.

"His name was Jason Henderson," I confessed.

Damon stilled against me as if he was afraid to move or I would stop speaking. He wasn't wrong in that assumption.

I closed my eyes as I placed my hand flat along his abdomen before speaking again.

"It happened sixteen years ago at college. My roommate and I went to a party at his frat house, but I'd known him for longer than that." My hushed voice flowed through the otherwise quiet room as I steeled myself to share the details of my sordid past with the only man I had ever desired.

I squirmed against him, unable to stay still any longer. I rolled and placed my back to his side. My head still lay against his chest but now his arm was around my shoulders. I grabbed his big hand and played with his fingers. Tracing his calluses.

"He had hit on me months before this happened. I turned him down and it must have made him livid, though he never showed how angry he was at the time." I swallowed around the lump in my throat before I continued. "Looking back, I can see that he used that time to try to become my friend as an opportunity to plot how he would get what he wanted." My chest jerked as my huff of a laugh left my body.

I tried to take a breath but it came in and out as a shaky mess. I focused on Damon's hand in mine as I continued.

"When his advances toward me failed, he drugged me the night of the party with the date rape drug," I blurted. Damon's hand twitched in mine and I heard his breathing pick up a notch.

"Normally, when you're dosed with Rohypnol you're supposed to go into an almost trance-like state. Most people don't remember anything that happens to them when they're given the drug. They wake up the next morning with a killer hangover and memory loss," I stated in a monotone voice as my vision zoned out. "But I remember everything," I whispered.

My next words came out of me almost like word vomit. I couldn't stop them from spewing out as if I was reliving the experience.

"I drank too much and I experimented with drugs I'd never done before that night. I remember dancing and feeling Jason behind me as he helped me finish the last of my mixed drink. He'd made it for me, so I'm sure that's when he slipped me the drug. One minute I was on the dance floor and the next he was pushing me up the stairs to his bedroom."

"Jill," Damon's ragged voice tried to break through my fog.

"When he finally had me behind locked doors, his hands were everywhere and I couldn't stop him. My arms and legs wouldn't work. I could hardly talk. When I tried to scream for help he covered my mouth and nose. I couldn't breathe," I choked.

"Jill, stop," Damon gruffly ordered as he moved.

"He held my hands above my head like I would try to fight back. I would have if I could've used my arms." My voice quivered as my body shook. "He lifted my dress and looked at me with such hatred. What did I do that made him hate me so much?" I whispered.

"Jill, *stop*!" Damon shouted from above me.

I blinked up at him, not realizing he had stood over my body and was trying to bring me out of my memory. He looked down at me with such pain in his eyes.

"Stop, I don't want to know anymore," he begged. "I can't hear anymore." He shook with rage as he stared at me.

"What did I do to deserve it?" I asked in a small voice as I trembled.

He clutched me to his chest and rolled us back over so I was on top of him again. He smoothed down my hair before he brought his lips to mine in a tender kiss.

"Nothing, Red. You did nothing wrong. It was his choice. It wouldn't matter if you had shown up to that party completely naked or drank entirely too much. He was the one that made the conscious decision to violate you. None of that was your fault," he assured.

He looked at me with such tenderness. "I'm so sorry that happened to you," he spoke softly against my lips. "I wish I could go back and make sure it never happened in the first place. I can promise you, I will meet that fucker in a dark alley one of these days." He had a dark gleam in his eyes.

I knew he was completely serious at that moment. If there was anything I learned about Damon in the short time I'd known him, it was that he would go to war for the people he *loved*. He would go to battle for *me*.

The thought of Damon loving me shouldn't scare me as it did. I knew when he showed up at my house today that he felt that way. You don't fight that hard for the woman that left you unless you love her. I hoped one day I would be able to let myself feel the same way, even though I knew deep down I already did.

I embraced him before I settled my head onto his chest once again. He rubbed my back in firm strokes, bringing warmth back to me. I took deep breaths as I released the rest of my memory.

I laughed despite myself. "You know, I may be fucked up now but I used to be much, much worse." I couldn't stop myself from sharing now. "I used to loathe myself even more than I do now, honestly. I didn't care who used my body or what I put into it after Jason." I lifted my arm to show him what I'd done all those years ago. "This is from my attempt at getting out." I swallowed heavily.

He grasped me below my elbow and ran his thumb across the faint white scar that marred my otherwise smooth skin. I sucked in a sharp breath as he brought my arm to his lips and kissed it. He kissed from my wrist to my elbow as he rolled me over onto my back again. He made a place for himself between my legs as he lowered his body onto mine.

His gaze seared me as he looked into my eyes as if searching for the words he needed to say. I bit my lip as he lowered himself and kissed me on my nose before speaking.

"I will forever be grateful that you didn't

succeed," he murmured.

I flashed him a sad smile. "Well, you can thank Kate for that."

"Remind me to send that woman flowers," he returned my smile. "If it wasn't for her, I wouldn't get to be with the most … beautiful … brilliant … smart-ass woman I know." He kissed me on my cheeks and nose between each word, causing me to chuckle.

I sighed against him, easily moving away from the darkness that lurked in the back of my mind. As he grinned down at me, I remembered something.

"Like I said, I don't do relationships." I paused as I watched his grin waver. "But, if we're going down this path, you need to remember I have neighbors. Unlike you." I frowned his way.

His grin widened and my chest felt like it was about to swell so much it would rip in half. I would do almost anything to see that look on his face.

His eyes sparkled before he buried his face in the crook of my neck. I shivered as his words rumbled across my ticklish flesh. "Don't worry, *Roja*," he mumbled against me and I bit my lip to stop the giggle that arose. "They won't be your neighbors for long," he finished his thought.

I was too busy soaking in his affections to hear what he was saying to me. He kissed me from my jaw down to my collarbone, making me hotter with each slide of his wicked tongue. He nipped me and I gasped as his words finally broke through the lust. I shoved my hands in his hair and pulled him away from my neck.

"What do you mean they won't be my neighbors for long?" I questioned with an arched brow.

He grinned down at me before he pulled my hands from his hair. He paused his upward motion as if he were afraid to trigger me. I met his eyes and nodded my head, giving him permission. I wasn't about to let Jason ruin something I had come to crave from Damon. Only from Damon.

His eyes sparkled as he moved, holding my hands above my head. I moaned as he then descended onto my outthrust breasts, licking and lavishing affection between the two. I squirmed underneath him.

"You're not going to distract me with that sinful tongue. Answer me." I gasped as he nipped me before consoling the ache with his sucking.

He chuckled against me. "I'm moving you in with me as fast as I can," he confessed.

"*What*?" I snapped, trying to straighten up. He released my hands and sat back on his heels as I sat to face him. I tried to ignore his hard cock dangling between his thick thighs. I swallowed thickly before I spoke again. "You want me to move in with you? Are you fucking crazy?" I asked.

Damon shook his head, playfulness still lingering on his lips. "Yes, Red. I'm completely crazy, bonkers, coo-coo, bananas … over you," he offered as he softly pushed me back down. I sighed as he trailed his hand up my torso and came to rest on my throat as I lay on my back. He brushed his lips over mine as he continued his slow seduction.

"Did you honestly think I'd be able to leave you after having you? I told you before we even started that if we did this, you were mine. I'm a selfish bastard and I want it all, baby. I already said I can't think of anything other than you. I can't go any longer without seeing you, being with you. Every. Single. Day. Red, I—"

I cut him off crashing my lips to his. I sucked his lower lip between my teeth and bit him gently. He groaned against me before I pulled away.

"Don't," I blurted. "Don't say it," I begged.

He looked down at me with glittering eyes and nodded his head before he leaned back down to my neck and continued his exploration.

"I won't say it until you're ready, *Roja*," he murmured against me. "But, don't ever doubt that I do feel it. Every time I look at you. Every time I think of you. I can't help but feel any other way," he confessed.

My breath shuddered out of me but I stayed silent. I leaned into him as he continued his exploration. He kissed and licked his way up from my shoulder. My hands were still caught above my head by his as that skilled mouth traveled up my arm, lingering on my scar before moving on to my fingers. He kissed each tip before moving back down, caressing my flesh as he moved. When he made it to my inner arm close to the apex, I giggled and flinched.

He looked at me sideways as he held me firmly. I saw the mischievous gleam in his eyes before he ran his tongue along the sensitive spot. I giggled fiercely as the tickling sensation intensified.

"Damon, stop!" I screeched as I twisted in his hold.

His boom of laughter rang out as he continued his torture. Releasing his hold on me, he used his fingers to tickle me then. I sucked in harsh breath after harsh breath as I wailed with laughter.

"What about this spot?" he teased. He shoved his face back in the crook of my neck and tickled my collarbone with his chin. I screeched louder as I giggled madly. I could feel his smile against my skin as he murmured. "I could listen to that all day."

My phone's shrill tone rang out, squelching our laughs. Damon rolled off me and handed me my phone from the nightstand. Lindsey's sunny smile shined from the screen. I grinned at him one last time before I swiped my thumb across the screen.

"Hey, Lyns, let me ca—" I started when Linsey's muffled voice came over the line. I sat up and threw the blanket from my legs as I listened as best I could.

"Ben, stop!" She sounded like she was choking. My blood ran cold.

"Lindsey?" Panic laced my voice. Damon sat up and looked at me, concern written on his brow.

"Stop, I'm gonna be sick," her muffled voice sounded so far away.

I stood in a rush and put my phone on speaker before throwing it on the bed. I ran into my closet and hastily put on shorts and a t-shirt. I could see Damon rush to put his jeans on.

I ran back to my bed, picked up the phone, and ran for the door with a very worried Damon hot on my heels.

"Where are we going?" he asked calmly.

"Lindsey's in trouble," was all the explanation I offered.

That's when the line went dead on me and I panicked. I grabbed my keys as dread flared to the surface and bolted out the door.

"Fuck!" I exclaimed.

I was blocked in by Damon's car. Before I could tell him to move it, he ran ahead of me and opened his passenger door for me to climb in before he ambled into the driver's seat.

He looked at me as he hastily started the car. "Where, Jill?"

Chapter Twenty-One

Damon swerved in and out of traffic lanes like a professional as we raced to the campus. I tried to get Lindsey back on the phone for what felt like the fiftieth time. When I was sent to voicemail I almost threw my phone against the windshield.

"Goddamnit!" I exclaimed in frustration.

"Jill, I need you to calm down and tell me where I'm going," Damon's composed voice consoled me.

I was lucky he was so calm under intense circumstances. His career in law enforcement assured that. I, on the other hand, was having a hard time keeping my shit together.

"I told you, I can't fucking remember what frat house she said she would be at tonight." I ran a frustrated hand through my wild hair. I scrunched my eyes closed as I tried to remember what Lyns had said earlier in the day. "Alpha something … fuck!" I blurted.

Damon glanced over at me before he squeezed my thigh reassuringly. "Hey, she's going to be okay. We don't even know what's happening. This could all be a big misunderstanding," he tried.

I scowled at him. "You don't know that," I grumbled. Then it hit me. "Kate!" I shouted.

I pulled up her contact and hit "call." Kate would remember where Lindsey was going tonight. Why didn't I think of her sooner?

The phone rang, and rang, and rang. Just when I was about to concede to her not answering, her groggy voice finally came over the speaker.

"Jill? Do you know what time it is?" she asked around a yawn.

"Where did Lyns say she was going tonight?" I

questioned quickly. Panic dripped from my voice.

"What? What's going on?" Kate seemed a little more awake now.

"Lindsey tried to call me and I think she's in trouble," I blurted.

"What!" Kate shouted in my ear. "What did she say?" she asked in a rush.

"I'll explain later, just tell me where the party is," I beseeched her.

There was a pause on the line and I almost thought I'd lost the call until Kate's voice came back over the speaker.

"Six-thousand-nine North University Drive. I'll meet you there." Then the line went dead.

I knew when Damon heard the address as the car lurched forward, speeding faster through traffic. He gripped the steering wheel with white-knuckle force as he steered with focused precision.

"You know that address, don't you?" I asked and immediately knew the answer by the way his jaw clenched. "Tell me what you know," I gritted between clenched teeth.

"The boys at the station have had to make multiple visits to that location. Illegal drugs, minors drinking excessively..." He glanced at me as if he didn't want to say the next thing on the list of violations. "There was a sexual assault charge on one of the members but he was acquitted. His daddy's a higher-up lawyer and knew the judge personally," he fumed.

I paled as I pictured all the bad shit that could be happening to Lindsey. Would we get there in time or would we have to pick up the pieces of my niece that someone destroyed? I shuddered as I thought of the possible outcomes.

I looked out at the traffic. "Can't this thing go any

faster?" I felt like I was going to be sick. I swallowed hard to keep my nausea at bay. I slapped the dash as a sudden burst of rage overwhelmed me. "Shit! Shit! Shit!" I yelled.

This couldn't be happening. Not to my Lindsey. I couldn't change my own past but I would be damned if I let her fate become the same as mine. "Drive faster, damnit!" I screamed.

Damon squeezed my thigh again. "We're almost there, Jill. I need you to calm yourself. I know you're worried but panicking isn't going to help Lindsey. Take a deep breath with me," he said softly.

I stared forward, trying to ignore the man who was making too much sense right now. I knew I needed to calm down but I was too far gone at this point.

"Jill," he tried again and I shook my head.

"Jill, look at me." His deep voice boomed through the car, demanding I take heed.

I snapped my head in his direction and scowled at him.

"Breathe with me," he bit out before he took a deep breath, looking between me and the road as we turned onto a side street.

His big chest moved in and out slowly and I found myself following his example. But it wasn't enough to quell the panic that had already dug its claws in.

I glanced back out the window as Damon slowed the car. I could see the house coming up on the right. It was absolutely packed to the brim with college students. People holding plastic red cups littered the front yard and gathered on the porch. I braced myself as memories swamped me

I bit the inside of my cheek hard enough that I tasted metal. I would not get sucked into my own trauma right now. Lindsey needed me.

Damon slowed to a halt but before he could fully stop I opened the door and sprinted for the house.

"Jill!" Damon yelled at me but I ignored him as I ran.

I'm sure I looked like a madwoman as I came crashing in the door. Strangers stared at me in shock as I searched faces looking for Lyns. The music thumped heavily through me the deeper I explored the house. I pushed my way through sweaty bodies as they crowded around, dancing and laughing.

We were so packed together I was having a hard time staying in the now. I swear I felt breath against my neck and clammy hands grip me as I shoved my way through the crowd.

"Lindsey!" I tried to shout above the noise.

My heart was beating out of my chest and my breath was leaving me in labored puffs. I felt my hands start to shake as the panic attack started to take hold.

No. I would not allow myself to shut down. I closed my eyes as I inhaled deeply and exhaled slowly. Thinking of the first night Damon had led me through the breathing practice. In and out. In and out. I pretended he was in front of me as I calmed myself enough to think straight.

When I opened my eyes again, I found an opening in the bodies that would lead me to my salvation, and I pushed for it. I finally made it out of the crowd and looked around at the lounge area I found myself in. Thick smoke permeated the air, making it hard to see anything. There were at least five couches in this room alone and they were all full. Young adults were piled on top of one another, kissing and rubbing.

The music abruptly cut off as I finally saw what I was looking for.

A pair of red Converse shoes jutted out from the side of one of the couches in a dark corner. I watched in disbelief as the bulky body on top of my niece ground down on her through their clothing. I couldn't see their faces, but I knew by the angle of his body that they were making out heavily.

Most of the people had stopped what they were doing after the music cut off, but the guy on top of Lindsey didn't halt his explorations. I watched his hand dip to her inner thigh as she pushed at his chest.

"What's going on? Let me up so I can see. Stop," she said as she pushed him harder.

"Come on, baby," his voice muttered against her before he gripped her more firmly.

"No, stop," she grunted as she tried to move away from him.

That's when I snapped.

I saw red as I took two big strides toward the asshole taking advantage of my niece. I gripped the back of his shirt and used all my strength to pull him off of her. His face registered shock as he was thrown back but quickly turned to anger.

"What the fuck is your deal, lady?" He loomed over me. He had at least a foot on me but wasn't nearly as bulky as some of his other frat brothers who stood around the room. He stared down at me harshly as if he was trying to intimidate me. I balled my fists at my side as I got in his face. My fingernails dug into my palm so hard I was sure I broke the skin.

"When someone says stop, it means stop. Get the fuck away from her," I seethed.

He looked around the room before he smirked at me. "She didn't want me to stop. Back the fuck up."

I saw Damon out of the corner of my eye as he reached the doorway but it was too late. I smiled at the asshole in front of me, reared back, and punched the kid straight in the nose. Pain exploded across my hand as I heard the sickening crunch of his nose breaking and immediately saw blood before he covered it with a long howl. He doubled over as he held the broken appendage. I shook my hand out as he stared back up at me, pain glowing in his eyes.

"You fucking bitch!" he bellowed.

Despite my hand throbbing, I smiled at him before kneeling down in his face. "Maybe next time you'll think twice before forcing yourself on someone," I taunted.

"Aunt Jill?" a familiar voice came from in front of me.

I looked up from Loverboy to see Lindsey standing in the doorway beside her mom. Heath and Reid both looming over the girls protectively. They looked over the scene I'd created with worried eyes.

Confusion marred my brow as I looked at my niece. She wasn't wearing red Converse under her black dress. Realization dawned on me as I turned to face the girl I thought was Lindsey.

There on the couch sat a girl who looked to be Lindsey's age, but that was where the similarities stopped. She was a thin little thing with mousey brown eyes and short purple hair. She wore a black dress similar to Lindsey's and red Converse on her feet.

The room was so silent, you could hear a pin drop as Lindsey and Kate came to my side.

"This is my roommate, Anna." Lindsey's quiet voice sounded so loud in my ears.

Anna fixed her dress as she stood from the couch. "Thanks, he was getting pretty handsy." she offered with a shy smile.

I closed my eyes as embarrassment washed over

me. I glanced back at the now recovering boy I had popped in the nose and then at my niece.

"So, this isn't Ben?" I cringed as Lyns shook her head no.

"Who the fuck is Ben?" the handsy frat boy asked. He stood back up to his full height, blood still dripping from his nose. "You know what, I don't give a shit. You're about to find out who the fuck I am," he threatened as he stepped toward me.

I readied to defend myself but before I could kick this guy's balls into his throat, Damon stepped between us and towered over the kid. If I thought the frat guy was big before, he paled in comparison to Damon. At least the boy had enough smarts to look submissive when he took in his size.

Damon pulled out his badge and flashed it around the room. "I suggest anyone who doesn't want me to start arresting people on multiple charges, including sexual assault"—he hovered over Mister Tough Guy, glaring down at him—"needs to get the fuck out of here … *now!*" His voice boomed through the house and kids scattered every which way.

Before I knew it, the room was empty, except for the seven of us. Watching Damon as he commanded the room left me speechless. That would have been way easier than the way I did it. Next time I would wait for him to come in with me. God, I hoped there was never a next time.

Reid strode over to me and took my right hand in his. I winced as he quickly examined it with a smirk on his face. "Doesn't look like you broke anything. You may want to ice it when you get home, though. That's one hell of a right hook you got there, Brookes." He chuckled as he winked at me. I felt a slight grin on my face from the compliment. He nodded at Damon before he released my hand and went back to my best friend, taking up the opposite side to Heath.

"Someone want to explain what the hell is happening?" Lindsey questioned over the silence.

I frowned as I looked at her. "You called me and I thought you needed help," I explained.

She looked at me like I had grown another head. "I didn't call you," she argued.

I nodded my head and showed her the call. "Yes, you did. All I could hear was, 'Ben, stop!' and then the call cut off. You had me thinking something terrible was happening to you," I clarified.

I watched Lindsey's face go beet red as she looked from her roommate then back to me. Anna dropped her head and sighed as if this whole thing was exasperating. Lindsey shook her head and worried her hands in front of her. She flashed me a self-deprecating smile.

"I'm so sorry," she sang. "My friend, Ben, was teasing me and he picked me up over his shoulder and started running around the house with me. My phone was in my clutch and it must have dialed you by accident. I was telling him to put me down." She cringed as she told me her story.

"Fuckin' Ben," Anna muttered under her breath as she rolled her eyes. I could tell by her reaction that her and this Ben guy didn't like each other.

I stared at my niece, befuddled, as I went over the events of the night in my head. I smiled to myself as I replayed my crazy actions over and over again. Then I started laughing hysterically as everyone stared at me. I laughed so hard my stomach started to cramp. I clutched myself around my middle as I howled.

Heath looked down at Kate and mumbled

something about it looking familiar. My bestie grinned before elbowing him in the belly.

Damon pulled his gaze from me and clapped his hands together. "All right..." He looked over at the group I had created out of my chaos. "It's late and all of us need to get some sleep. Can you guys make sure Lindsey and Anna get back to their dorm? I'll get Chuckles here back to her house," he finished.

Kate nodded her head and grabbed Lindsey's hand. "Jill, I'll talk to you tomorrow, okay?" She didn't wait for a response as she led her daughter out of the frat house, the boys following close behind.

Damon turned and gathered me in his arms. He hugged me tight as my laughs finally quieted. I had tears in my eyes as I burrowed my face in his shoulder.

"I'm a fucking lunatic," I mumbled.

Damon chuckled against me as he rubbed my back. "No, you just love hard." He paused to kiss the top of my head before speaking again. "Although I did enjoy watching you punch the shit out of that kid, next time why don't you let me take the lead?" he retorted seriously.

"Deal." I smiled against his shirt and inhaled calmly for what felt like the first time in hours. I let his scent surround me as I relaxed under his firm hands. I looked up at him as I offered him my lips. After the rush I had from this whole night, I needed him to ground me.

His kiss was tender but firm, dominant but loving. It was just what I needed. I pulled away from him and looked up into his chocolate eyes. They shimmered like moonlight off the bay.

"Take me home?" I requested.

He grinned down at me as his voice rumbled deeply, "*Siempre, Roja.*"

Chapter Twenty-Two

Jason towered over my body as I lay in the bed. But this time it was different. This time I was in my own bed. In my own house. With my lover laying next to me, asleep.

I glanced up at my abuser and felt my heart lurch in my chest. He was just standing there, waiting. For what, I didn't know.

He looked different than before. He was older, harder. Still intimidatingly tall and it was as though he had tacked on about twenty pounds of muscle to his thick frame. His hair was longer than it used to be but his blue eyes were just as piercing. They seemed to penetrate my soul the longer he stared down at me.

The only thing that was the same was the fact that I couldn't move anything other than my eyes. I felt my panicked breath leave me in harsh rasps as my chest rose and fell rapidly. Not able to open my mouth, I tried to breathe with only my nose. I felt like I couldn't get enough air through the small holes. I tried to call for Damon but the only sound that came out was a small whimper. Too quiet. Damon continued to sleep next to me. I could feel his even breaths as he slept soundlessly, unburdened.

This was a dream, my Damon would wake up if this was real. I knew he wasn't that deep of a sleeper. He would've known something was wrong. He would help me.

I could do nothing as I watched Jason bend his knees, squatting in front of me. I choked as I tried to call out for help again. Damon shifted but didn't wake. Jason's hateful eyes glared at my lover before returning to me.

I whimpered as he brought his hand to my cheek, gathering a tear that leaked out. His cold touch sent disgusted shivers down my spine. I squeezed my eyes together hard.

Wake up! Wake up! Wake up!

His hand slid farther down, briefly tracing my lips before moving on. I twitched as his hand dipped below the blanket. His eyes flared as he pulled it down to expose my breasts. I whimpered as I felt my fingers and toes start to come back to life.

He hissed as if I'd burned him as he jerked his hand away, then it disappeared. I watched with watery eyes as he pulled a knife from his pocket. A long slender blade gleamed in the moonlight that streamed through the window. The plain black handle was so dark it seemed to be void of all color as if the light was afraid to touch it.

My hands and feet were working now and I tried like hell to hit the sleeping form next to me. I dug my nails into my palm, hoping to wake myself through pain.

He held the knife between his hands as he watched me and then Damon. He played with the tip against his finger as he glared at him. Fear for not only myself but now my lover coursed through my veins heavily. Would I be forced to watch him gut the man I loved, as I lay there unable to move? Was this my fate? To always be an unwilling bystander in my own trauma?

I watched as he winced when the sharp point punctured the skin on his fingertip. He stared at the droplet of blood as it fell to the floor. Another thick drop gathered before he rubbed it between his index finger and thumb.

He glared at me with lustful eyes as he leaned forward. His face was so close to me now. I squeezed my eyes closed again as his mouth dipped to my wet cheek. I whined loudly as his tongue darted out from between his lips and licked the tear that lay there.

I could move my arms below my elbow now and jerked them wildly. Trying like hell to get Damon to wake up. But all he did was shift beside me and I groaned deep in my throat.

Jason moved further down to my ear. His breath was hot against me as he spoke for the first time.

"Hey, beautiful." The same silky voice from all those years ago raked over my sensitive skin. The smell of vanilla mixed with his heady musk surrounded me. I clenched my eyes together and I screamed.

****

I jerked upright with a loud wail on my lips. My chest heaved harshly as I tried to catch my breath. Cold sweat dampened my skin. I clutched the blankets to my chest as I trembled in the recesses of my dream. I swore I could still smell the scent of vanilla clogging my nose. My eyes trailed to my side of the room and I vaguely thought about looking under the bed.

I jerked violently when I felt a hand touch my arm. Whipping my head in the direction the touch came from, I came face to face with a very worried, very drowsy-looking Damon.

He held his hands up as if to show me he wasn't going to hurt me. "Hey, it's just me. Are you okay?" he soothed sleepily.

I pushed my hair out of my face and regarded him as I tried to calm my speeding heart. Unlike before, I told myself not to run from him. We had been doing this same routine for over a week now. I would wake from a nightmare and then fight the urge to shut him out. It was getting slightly easier each time to lean on him. I let the blanket fall to my waist and lunged for him.

He caught me and dragged me to him, squeezing

me tight. I nuzzled into his neck and breathed in his scent. Hoping desperately he would remove the smell that still haunted me.

"It felt so real," I mumbled as I shivered.

"Shhh, I know, Red," he soothed as he rocked gently and rubbed my back.

We sat like that for long minutes as my adrenaline slowly lowered. I listened to Damon's even breathing and eventually mine matched his. My shaking ceased and my skin warmed under his ministrations.

"Do you want to talk about it?" he whispered against the top of my head.

Tremors wracked my body as the words Jason spoke came roaring back through the fog. *"Hey, beautiful."*

"This one was different from the rest," I admitted. "I swear, it felt like he was right here. I felt his breath against me. I heard the words he spoke as if he was sitting right next to me. I can still smell him. Still feel his cold fingers against me." I shivered. "I couldn't move. All I could do was try to wake you without being able to touch you or speak." My voice cracked as I nuzzled further into Damon's neck.

He held me tight. "It sounds like you were having a night terror," he explained. "I have known a few guys on the Force to have them. They say it's as if you're paralyzed and have no choice but to watch as your worst nightmare manifests itself in front of you. They say it's like watching your own body in real time, but the illusion is just that—an illusion." He yawned as he finished. I could feel his arm becoming heavy on my back as if he were about to fall asleep despite his need to comfort me.

I quivered as he spoke. God, I hoped this would only be a one-time thing. I don't think I could handle constant night terrors alongside my normal dreams. I would never sleep again.

It had been like this almost every night since the night I'd rushed to the frat house with Damon. I wasn't sure if it was that night that brought back such fierce memories of college, but ever since, my dreams had only gotten worse. I would wake up in a panic still able to smell vanilla as if Jason had been right next to me. Almost every night Jason found me in my nightmares, but none of them had been like this one. This one felt way too real.

I briefly wondered if the glass of wine I had before bed was the reason for the terror. I quickly dismissed that as the culprit when I remembered Damon usually indulged in a glass as well. That, and the fact that I drank the same wine almost every night. I never had more than one or two glasses, though. Just enough to hopefully calm my nerves for sleep.

Oh, how badly I wanted him to take me away from all of this. I used to love this house, but now it felt cold compared to his home. I'm not sure when it happened, but at some point this house that I worked so hard for stopped feeling like home. Maybe it was the fact that these walls hid so many of my late-night screams. This room was where my nightmares always found me time after time.

I also felt as if I were going insane here. Things went missing more and more frequently as the days went on. I would discover my clothes, which I always kept meticulously organized, in places I would never think to put them. I would leave a room and turn the light off, only to find it on when I returned later. Every time these things happened, I was always alone in the house. Even when Damon had brought Boone over to stay the night a couple of times, the dog had acted jumpy and anxious about something neither of us could see. It was like this place was haunted.

I knew if I asked, Damon would take me away from here. But how could I ask him when I knew that was the very thing he desired most? I couldn't promise him forever right now, so it wasn't fair to ask for such things and not be sure of what I wanted.

We had fallen into a routine this last week. Damon had stayed with me every night and woke with me every time I'd had a nightmare. He had soothed me with his soft words and calming touch, always allowing me to take my time to talk about the nightmare. Although I hated the fact that I was still having nightmares, it was nice to have someone help me work through them. Most of the time I was even able to go back to sleep for a little while.

I laid on Damon for a while longer until I felt him twitch under me. He snuffled softly as I raised my head to look up at him. His eyes were closed and his breathing was even. I couldn't help the grin that barely formed on my lips. He was asleep.

Glancing at the clock, I felt guilty for a moment. It was a little after four in the morning and we had only gotten to sleep a few hours ago. I found it odd that he had fallen asleep so easily after the way I had woken but I understood why. Poor guy had to be exhausted from constantly being woken up by me.

I pulled the blanket up and around us before I tried to sleep again. I laid my cheek against his chest and listened to his deep inhale and exhale. In and out. In and out. Relaxing further against his warmth.

I closed my eyes and was immediately assaulted by the sight of blue eyes staring back at me. My eyes sprung open as I lifted my head. Sleep was clearly not going to happen.

I looked up at the vision Damon made as he slept

soundly. I leaned forward enough to kiss his lips softly before I pulled the blankets back and eased out of the bed. I padded silently to my closet where I put on a pair of leggings and a sports bra before exiting back into the bedroom. I walked back to the bed where my Latino lay, and kissed his forehead before turning to go.

I was halfway to the door when I turned back, feeling the hairs on the back of my neck stand at attention. I had to be sure.

I came to my side of the bed and got on my knees. Taking a deep breath, I lowered to the floor and looked underneath. Nothing.

I released my breath in a rush and shook my head at myself. "It was just a dream, Brookes," I muttered to myself as I stood. With one last look at the man slumbering in my bed, I walked out the door.

Looking back, I wished I would have been more thorough in my search for something askew. I wished I would have listened to my instincts and asked Damon to take me to his home and never return here. Because as I'd laid on that floor looking for a person under the bed, I'd been too shortsighted. I hadn't seen the drop of blood on the floor next to me.

Chapter Twenty-Three

I grunted as I squatted my last rep of the morning. My legs trembled with the effort it took to lift the weight on my shoulders. I released my breath as I straightened my legs and placed the barbell back on the rack.

Stepping out from under the bar, I grabbed my towel and dried my face off. I had been in my home gym for the past hour and a half trying to burn off the feeling of dread that followed me around since my night terror. I wasn't having much luck.

I figured I would be exhausted enough to shut my brain off after my run on the treadmill, but that proved not to be the case. I had finished my run just to jump into the next exercise and then the next and so on. No matter how much my muscles protested, I couldn't shake my dream. Everything about it seemed so real. The fact that Jason even looked like he had aged didn't sit with me well. It was as if my brain had made up a new version of him just to correlate with the number of years it had been since my assault. It was unsettling, to say the least.

I gulped my water before I leaned against the barbell rack. Placing my forehead against the cool metal did nothing to cool the boiling emotions rolling inside of me.

When was this going to stop? The constant nightmares of things I couldn't change. I thought after the first night with Damon I had found the cure to my sleeplessness. He had successfully calmed me enough to sleep all night for the first time in months. But as the nights went on, the dreams slowly resurfaced. I had to wonder why they seemed to be getting worse. Maybe it was my body's way of telling me I had unfinished business.

But how did you finish business with somebody who had already paid for their crimes against you? Wouldn't the fact that he had already been to prison mean justice had been served?

I pushed away from the rack with a huff and headed to the free-weight stand. Picking up the twenty-pound hand weights, I bent at the waist and started my kickbacks when I heard a deep voice come from the doorway.

"You better save some of that energy for class tonight," Damon teased as he leaned against the doorframe.

I hid my grin from him as I placed the weights back on the rack. I looked back at him and felt a rush of arousal course through me. He stood in nothing but a pair of tight boxer briefs. His big torso was on full display as he gripped the top of the doorway. I squeezed my thighs together when I focused on his growing erection. It looked like he was enjoying the show I hadn't known I was performing

"Is that so?" I questioned as I strode over to him. I watched as his gaze raked my body appreciatively, his eyes darkening with each second.

When I stood in front of him I pushed up to my tiptoes and teased his lips with mine before pulling back. He stepped forward to grab me, pulling me against his hard body.

"That is so," he murmured while looking at my lips. I licked them slowly and reveled in the way my confidence spiked as his eyes flared. "I'm your partner again tonight, Red. I have some moves I'd like to go over with you."

I smiled up at him with a challenging gleam in my eyes. "Jo will be devastated that you're taking her partner away," I teased

Joanna was one of the other women in my class for beginners. She and I had found an easy friendship after I had returned to class last week. She accosted me in the locker room with an exaggerated high five that still made me smile. She'd told me she wanted to partner up with the badass that took out Vince. Apparently, I wasn't the only woman he had tried his overpowering maneuver on.

I pulled out of his arms and walked past him, toward my bathroom. I glanced back as I removed my sports bra, tossing it to the ground as I kept walking.

"Why don't you show me some of your moves now, Detective Santos?" I threw over my shoulder as I made my way to the shower.

I had fully stripped out of my clothes as I walked to my room, leaving them where they lay. By the time Damon made it to the bathroom I was already under the hot spray. I watched with anticipation as he shoved his boxer briefs down from his hips and his erection sprang free from its constraint. He stood outside the shower door watching me. His cock was so hard it almost looked painful.

"Come in here and I'll help you with that," I offered while shamelessly staring at him.

He chuckled before he grabbed himself. I squeezed my thighs together to soothe the ache that was building. I watched with hot eyes as he stroked himself from tip to base with a firm grip.

"I want to watch you for a bit." His breathy reply turned me on further. "Wash yourself, Red," he ordered as he stepped into the big shower. Never taking his hand from his heavy cock.

I grinned at him as I grabbed my favorite body wash. I squeezed a liberal amount of the sweet cucumber-smelling soap onto my loofa and lathered it with my hands. I watched him slide his fist up and down his shaft as I washed myself.

Starting at my neck, I made my way down my arms with the soapy sponge. Coming back up to my shoulders slowly before dragging the rough material over my heavy breasts. I washed over the tightened peaks, slowing to roll my fingers over them. I watched Damon's fist tighten as I traveled further down my body. When I reached the apex of my thighs, I dropped the loofa in favor of using my fingers.

I leaned against the shower wall as I dragged my soapy fingers through my labia, over my engorged clit, and into my aching channel. I moaned and threw my head back as I let my other hand pinch and roll my nipple.

"I touched myself, just like this, to the fantasy of you in this shower," I admitted as I swirled my fingers around my clitoris.

"Is that so?" Damon's rough question had my eyes moving in his direction.

I nodded my head as I sped my fingers. "You were standing behind me with your cock pressed against my ass," I offered around a moan. "And it was your fingers touching me, making me come," I finished as my legs started to shake. "You asked me to tell you this pussy was yours," I confessed.

His groan let me know my words were affecting him the way I'd hoped. "And what did you say?" he asked.

I grinned at him. "Come over here and find out."

That was all the permission he needed as he rushed me. He grabbed onto me and put us both under the hot spray of the water before sealing his lips to mine. I locked my arms around his neck as he pushed me against the glass wall. He moved his lips to my jaw and then my neck, blazing his way to my breasts.

When he got on his knees in front of me I nearly whimpered. He lavished my breasts with his rough dominance. Biting onto the hardened peaks, drawing hisses from my mouth that turned into deep groans. His hands pinned my hips to the glass at my back as he tortured my sensitive flesh.

When I thought he would never touch me where I craved him the most, he released me and traveled lower. He was a madman as he pulled my leg over his shoulder and latched his mouth onto my pussy.

I cried out as he tongued me rapidly. I pushed my hands into his wet hair and held him to me as I ground down onto his mouth. He removed one hand from my hip in favor of thrusting two big fingers inside of me. He curled them at the same moment he sucked at my clit and I went flying. I screamed his name loudly as I came. He didn't slow as he prolonged my orgasm as long as possible.

When he finally released me from his mouth and stood, my legs nearly gave out on me. He crashed his lips back to mine. The taboo flavor of my own arousal washed over my tongue. I moaned into his mouth as he grabbed my throat. I didn't realize he had grabbed my removable showerhead until he placed it against my engorged clit.

I shouted as he switched the nozzle to the massage setting. The powerful jets slammed against me and before I knew it I was on the cusp of another orgasm. Damon grinned down at me before his eyes traveled lower to watch what he was doing to me. I gripped onto his forearm that held my throat, my nails digging into his skin. I moaned loudly as my hips moved of their own accord.

"That's it, *Roja*," he growled. "Take your

pleasure. Come for me," he ordered.

I cried my release as he slammed his mouth onto mine once more, swallowing down my wails of pleasure.

Before I fully came down from my high, he spun me to face the glass. I could see myself with him standing behind me in the mirror of my vanity. He was dripping wet and looked at me so longingly, I almost lost it. We made eye contact through the foggy mirror and he grinned my way savagely.

He gripped onto my hips before he slowly dragged the head of his cock across my center, never taking his eyes from mine.

"I want you to watch yourself as I fill you up, Red. Watch as I take this little cunt roughly," he growled.

He brought his flattened hand down on my ass as he slammed into me. I cried out again as he took me roughly. He gripped my hips, pulling me back to him as he pushed forward.

"Fuck!" he roared as he fucked into me.

I watched the vision we made in my mirror. He looked absolutely feral as all of his muscles worked in unison. His abs flexed with every forward thrust and his biceps clenched as he pulled me back to him. His brow was furrowed as if in concentration as he focused on his one goal—giving me as much pleasure as possible.

He shoved his hand in my hair and pulled me back so he could take my mouth again. His tongue plunged in deep as he kept up his grueling thrusts. He bit down on my lower lip before releasing me.

"Whose pussy is this, Red?" he asked harshly against my lips. We both knew the answer, but I gave him what he wanted.

"Yours!" I screamed.

He pulled my leg up and to the side with his other hand, giving himself the room he needed to fuck me deeper. He groaned deep in his chest.

He turned my head back toward the mirror. "I want to feel your pussy squeeze around me. See what I see, watch yourself as you come with me inside of you. Milk my cock with that greedy cunt, *Roja*!" he demanded.

He angled himself just right to rub over my G-spot and I was a goner. I watched myself crumble in his arms as I came around him. My pussy convulsed and squeezed him hard. His groan was long and ragged as he found his release. I watched his mouth fall open as he took rough inhales. All the while he never took his eyes off of where we were joined together. His thrusts slowed as he rubbed the rest of his orgasm out inside of me with long hot jets.

He released my leg gently and spun me in his arms when he finished. I flashed him a lazy sated smile as he brought us both under the now cooling water. He washed my hair with skilled fingers before rewashing my body lovingly. He kissed me softly as he washed.

"I need to apologize for last night," he said as he cleaned me.

I furrowed my brows. "What do you mean?"

He dragged his soapy fingers over my belly and breasts as he made eye contact with me. "I should have been able to rouse myself while you were having your nightmare. I should have at least been able to stay awake with you after to help talk you through it." He swallowed hard as he pinched his brows together in frustration.

"I don't blame you. You were tired and I can't foul you for that. You haven't exactly gotten much sleep here lately," I offered with a self-deprecating smile.

His frown deepened before kissing me softly. He pulled back and continued to wash me. "But that's the thing." He looked worried. "I'm used to not sleeping a lot and I have never felt the need to crash like that. It was like no matter how hard I tried to keep my eyes open, I just couldn't. You needed me and I failed you," he finished with sadness in his eyes.

I had never felt the need to comfort a man in my entire life until that very moment. I stepped into his body and wrapped my arms around his muscular waist before going on my tiptoes to take his mouth. I licked at his lips until he allowed me entrance. Our tongues danced together before I sucked at his. He groaned roughly and I could feel him hardening against my belly.

When I pulled away, he looked at me with such heat I nearly melted into a puddle at his feet. I smiled up at him. "You didn't fail me. It was just a bad dream," I clarified before giving him a short peck.

He grinned down at me but it almost looked forced. He had disappointed himself and needed time to deal with it. He stepped back and finished washing me with loving touches.

When he was done with me, he quickly washed himself before shutting the water off. He dried me slowly and thoroughly. I let him take care of me, reveling in the attention he lavished on every body part he touched. When he got down on his knees to dry my legs, I threaded my fingers through his still dripping wet hair. I leaned down and kissed him tenderly.

"A girl could get used to this," I teased.

"That's the point, Red." He flashed me his crooked grin before returning to his task.

****

After our steamy shower, I dressed for work. Forgoing a bra altogether, I put on a white silky thong before my garter belt and stockings. Choosing a light-blue crisscross halter top, a cream-colored pencil skirt, and a pair of Louboutin's to match.

I felt hot as I dressed but it had nothing to do with the temperature in the house and everything to do with the Latino that watched me. He sat, sprawled on my chaise, with only a towel around his lean hips as he watched me with a scalding gaze. I could see the evidence of his excitement from watching by the tent of the towel.

He had only moved once. Leaning forward to pull me to him after I attached my stockings to my garter belt. He'd run his fingers under the material against my skin before looking up at me.

"I like this," was all he said before he lightly rubbed his thumb across my clitoris above the silk of my panties. He'd then grinned a deviant grin before smacking my ass and stood to get dressed himself.

I was reminded of the first morning after he'd stayed the night. We had just gotten out of the shower when I asked him about his clothes. He simply smiled and walked out the front door. I'd hoped my elderly neighbor, Mrs. Howel, wasn't outside tending her garden that early. The poor woman would've seen Damon in nothing but a towel and promptly had a heart attack.

He returned within minutes, gym bag in hand. I couldn't keep the giggle out of my voice as I said, "Confident in your ability to win me back, were ya?" He kissed my nose before walking to the bedroom, bag in tow. "Very," was all he said as he disappeared.

When he reappeared fully dressed, I had a hard time not wanting to undress him all over again. He filled out that pair of blue jeans like a model in a Calvin Klein ad. The black t-shirt he wore molded to every muscle on his big torso. The sleeves looked drawn tight as they formed around his biceps. He had on a brown shoulder holster that held his firearm. His long chain holding his badge shined like a beacon around his neck. I didn't know I was one of those women who had certain feelings for a man in uniform, but damn, I was quickly becoming one.

He'd caught me staring and gave me that crooked grin. "I normally wear a suit to work, but I didn't want it to wrinkle in my gym bag so I brought this. If you keep looking at me like that, I'll never wear a suit again," his deep rumbling voice broke my stare.

Ever since that morning, he had dressed similarly almost every day. The fact that he did it just because he knew I liked it made butterflies flutter around my stomach.

This last week had been the change I didn't know I needed. Every morning we would get ready for work together, most of the time starting our day with a frenzied romp in bed, or the shower, or the living room, or any room really. We fucked like horned-up teenagers daily and I loved every second of it.

After we found our ecstasy in one another, we would leave for work at the same time every morning. Afterward, we would meet up at either my house or Krav Maga. In class, Damon would partner up with Jo and I each time and teach us new moves. He was an intense instructor but I loved a challenge. I always left class sore but feeling just a little more strength each day.

At the end of every day, we would return to my house and find solace in one another's arms again. It was like we couldn't wait to get our hands on each other again.

When we had first started this relationship, I thought for sure that Damon would get sick of me after so long. After all, I was nothing if not a little neurotic. But, to my surprise, we had only seemed to grow closer this last week. I couldn't help the giddy feeling I always got around the end of the day. My excitement to see him felt strange but good. Coming home to someone every day elicited feelings in me I had never experienced.

When he didn't bring him here for the night, Damon would go home to check on Boone. Feeding and spending a few hours playing with him. I hadn't gotten up the nerve to go back to his house with him yet. I just knew that if I returned, I would never want to come back here. That thought still scared me enough to make excuses as to why I couldn't go with him. I was still a coward but he was gracious enough not to push me.

The worst thing about this last week, other than the constant nightmares, was my increasing anxiety over not being able to find Fiona. The fact that she had stopped greeting me when I would get home was reason enough to be worried, but she had also stopped doing the things that had become her routine as well. Like rubbing against my legs while I got ready every morning. Or, how she normally slept at my feet every night.

I had myself half-convinced in the beginning when she had stopped doing those things, it was because Damon was here. She was a one-person type of cat, meaning she didn't really like other people invading her space. Not that she really ever had to deal with it, seeing as I never let people come to my house in the first place. But on the off chance that someone did come over, she would often hide until they left.

I let it go for the first couple of days until I noticed that her food bowl hadn't been touched. Surely she would have snuck out of her hiding spot when Damon wasn't around to at least eat, but it seemed she hadn't in the last week and I was really starting to get concerned.

I'd walked all through my house calling for Fiona to no avail. I'd even resorted to walking around shaking her favorite bag of kitty treats. Nothing. Not even a single meow. Each day that passed with no sign of her only caused me to worry even more. Soon, Damon was helping me, even checking my basement for signs of her.

"Where could she be?" I'd questioned.

"Maybe she got outside somehow and is just exploring," he offered reassuringly.

I nodded my head but didn't really think that was the case. Fiona was a pampered house cat in every sense. She never wanted to go outside. In fact, the only time she had been out was when she got out of the car after my panic attack. She had promptly bolted back inside the house at the earliest opportunity.

I pulled myself back to the present as I made us both a breakfast of my usual and we sat in comfortable silence as we ate. We took turns every morning cooking breakfast. I had to admit that it felt nice to break from my normal routine. It also felt nice to have someone sitting at the big table with me.

When we'd finished, Damon took our plates and washed everything while I got our travel coffee mugs ready to go. Before I knew it, it was time to leave for work. Damon pulled me in for a scorching kiss then opened the door for me. When he kissed me like that I couldn't wait for the day to end just to see him again.

I came to a stuttered halt when I looked in my driveway, furrowing my brows in confusion as I looked over my car sitting there. I had finally gotten it back this last week but as I looked at it, I noticed something was amiss.

Damon's hand slid around my waist as if to pull me back at any second as he looked in the same direction. All four tires on the car were flat. It would have been one thing if only one of them were flat, maybe an unlucky coincidence. But all four? Someone had done that on purpose. Someone was messing with me.

Damon walked past me to inspect the car. He knelt in front of one of the tires and ran his hand all along the sidewalls, searching for holes.

I felt the hairs on my neck stand on end as if someone was breathing on me. I looked all around the houses that surrounded my subdivision and saw nothing. Nobody was out on their lawns or getting in their cars. Most had already left for work by this time. I swiveled to look back at my closed and locked front door. I felt the need to leave this place.

"It looks like someone just let the air out of them. Probably some neighborhood kids joking around." Damon's voice surprised me and I jerked around to face him.

"Are you okay? You look pale, do you need to sit?" he asked, concern lacing his voice.

I looked at him with wide eyes before glancing back at my door one last time. I shook my head. I was being ridiculous.

"I, uh, yeah, I'm fine. Just a little frazzled," I allowed. He regarded me seriously for a moment before nodding his head.

"Come on, I'll give you a ride to work before I head to the station. I'll send someone out to get your tires aired back up later today." He grabbed my chin, pulling my lips to his for a tender kiss. "Can I pick you up after work before we head to class?" he asked against me before brushing his lips to mine. I sighed, it was always hard to think when he did that.

I nodded rather than try to speak. He grinned at me before taking my hand, leading me to his car. He opened the door for me and I clambered in.

A short while later we pulled up in front of Brookes Publishing. Damon put the car in "park" and looked at me expectantly. He said nothing as he raked his gaze down my body. I felt heat flush to wherever he was looking. When he made it back up to my eyes, he paused.

The silence dragged so long that I felt the need to fill it. "What?" I asked.

Damon grinned before responding. "Show me," was all he said in a deep sultry voice.

I raised my eyebrows. *Was he serious? Here?* I looked around the parking lot filled with cars but saw nobody walking around. Still...

He drew my attention back to him by cupping my chin and turning me to face him. "Show me," he repeated darkly.

I flushed with heat at his command as I leaned back in my seat. Lifting my hips slightly, I raised my tight skirt slowly. Making a show of exposing myself to him.

I watched his eyes darken further as I lifted the skirt to my hips, showing him my thin panties and garter belt. He ran his finger down the snaps that held my stockings in place before pulling it away from my skin just to let it go. The strap snapped me, leaving a sharp sting in its wake. I inhaled harshly at the sensation.

Damon groaned before he adjusted himself. Those jeans he wore must have felt pretty tight at that moment.

"Me estas matando, Roja," he rasped around a growl.

I chuckled as I lowered my skirt, smoothing the material back down. I leaned in and kissed him one last time, swiping my tongue teasingly across his lower lip before I opened my door and climbed out. I still had a stupid grin on my face as I bent to face him again.

"Just wait, Detective Santos. If you think I'm killing you now, you haven't seen anything yet," I teased. "See you after work?" I asked.

At his nod, I shut the door and walked into my building. I glanced back and felt that warm feeling in my chest as I watched him pull away. He had waited until I was safely inside before leaving.

I couldn't keep that smile from my lips as I made my way to my office to start the day.

Chapter Twenty-Four

I kicked out, trying for his thigh this time, but Damon gripped my ankle before I could make contact. He moved fast as he twisted my foot, completely twisting my body in the process. Somehow, I ended up facing the opposite way with my leg still firmly in his grasp. I glanced back at him in time to see his wicked grin. I braced myself as he pushed me forward. I barely had enough time to catch my balance before he was back in the starting position.

I scowled at him as he smiled, showing me those pearly whites. I took a moment to look him over. He was shirtless and covered in a fine sheen of sweat. His hair was pulled up high in one of those manly buns. I could still see the heat in his eyes as he watched me.

I put my hands back up in the position he demonstrated and waited. He continued to grin at me before he made the "come here" motion with his fingers. I rushed him and tried to sweep his legs out from under him but failed miserably as he moved away quickly.

I'm not sure how he managed it, but somehow he grabbed me and had me twisted around and trapped against him in seconds. My back was to his front and he held both of my arms to my sides in a familiar position. Only this time, my capturer kissed my neck, making me hot for another reason altogether.

"What are you going to do now?" he murmured against my ear, sending shivers down my spine.

I tried to break his hold on me to no avail. When I huffed an exasperated sound he nipped my ear. I bit my lip to stop the yelp that rose.

"You know what to do, Jill. Do it," he breathed.

I leaned forward, trying to take his weight off the

ground but my legs trembled with the effort. I grunted as I felt him grip me tighter.

"I can't," I panted.

"Bullshit." He rejected my excuse. "I've seen you take out two grown-ass men since we've met. Both of which were much bigger than you. You can do this, so do it," he ordered harshly.

I rolled my eyes. "I broke their noses and if you haven't noticed,"—I wiggled my arms—"my arms are a little preoccupied," I huffed.

"Stop making excuses and fight for yourself, Jill," he growled.

"What? All I have ever done is fight for myself. Nobody has ever come to save me, it's always been just me. I've always had to save myself!" I seethed, feeling my face redden with anger.

"Prove it," he taunted.

I thought vaguely about trying to kick him in his manhood but I doubted that would work. So, I took a deep breath and widened my stance. I used every bit of strength I had to bend forward. I felt a rush of victory when I saw his feet leave the ground before my world turned upside down.

I pushed off the ground as hard as I could as I flipped him up and over my body. His hold on me broke when his back hit the mat with a solid thud. His grunt was enough to make me want to celebrate. I scrambled up and twisted around to face him. I straddled his hips in a crouched position as I raised my padded fist back.

I scowled down at him, posed to strike his beautiful face when he started to laugh. He gripped my hips firmly as his deep belly laughs jostled me. His delighted sounds smoothed my features as I grinned down at him. I chuckled with him before I leaned forward to take his lips.

His smile broadened before he flipped us both so I was under him. He used his padded hands to grip mine and bring them above my head. His smile vanished as he looked down at me seriously before sealing his lips to mine.

I arched into him as he thrust his tongue past my lips. I bit back my moan as he lavished me with his attention. Feeling dazed when he pulled away. He rubbed his nose against mine as he led my hands around his shoulders.

"Good job, *Roja*," he whispered against me.

I breathed in his manly scent and leaned up to capture his lips with mine once more. Then someone cleared their throat.

"I don't believe I've seen this form of self-defense before." Hugh stood above us with a knowing grin on his face.

Damon grinned down at me as he pushed up to stand, extending his hand out to help me up. I flushed slightly as I looked at my instructor.

"I figured I'd let you lovebirds know that class is done for the day. Everyone else is packing it in for the evening." Hugh shook his head as he looked between the two of us with a smile on his lips.

Damon shook Hugh's hand in a manly way as I nodded my head.

After Hugh walked away from us, Damon grabbed my hips and pulled me to him. I sucked in a sharp breath as he gazed down at me.

"I'm going to wash up real quick and then I'll take you home. I need to run to my house and grab Boone. I left him outside with plenty of food and water earlier but I think he's starting to get lonely. Do you mind if he stays with us at your place tonight?" he asked hopefully.

I shook my head. I didn't want to go home. I swallowed hard and shoved away that dread that coiled in the pit of my stomach. It was time to shove my fears aside.

"Actually, can we stay at your house tonight?" I asked quietly. I didn't look back up at Damon as I waited for his answer, afraid of the look he would give me. I immediately questioned whether I should have asked that of him. Was it rude to ask to go to his house instead of mine?

I closed my eyes as he grabbed my chin, forcing me to look at him. When I opened them again he was smiling at me. His eyes were bright as he answered.

"*Siempre, Roja.* I thought you'd never ask," he assured me before his eyes darkened. He pulled me to him and whispered against my ear. "I plan on eating you up at the earliest moment so go get your things and I'll meet you back here in a few." His promise sent shivers through my body.

I turned as I started for the locker room before Damon smacked my ass, drawing a yelp from me. I heard his chuckle as I picked up my pace.

****

Damon drove me to my house to get a few things so I wouldn't have to come back for a while. After collecting my things and checking to see if Fiona had resurfaced—she still hadn't—we made the journey out of town to his carved-out oasis. I pushed aside my anxiety over my cat as he drove along the secluded roads. I couldn't wait to be back at his cozy home and see the peaceful view it offered.

He held my hand as he drove with the other. He smelled clean from his quick shower at the studio but he'd dressed in the same clothes he had on this morning. The sight made all my girl parts perk up and take notice.

He had put his hair back up in its constraint so I could see all the harsh angles of his chiseled profile. I caught myself smiling as I watched him.

He spied me staring and smiled before returning his eyes to the road. A naughty thought came to my mind and I couldn't stop myself. It was dark outside the car so it wasn't like anyone would see.

I took my hand from his and turned in my seat. Getting on my knees, I prowled toward him. I leaned forward and kissed his neck, traveling up to his ear. He groaned and shivered as I nipped him.

I rubbed my hand down his chest, past his stomach, right to the front of his jeans. He hissed as I grasped him through the thick denim.

"Jill," he growled a warning.

I smiled and chuckled against his ear, eliciting another chill to race down his body. With deft fingers, I unbuttoned his jeans and slid the zipper down. My breath hitched when I saw he was going commando underneath.

"Oh, how lucky am I?" I whispered seductively as I gripped him, pulling him past the fabric.

He twitched heavily in my palm as he groaned. His hand tightened on the steering wheel as I stroked him. I grinned before I kissed and nipped at his jaw. I could feel myself getting wetter and wetter the longer I stroked him.

I saw a pearly liquid gather at the head of his cock that had my mouth watering. When I couldn't fight temptation any longer, I leaned down and swiped it with my tongue.

He jerked against me and groaned deeply.

"Fuck," he gritted out.

A rush of feminine power surged through me as I sucked his bulbous head past my lips. Swirling my tongue around him before bringing him deeper. He gripped the wheel with one hand as the other hand traveled under my hair to the back of my neck. He held me there as my head bobbed up and down.

I sucked him further and further with each swipe. His cock seemed to get thicker with each passing moment. He would jerk under me when I focused on sucking his head in fast motions before plunging him deep. The only sounds in the vehicle were his labored groans of pleasure and my crude sucking noises.

His hand squeezed my neck as I pulled him to the back of my throat. "Oh, shit!" he grunted as I swallowed around his thickness. I could taste his pending orgasm as I pulled back with a gasp before swallowing him again. His legs started to shake as I bobbed furiously.

I felt the car lurch to a stop as Damon parked. I briefly thought about stopping but quickly dismissed the notion as he grabbed my hair with the hand that had been on the wheel. He groaned deeply as I sucked harder. His hand tightened in my hair, spurring me on.

He helped me bob faster as he swelled. I pulled him to the back of my throat and swallowed one last time as he spilled his seed with a long curse. I drank him down desperately, not wanting to lose a single drop.

He shook with aftershocks as I licked him clean. Before I could sit back in my seat, he lunged for me. Pushing me against the passenger door as he leaned over the console. He crashed his lips to mine with bruising force as he shoved his hand up my skirt.

I spread my legs for him as he explored my mouth. He shoved my panties to the side before spearing me with his fingers. I gasped against his mouth as he smoothly thrust into me. He groaned and leaned his forehead against mine.

"Your pussy is drenched, baby. Do you like tormenting me?" he asked darkly before curling his fingers against my G-spot.

"Oooh!" I exclaimed as he chuckled.

Suddenly he released me and stepped out of the car. Before I knew it, he was on my side tossing the door open forcefully. He pulled me from the car and lifted me easily. He pushed my body against the car, lifting me up so I was damn near sitting on top of the cab.

In the distance, I could hear a dog barking but I paid no attention to it as Damon shoved my skirt up my hips. I felt the familiar tug and heard the snap of my thong being ripped before his mouth was on me. I held on for dear life as he lifted my body so I was at the right height for him to eat my cunt as he pleased.

He pulled one of my garter straps away from my thigh, gripping it tautly before releasing it. I hissed as the sharp sting settled on my tender flesh. He alternated between the straps, never snapping the same one twice in a row. I relished in the burning sting it left behind. He always knew what side of pain to keep me on, never pushing me further than I wanted to go.

I leaned back against the roof of the car and gave over to him completely. The vision of his dark head of hair between my legs had me on the cusp. He speared me with his tongue before nipping my clit between his teeth.

I screamed as I came in a rush. I could feel the flood of fresh arousal as he sucked at me around a deep rumble. The vibration against me intensified the orgasm that coursed through my body.

When he pulled away, his lips and chin glistened with my release and I felt a deep heat settle in my core.

The dog was still barking as he lowered me to the ground. I didn't have time to think much about it before Damon's lips crashed into mine once more. I moaned as I felt his still hard length grind into my belly. Without thinking, I gripped him hard. He hissed before jerking in my hand.

He gazed down at what I was doing to him before he grasped my hair, craning my neck back so he could look at me. He was a wild beauty as he flexed his jaw and briefly closed his eyes. When he opened them, there was nothing but scolding desire.

"I want to play a game," he growled. "I want you to run and hide. And when I find you, because I will find you, I'm going to tie you up so you can never get away from me again," he said as I shivered with anticipation.

"What happens then?" I asked in a husky tone.

He smiled darkly. "That's for me to know and you to find out," he rasped before he stepped back from me.

I felt a giddy energy buzz through me as I slid my heels from my feet before I took off as fast as I could. My adrenaline spiked as I felt the wind whip past me. I squealed with delight as I heard him take off after me.

I picked up speed as I rounded the darkened cabin. The dog's barking got louder the closer I came to the side entrance of the house. I slowed as I saw Boone.

Confusion set in as I slowed to a walk. He was looking at the side door, barking his head off. My heart rate ticked up as I slowly approached. Boone saw me but continued to bark at the door. I saw a flash of white on the door before Damon grabbed my waist.

"You didn't try to hide very well," he murmured as he pressed his lips to my neck.

I pushed out of his embrace as I continued to walk toward Boone. Damon picked up on my investigation and quickly grabbed me, pulling me back. He looked between me and the door before speaking.

"Stay here, Jill." Gone was the playful lover and in his place was a cold detective.

I watched as he slid his firearm out of its holster,

palming it with both hands at the ready. His steps were silent as he signaled something to Boone that had him ceasing his barks. Damon stepped closer to the door and then stopped suddenly at what he saw, lowering his gun.

Dread coursed through me as I stepped closer, and then closer still. I had to see what I already knew was there. My steps quickened as I approached. Damon turned in time to see me and quickly holstered his gun before grabbing for me.

"Jill, don't," he tried but it was too late.

My blood ran cold and my breath hitched as I stared at the corpse stabbed to his door. I cried out as I stumbled forward. Her normally long white fur was matted with dark blood. The life that normally filled her small body, snuffed out. I couldn't find Fiona for the last week because she was here. Dead.

"No!" I cried around a harsh breath.

Damon grabbed me and pulled me against him, pushing my head to his chest as I sobbed. He tried to soothe me with his firm strokes and soft words but nothing could calm the storm brewing inside of me.

I pushed away from him so I could step closer to Fiona.

"Jill, stop. You don't need to see this." He grabbed for me again but I shook off his touch.

"Yes, I do," I cried before reaching the door.

My poor girl must have been so scared. To most other people she may just be a cat, but to me, she was my friend. Sometimes she was the only living thing I shared my thoughts with. And now she was gone.

Tears clogged my vision and my hands shook as I touched her cold body. She had been here for a while, her blood long dried. I looked up to see what was holding her little body to the door and my breath caught in my throat at what I saw. I backed up and felt my chest squeeze.

"Jill," Damon's worried voice cut through the panic as he rushed for me.

My lips started to tingle as my breathing intensified. He gripped me tightly as he took in my shocked gaze.

"It's him." My whispered voice was barely audible as I stared at the long blade that held Fiona. Tunnel vision kicked in to where all I could see was that damn knife. *The plain black handle was so dark it seemed to be void of all color, as if the light was afraid to touch it.* It was the same blade that haunted me last night. My fingers felt numb as I gripped Damon's shirt as if my life depended on it.

"Jill, you need to breathe." Damon gripped my face between his hands to get me to look at him. I gasped as my vision started to fade around the edges. Panic clogged my throat making it impossible to get a full breath.

"Jill, breathe!" Damon's loud voice sounded like he was shouting at me through a tunnel as I stared at the knife jutting out through the door.

"Jason," was all I managed before everything went black.

Chapter Twenty-Five

"I want to know everything about the fucker. Where he's been staying, who he talks to, when his next court date is, everything. Do you understand me?" Damon's harsh tone cut through the darkness that clouded my brain.

"I understand what you're saying, Santos, but it ain't that easy. When Henderson got out of prison, he completed his parole like an upstanding citizen. He's had a clean record ever since. When it looks like the sexual offenders have been rehabbed into normal society successfully, they tend to fall through the cracks. It might be hard to find him," said a voice I didn't recognize.

They were talking about Jason. I kept my eyes closed, needing to hear the rest.

"I don't give a shit what you have to do, Cruz." Damon's voice dipped dangerously low as he spoke. "Find him." His tone held a silent threat in those two words. *Find him, so I can kill him.*

The two men left the room as they were still talking. Their voices became fainter with each passing second. I wondered briefly if it was safe to open my eyes yet. I wasn't ready to talk to Damon about the events of the night. It was extremely embarrassing to pass out every time I had a panic attack. I didn't feel like talking about it.

"They're gone now, you can open your eyes." Kate's soft voice surprised me and my eyes sprung open. My bestie sat on the chair next to where I lay in my living room. Damon must have taken me back home after finding Fiona. He probably assumed this place was safer than his right now.

I sat up, letting the blanket that covered my body

fall to my waist. I noticed Boone perk up and look at me from his place on the floor. He thumped his tail happily before nosing my hand for pats. I stroked the dog's fur as I looked at Kate.

"What are you doing here?" I asked in a rough voice. My throat felt like I had swallowed a hundred nails.

Kate offered me a small smile before grabbing my cold hand. She rubbed it between hers, bringing heat back to my skin.

"Damon called us." She tilted her head in the direction he'd disappeared. "Em's on her way," she finished.

I nodded my head in acceptance as I thought about the implications of this night. Emily and I were about to become a lot closer after this.

"You wanna tell me what happened?" Kate asked softly.

"He didn't tell you?" I responded with shock in my tone.

Kate shook her head. "He said it would be better if you talked to me about it. I think it was his way of getting you to talk about it in general. Men can be sneaky like that." She offered a small smile. "So, do you want to talk about it?"

That was all it took for the dam to burst. I buried my face in my hands as I sobbed. Kate moved to my side then. She pressed against me and wound her arms around mine, pulling my head to her so I could cry on her shoulder.

I wasn't sure why, but I had become such a crier in these last few weeks. Before Damon, I had always kept my emotions bottled up. Whether or not that was healthy was still debatable. But now? I was way more in touch with my feelings and I didn't know how to deal with them.

I heard my front door open and slam closed suddenly. Kate and I looked up in time to see a frazzled Emily walk in. She spotted us immediately and rushed for us. When she sat down next to me, she leaned in to soothe me as well. That made me cry even harder. I hadn't known she cared that much about me.

"Oh, honey, what happened?" she asked as she rubbed my back.

I calmed my sobbing enough to tell them about the last week. I let them know about Fiona going missing before I explained all the details about my night terror and the knife Jason held. I'd looked at Em as I promised to tell her about him later. Then I moved on to the events that happened tonight. I told them all about how I found Fiona against Damon's door with the very knife Jason held in my dream.

When I was done telling my story, both girls were quiet as they contemplated how best to help me. It was Em who spoke first.

"Nothing I say is going to make any of this better, hun. But I just want to tell you how sorry I am. We will figure this out, you're not alone," she offered.

Kate spoke next. "You're damn right, she isn't alone," she said as she hugged me again.

I dried my tears and sniffled before hugging her back. Emily's arms wrapped around me too. Soon we were all embracing each other. At that moment, I was extremely grateful for those women. I didn't know where I'd be in this world if I didn't have either of them as friends. As sisters.

"I hate to interrupt this, but I need to speak with Jill," Damon's hushed tone broke the moment.

Both girls leaned back as they looked over at the detective that stood in the doorway of my living room. I nodded my head as I stood and walked toward my lover. He seemed to soak in the sight of me as he held out his hand for me to follow him to the bedroom. Once there, he shut the door behind us.

I opened my mouth to speak first when he hauled me to his body in a fierce embrace. His hands were everywhere as if to see if I was broken. When he found no damage, he held my face between his hands as his eyes searched mine. I leaned into him and enjoyed the feel of him caressing me.

"I'm so sorry." He released a pent-up breath harshly. "I should have done more, I should have looked into that son of a bitch as soon as you told me his name. I would have known to be more careful then. I would have kept tabs on his movements. I would—" I shushed his self-deprecating ramblings with my finger pressed against his lips before I replaced them with my lips. I kissed him softly until I felt him relax slightly, then I pulled away.

"None of this is your fault," I whispered as I hugged him. He wrapped his arms around me and squeezed me tight. I let him hold me for long moments while we both decompressed. He sighed against me as he kissed the top of my head.

"You scared the shit out of me, Red," he mumbled and I felt my heart clench.

"I'm sorry," I allowed. "I'm getting really good at passing out when I'm stressed," I joked.

Damon chuckled quietly before he pulled away from me. When he tucked my stray hair behind my ear, I thought he was going to kiss me again. When he didn't, I deflated slightly.

"I called a friend of mine who's a PI to help find Jason. Apparently, he didn't go to his last six-month check-in with the local sheriff. When they visited his place of residence, he wasn't there. You would think the idiots up in Georgia would have given you a heads-up that he might have been nearby. I'm going with Cruz to the station to see if we can look further into him, maybe find out where he's been staying," he told me with a serious tone.

I shook my head. "I don't want you to leave," I said in a small voice. I wasn't used to asking for help so this was all new territory for me.

His brows furrowed as the look of sorrow crossed his eyes. I could see that he was torn between his need to keep me safe and the need to see me happy. I immediately felt guilty for putting him in the position where he felt he had to choose. I shook my head and cleared my throat.

"It's okay, I'm okay. You go and do what you need to do and then come back here to me." I tried to give him what I hoped was a reassuring smile.

He searched my eyes for a minute before pulling me back to him. I sighed as he squeezed me. I appreciated him so much at that moment and felt the overwhelming need to tell him just that when I heard shouting coming from my living room.

"What the fuck are you doing here?" Emily's loud voice carried our way. I looked up at Damon before we bolted for the door.

Emily was standing by the couch in an angry stance. Her face was red and she clenched her fists together so tightly I was surprised she didn't cut herself with her nails.

She was squaring off with a man I didn't know but assumed his last name was Cruz. He looked to be in his mid-thirties but was in exquisite shape. His shaggy hair curled slightly around his ears and partially covered his honey-colored eyes. I could see streaks of natural highlights in the brown mop from long days spent in the sun. His beard looked well-maintained and soft. He stood a good half foot over Emily and carried solid muscle under that tight white shirt he had on. He also filled out the faded pair of jeans that clung to his lean waist. I took a moment to look over his tattoos that wrapped around both arms, disappearing beneath his short sleeves as he held his hands up toward Emily. As if that was going to stop her from exploding.

"Now, Emily, you need to calm down," he cooed in her direction. Not the thing to say to an infuriated female, which he was soon to learn.

Em laughed but the sound held no humor. "I need to calm down? How about you get the fuck out! You have a lot of nerve showing up here, Leo," she yelled at him.

Leo apparently was really bad at following directions as he stepped toward Emily. "Where is all this hostility coming from, Emy?" He stepped closer still. I hid my smile behind my hand as I assumed what would happen next.

"Don't call me that," Emily gritted out behind clenched teeth. "And don't play dumb with me, Leo. You know damn well you betrayed my trust back in New York. Because of you, most of my family thinks I'm a good-for-nothing liar. I had to move across the country just to get away from their scheming ways," she seethed.

Leo looked increasingly confused as he stepped into Em's space. "What? I didn't lie. Emy—" His next words were cut off as Emily reared back and smacked him right across the face. I flinched back but smiled at the same time. What could I say? I was a sucker for good drama.

"I told you not to call me that!" she berated him as he rubbed the side of his face.

I could have sworn I saw him smile at her before he crowded her once more. She didn't back down from him as she kept the deep scowl on her face. He towered over her. If I hadn't felt the sexual tension between the two, I would have assumed he was threatening her.

"Oh, I'll do more than call you a name, Princess," he growled at her, and I almost giggled like a schoolgirl.

She opened her mouth to say something I'm sure was venomous when Damon intervened. He clapped his hand together, gaining everyone's attention.

"Fun sponge," I muttered. He grinned down at me before pinching my ass. "Sexual deviant," he murmured before walking toward the couple still holding a staring contest.

"All right, Cruz, we need to get going. Kate, Emily, always a pleasure." He slapped Leo on the back before looking at me. "I'll be back as soon as I can, Red. In the meantime, Boone will keep you company." As if on cue, Boone trotted his way to me and nudged me with his snout. I knelt to pet the furry beast.

I watched Leo step away from Em and break the spell they both seemed to be under. Damon kissed me goodbye and they were out the door the next second. I fanned myself as I looked at Emily expectantly.

She huffed loudly before settling on the couch with a plop. "It's a long fucking story, girls."

Chapter Twenty-Six

"I swear, I'm fine. It's late and you need to get home before those men of yours come knocking down my door." I smiled at Kate as I walked her to the front door. It was just past midnight and I felt the events of the day laying heavily upon my shoulders. I was ready to take a hot shower and crash.

Emily had gotten quiet after she had her blow-up with the hot PI in my living room. I could tell she didn't want to talk about how she and Leo knew each other, so we changed the subject. She stayed for a little longer before I convinced her it was okay to go. Now, I just had to convince Kate of the same thing.

"Are you sure? I can stay until Damon gets back. Reid is working tonight anyway and Heath won't mind," she offered.

I smiled as I walked her to the door. "Go. I'm just going to crash. It's been a super long day," I admitted.

I opened the door and Kate turned to look at me. "I feel like we should have a sleepover, like old times." She grinned at me with playfulness.

I chuckled before I rolled my eyes. "Really? Cause I feel like I need to fuck Damon's brains out when he gets home. You want to be around for that?" I challenged.

Kate turned on a heel and started down my sidewalk at that. "Call me tomorrow!" she yelled over her shoulder as I laughed.

After I watched her back out of my drive, I locked the door and shut off all the lights except for the porch light. I left it on for Damon.

I walked through my suddenly quiet home, shutting the lights off as I went. Boone followed close behind me as if guarding me. I found it comforting.

When I finished, I walked into my bedroom and sat on the edge of the bed. I let myself decompress for the first time since finding Fiona. I felt the back of my eyes burn as I thought about how scared she must have been. I released a shaky breath as I tried to calm myself.

Boone licked my hand, consoling me in his own way. I looked at the yellow dog with a soft smile on my lips. "Hey, buddy," I said as I pushed my fingers into his fur. He thumped his tail against the floor as if to acknowledge my greeting.

I slid down the side of the bed and sat on the floor with the loving animal. I let him lick me and love on me until my frown turned into a smile. He let me stroke his soft fur while I calmed my rolling emotions.

Some people say that animals know instinctively when we are in distress. I believed it at that moment as Boone soothed me without words.

"You're just a good boy, aren't you?" I cooed at him as he wiggled his tail before licking my face.

"Oh, yuck!" I giggled as I pushed him away from my face. I may want his comfort, but he could keep his stinky dog breath.

I patted him on his hind end before I stood. I started to walk to the bathroom and he followed. I turned around to face him as he sat back and stared at me like he was waiting for his next command.

I laughed again. "I'm going to take a shower, you stay here." I talked to the dog as if he could understand me. I shook my head to myself as I walked through the doorway, shutting the door behind me. I didn't need a dog watching me take a shower.

I flipped the water on and stripped out of my clothing. I grinned when I realized I was still wearing what remained of my ripped thong. Oh, how this night could have gone so differently. I would probably still be in Damon's bed if the night hadn't gone to shit. I'm sure we would have made love for hours, only to come apart for brief moments of reprieve before finding our bliss all over again.

I sighed as I discarded the ruined thong in the trash can. If only that's how the night had gone.

Now, I was stuck in this haunted house by myself, yet again. In such a short time, I had become used to being around other people. Whether it was Damon or one of the girls, I hadn't been alone for days now. I used to love my solitude and now I almost despised it.

I shook my head. "He'll be home soon," I said to myself as I stepped under the shower's hot spray.

I groaned as the hot water hit my sore muscles. I didn't know if it was from class or stress, but I was achy all over. I let the scalding water run all over my body as I felt myself relax more and more. I'd spent good money on the pulsing jets and I was going to get my use out of them tonight. I laughed at myself. I was going to get my use out of them *again*. This morning when Damon had used them on me flashed in my memory and I heated. I briefly thought about using it like that on myself but then quickly dismissed the idea. Sure, an orgasm would release some of my stress, but I was craving more.

It was crazy to me how my attitude toward sex had changed so much just in the last week and a half. Before Damon, I damn straight would have gotten myself off, or even found someone to do it for me before going on about my night. After Damon, I wanted his touch more than a quick release. I was unnerved as well as comforted by that fact. He had shown me in such a short time what it was really like to be loved and cherished by another person. Sure, we indulged in filthy hot sex on a regular basis, but that didn't mean he didn't do so lovingly.

I had tried to forget the part of my dream where I admitted to myself that I loved him. I blocked it from my thoughts as if that would make it any less true. But, there was no point in trying to forget it now. I loved that man so hard that it scared the shit out of me. Not because I thought he would use that love against me, but because I didn't think I would survive if it was ever taken from me.

I sighed as my water started to run cool. I quickly washed my body and exited the shower. I dried and wrapped my robe around my naked body. Using my towel, I wiped away the fog that collected on my mirror.

I stared at the woman who filled my vision. She was beautiful in the traditional sense of the word. I used to hate the face that stared back at me. Secretly wishing she wasn't pretty so maybe she'd be happy instead.

Now when I looked at her, I saw the woman that Damon loved. The woman I was slowly learning to love again. Sometimes all it takes to see your own worth is to watch that worth grow in the eyes of the person you love most. I had to learn how to love myself by experiencing that love from another.

It was time I stopped pushing Damon away and started soaking in every moment we had together. Tomorrow wasn't promised and it was almost sad how long it had taken me to figure that out.

A sudden noise jarred me from my thoughts as I jumped. I smiled at myself before throwing my towel in the hamper on my way to the bedroom. It sounded like Damon was home, and I couldn't wait to show him how much I needed him tonight.

I opened the door that led to my room expecting to see Boone still sitting where I'd left him. When he wasn't there I figured he went to greet Damon. I padded further into my room before I heard rustling come from the kitchen.

"Damon?" I raised my voice, hoping he would come to me. When he didn't answer, I stepped into the hallway.

The noise in the kitchen stopped as I stood next to my doorway and listened. A tickle at the back of my neck told me to go back to my room and lock the door.

You're being ridiculous, I scolded myself. Maybe it was just Boone getting into my trash. I sighed as I walked down the hallway.

"Boone, come here, boy," I called.

I stopped again as I listened for his paws to clank over the wooden floor. Nothing.

My heart rate ticked up as I came closer to the end of the hallway. Something wasn't right. I knew Boone enough to know that he came when he was called. Maybe he hadn't heard me.

"Boone!" I hollered for the canine louder this time. Nothing.

That's when I saw it. The faint trickle of light streaming in through the dining room doorway. My breath left me in sharp pulls as I padded closer and closer to the kitchen. Dogs could do miraculous things, but I doubted Boone could turn on a light switch.

I was silent as I approached the dining room. The closer I got the more I heard Boone growling. *What was he growling at?* Maybe he could see something out of one of my windows. That still didn't explain the light, though. I knew I turned it off before I went to my room.

As I came to the doorway, I held my breath as I peered past the frame. It took me a moment to see anything at all as panic started to cloud my vision. I pulled back, closed my eyes, and took another deep breath as Damon had shown me before I tried again.

At first, it looked as though Boone was just standing in the archway to the kitchen. Then I realized he was in an attack stance as he blocked whatever was in the kitchen from the rest of the house. He growled fiercely at what was in there, baring his teeth viciously.

I stepped into the dining room, still out of view, and grabbed the first blunt object I could find, which happened to be one of my heavy candlestick holders. I hastily removed the candle and placed it on the floor.

I raised it over my head with my right hand as I stepped further into the room. Each silent step I took brought me closer to the intruder in my kitchen.

My blood turned to ice in my veins as I got close enough to hear whispering.

"Good dog. You want a treat, buddy?" a deep voice whispered to the vicious dog blocking his advance.

I inhaled sharply as I recognized the voice that had haunted my dreams for years. I numbly brought the candleholder down from above my head as I stepped forward.

He was crouched over, talking to the dog but he looked exactly like he did in my night terror. If it had been a night terror at all. He didn't notice me right away as he continued to talk to Boone as if the dog would let him pass.

When he finally looked up from the snarling beast, we made eye contact. He grinned up at me as he straightened and I was thrust back in time. I sucked in a shaky breath. I smelled musty sheets and vanilla as if I was still trapped in that room. I felt my eyes start to burn and my throat start to clog as I choked.

"Jason."

Chapter Twenty-Seven

"Hey, beautiful." Jason's voice sounded so loud in my ears. He stood up to his full height now and looked just as he had in my dream. Only, I was pretty sure at this point it hadn't been a dream.

He was still just as imposing as ever as he stood in my kitchen. His blond hair was shaggier and his blue eyes just as bright. The differences between now and then were subtle. Like the way his eyes creased at the corners, they hadn't done that sixteen years ago. Or the way his skin looked as if time on the inside had made his elasticity less operable. He looked bigger too, more muscular. I would assume being in prison so long would've given him plenty of time to bulk up. I glanced down to his feet and saw a small puddle of blood that seemed to trickle out from his pant leg. I furrowed my brows before looking away.

The way he stood there and glared at me had my heart rate tripling in beats. Although he may look slightly different, prison couldn't change the way he leered at me. It was obvious he had a vendetta against me and he meant to take care of that now.

I should have turned around and run the moment I figured out he was in the house. I kicked myself for not grabbing my phone before I came exploring the noise I'd heard. Now, no matter how hard I told myself to back away, my feet wouldn't work.

I looked down at the dog still snarling at Jason and knew without a doubt that he wouldn't let Jason get anywhere near me. But, I was still frozen. I opened my mouth to speak but all that came out was a choking sound. Jason grinned at that, like he found my inability to talk funny.

Get a goddamn grip, Brookes, I scolded myself.

"What are you doing here, Jason?" I finally managed in a shaky voice.

Jason walked over to the opposite end of the room, trailing blood as he went, and leaned against my stove. When he faced me again he looked cool as a cucumber. Like invading someone's home was just another mundane thing on his to-do list. When he smiled at me again, I was immediately sucked back in time to that party.

"I'm here for you, Jill," he said calmly as he continued to leer at my body in appreciative glances.

I was suddenly all too aware of the fact that I was still in just my bathrobe. I felt the need to wrap the material further around my body but I made myself hold still. He smirked as though he knew my thoughts and I felt a flare of anger.

"How did you even find me?" I fumed.

He tilted his head back and laughed. His boom of sudden laughter made me jump where I stood and Boone took a tentative step toward him, lowering his head and still baring his teeth. If I hadn't been so petrified by fear, I would have smirked at the way Jason immediately stopped laughing when he saw the dog's advance.

He scowled down at the canine before answering me.

"*Brookes Publishing*... That's real original, Jill. You act surprised." He paused. "Like I wouldn't come looking for you in the end. What? Did you think I would just let you get away with what you did?" he sneered.

I scoffed in outrage as I widened my stance, becoming more and more pissed off and less scared. He wasn't the boogeyman. Jason was just a man and nothing more. And I had never cowered in front of a man. I didn't plan on starting now.

"What I did? You mean what *you* did. You raped me, Jason," I said, surprisingly calm.

Jason's face reddened and he took two big strides in my direction, pointing his finger at me. Boone snarled loudly and lunged for his ankles. He had enough common sense to jump away from the dog, but kept his hatred for me locked in his eyes.

"I did not rape you!" he shouted at me and I hated that I flinched. He looked like a madman standing there. His face was crimson and his muscles were primed for a fight. I'm pretty sure if he could get to me he would have strangled me at that moment.

I laughed but there was no joy in the cold sound. "Wow, after all these years, you still can't own up to the fact that you raped me?" He looked away from me for the first time and I stepped forward. "You put a drug in my drink, Jason. You forced me up those stairs to your room." Another step. "You held me down and fucked me without my consent." Another step, now I stood right behind Boone in the full light of the kitchen. "I don't know if anyone has ever told you this, but when a girl says stop and you don't, that's rape." My chest heaved and my eyes watered as I stared at him. "You took something from me that night. I didn't ask for any of it. *You raped me!*" I screamed so loud my throat protested.

"What was I supposed to do, Jill? I wanted you so bad and you didn't want anything to do with me," he whined. He almost acted like he was the victim and it made me sick. "You flaunted yourself in front of me, you teased me. I knew you wanted me but you just wouldn't admit it. I had to make you see that you wanted it. You gave me no other choice, beautiful." He cooed at me.

I was nauseous when he finished. Did he really think his actions were justified? I never once flaunted or teased him. Even if I had, that didn't give him the right to take what he wanted from me.

"You're a fucking psycho," I whispered.

"I'm not crazy!" He shook with rage. His reaction made me wonder how many times he had been called that.

I realized I was still holding the candleholder as I crossed my arms over my body. I needed to de-escalate this situation before he fully snapped. Damon would be back soon and I would let him take care of this crazy fucker. I just had to keep Jason preoccupied in the meantime.

"Okay, even if you're not coo-coo bananas, what do you want? It's been years. Why didn't you just go on about your life? Start fresh somewhere else. Why track me down?"

He smiled that same cruel smile as he glared at me. "I don't want a fresh start. I want my life back but you took it away from me!" he yelled. He pulled the knife he had used on Fiona out of his pocket and smiled at me. He twirled the blade between his fingers as he had in my dream. My hands started to shake as I looked for a way out of this situation. I furrowed my brows in confusion. How did he get it back?

"Your lover was stupid enough to leave this in his car after he brought you back home." He answered my unspoken question as I stared at the knife. "You took something from me, so I took something from you. You should just be lucky I took your cat and not your lover." His smile proved just how insane he had truly become.

I couldn't stop the question that rose from me. "Why did you take her to Damon's house?" I choked out behind the thick emotion clogging my throat.

He chuckled as he played with the blade. "I had to make sure you'd come back here to me. I could see how much you were starting to hate being here. I knew it was only a matter of time before you asked that fucker to take you to his home. So, I brought the cat to his house to scare you back here." He snarled in Boone's direction as he spoke again. "The dog did take a chunk out of my leg before I could get away, though. Damn thing was lucky my knife was otherwise preoccupied," he admitted as he lifted his pant leg. A nasty-looking gash in his leg made me want to give Boone the biggest steak I could find.

When he walked over to the door that led to my backyard, I thought he was going to leave. But all he did was open the door and walk back toward me. Boone's snarl of outrage became louder the closer Jason came to me.

All at once, his admission smacked me in the face. I felt all the color drain from my face as I shook with adrenaline.

"What do you mean you could see how much I hated being here? How would you know?" I asked the question I already knew the answer to.

He snickered at me as he used the blade's tip to scratch his temple. His smile would have been endearing if he wasn't so fucking crazy.

"Funny thing about home invasions, most people don't think to check the attic." He laughed as I stopped breathing. "I've been your roommate for quite some time now, Jill. You just didn't know it until I was ready for you to," he admitted before he rushed for me.

I jumped back and tripped, falling flat on my ass and dropping the heavy candleholder. I thought I was done for, as I watched his large frame hurtle toward me, only to be stopped by a seventy-pound golden retriever. Boone launched himself in the air at Jason. I cringed as I heard the sickening sound of flesh being shredded.

Boone snarled as he clamped down on the intruder's arm. Jason wailed in pain as the dog pulled all his weight down and shook his arm viciously, causing him to drop the knife. I scrambled across the floor for it. I was just within arm's reach when Jason brought his booted foot down on my ribs with a harsh kick.

All the air in my lungs left me in a whoosh as I screeched to catch my breath. Pain flared across my torso as I curled in a ball at his feet. I watched in horror as Jason used his free arm to hit Boone along his side, trying to get him to release his arm. His face was red and brutally hateful as he hit the dog hard enough to elicit a yowl from him. Boone dropped to the ground next to me with a thud and Jason kicked him just as hard as he'd kicked me.

"*Stop!*" I screamed.

Jason pulled the temporarily incapacitated dog by his collar to the open door. Once he was clear, he slammed the door hard enough to rattle the glass. Boone was immediately on his feet, clawing, barking, and growling at the door. Trying desperately to get back to me.

Jason leaned against the door for a moment before his hateful gaze turned back to me. He was covered in blood and it was pouring out in a steady stream to the floor. As he stalked toward me, I scrambled for the knife one more time.

I was on my hands and knees by the time he made it to me and had just gotten my grip on the knife as I felt him pull my hair. He ripped me up from the ground and pain flared along my scalp as I screamed. I nearly dropped the knife to hold my hair as he jerked me upright.

He released me long enough to grab me around my torso. He held my arms to my sides and squeezed me so hard I couldn't breathe. I cried out as my bruised ribs screamed in protest. His blood still gushed from his arm, smearing all over me.

"Please!" I gasped as my air was cut off.

He lifted me off the ground briefly and I kicked wildly. A small victory rushed through me as I landed a blow to his thigh and he lurched backward. He recovered quickly, though, and tightened his grip once more before placing my feet back on the ground. I tried to breathe as I gripped the knife so hard in my palm that I thought my hand might break.

"I should have ended this the other night! It would have been easy," he snarled against my cheek. "I've watched you for weeks, I learned your routine at home. You drink the same wine every night before bed. Every night!" he yelled against me and I gritted my teeth. "It was easy to crush up some Ambien and dissolve it in the wine," he admitted and I paled.

He'd drugged not only me but Damon too. That was why Damon couldn't stay awake. I shook violently as he continued.

"Loverboy laid there while I stood over you, Jill. He didn't care enough about you to wake up and protect you. I would have woken up!" He was delusional.

"You drugged him, you crazy fucker!" It took all my air just to get the words out as I thrashed against him. If I could just get my arm free I could end this.

Jason's heavy breath slithered across my ear as he spoke. "Stop fighting me, Jill. Can't you see that I just want to be with you? I love you so much, baby." His voice sounded desperate as he shoved his face in my hair.

I shivered in disgust. "Jason, let me go." I wheezed. My air supply was slowly disintegrating the longer he gripped me, and my vision darkened around the edges.

"No! Don't you get it? You're mine and I'm not going to let anyone else have you," he gritted angrily as he pushed me forward. I couldn't let him get me out of the house.

I swore I heard my name being called suddenly. Jason stopped moving as if he heard it too.

Damon.

"He can't have you," Jason's harsh whisper against my ear sent panic through my body. I couldn't allow him to take me.

I *wouldn't* allow him to take me.

All of my memories flashed back to me in a rush. Starting with the first time Jason held me from behind and I hadn't been able to fight him off. Then came Tom holding a gun to me as he gripped me harshly. Vince was next in the long line of men that tried to take advantage of me in a vulnerable state. Last was Damon, but I didn't feel helpless when he had done it. No, he had done it to help me learn to protect myself.

I took as deep a breath as I could as I planted my feet firmly, just like Damon taught me. I used all my strength to lean forward, bringing Jason's feet off the ground.

"Jill?" Damon's voice sounded closer as I bent forward as far as I could.

Jason growled and squeezed me even tighter, but it was too late.

I pushed up and off my feet, flipping over and taking my abuser with me. He landed with a thud and I heard him sputter as his breath was knocked out of him. I spun just like Damon showed me, only this time I wasn't going to pull my punches.

I crouched on his chest and pulled the knife up and over my head with both arms. I watched his eyes go wide with shock as I screamed and slammed the knife down as hard as I could. My aim was dead-on as the blade hit hard resistance before sinking into his chest.

My breath shuddered out of me as I looked down at the man that had tormented my nights for years. His eyes were still open when he took his last breath before he went limp. I shook as I covered my bloodied hands over my mouth to stop the sob that tried to escape.

"Jill!" I heard Damon's voice as he ran into the kitchen and slid across the ground to get to me. I glanced up into his chocolate eyes as I quivered. He searched me for evidence of any injury. He studied the blood all over me before looking down at the body that lay beneath me.

He looked on the verge of rage as he held his hands out to me. I released a harsh breath that ended in a cry as I flung myself into his arms. I could feel the sticky warm blood all over my arms and legs as I grasped onto him.

I shook as he called 911, before he picked me up, cradled me to his chest, and walked us out of that house.

Chapter Twenty-Eight

Six Months Later

I smiled brightly at the older woman that sat across from me, as the man I was madly in love with sat next to me. He squeezed my hand and I glanced at him with a knowing smile before leaning in to give him a quick kiss.

"You look like you're doing well, Jill." Dr. Yorker grinned at me over her glasses. I turned my gaze away from Damon as I smiled at the doctor who had helped me so much over the years.

She was correct in her assumption of me doing great. It took some time, but I felt better now than I ever had in the last sixteen years.

After the altercation with Jason, Damon had called the police and they'd arrived within minutes. I was promptly taken to the hospital to be evaluated, despite my protesting. Damon had refused to take no for an answer. He wouldn't even let us take the car. He had marched right up to the ambulance with me in his arms and told them to drive. It was just my luck that Reid happened to be the one on call that night.

Soon I was in the ER surrounded by all the people I loved. Kate had flown through the doors with both Heath and Lindsey in tow. Then, Emily had shown up looking like she had been run over by a train.

I'd been in shock at the time but I still remember when the doctor had asked everyone to leave the room. Damon had flat out declined to leave my side and he hadn't budged. When the nurses threatened to call Security, he had simply flashed his badge and everyone had gotten quiet. Needless to say, he stayed in the room with me the whole time.

I had gotten X-rays, tox screenings, and a nurse had helped me wash all of Jason's blood off. They had, in fact, found a large amount of Ambien in my system from the wine Jason had spiked. The doctor explained to me that that drug did have the horrible side effect of producing night terrors. She explained that some complaints about the drug included the users' inability to move upon waking. It was clear the night terror had been real.

The fact that all of it had really happened left me very unsettled, to say the least. How easily he had been able to drug not only me but Damon too was a scary thought. Damon had felt guilty after hearing what had really happened, even though he had been unable to do anything about it.

After the doctor had returned with my scans, she proclaimed I was fit to go home at any time. I had some severe bruising but nothing had been broken, thank goodness.

I was still shaking and out of it when Damon promptly whisked me away to his private oasis. My house had been labeled as an active crime scene, so I hadn't been allowed to return to it for a long while after. That had been fine with me, though. I could have waited ten years to go back there and it still would have been too soon.

Damon had taken his time that night. He'd soothed my achy soul with his loving ministrations. We hadn't slept at all that night, not wanting to stop holding each other even when our brains tried to shut down.

"I'm so sorry, Red," he'd whispered against my hair as the early morning light streamed through his bedroom windows. "I should have never left you. I should've listened to you when you asked me to stay." He trembled as he spoke.

"None of this is your fault, Damon." I'd looked up into his eyes. "Jason would have made his move against me whether you had been there or not. He was psychotic and there was no way you could have known he would go after me in the first place," I whispered against his neck as I buried my face there, breathing him in deeply.

Damon said nothing as he held me tightly. I knew he was having a hard time taking my words for what they were.

I rose above him after that and straddled his hips, still in the robe the hospital had sent me home in. I traced the hard lines of his face as I gazed at his frown. I leaned forward and kissed the crease between his eyes and then his harsh lips. I'd kissed all over his face until he finally sighed against me, squeezing my bottom as he did.

I'd kissed him deeply and begged silently for him to move his mouth with mine. When he did with a long, tortured groan, I melted against him. I pulled back from him enough to pull the knot on the robe free and exposed myself to him before crashing my lips back to his.

He squeezed my hips before letting his hands travel upward. When he came to my ribs, I winced as he lightly ran his fingers over the bruise that marred my skin. He pulled back with a hiss as he looked over my body. I let him explore and watched his eyes assess the damage he found there.

When I saw the moment his mood was about to turn, I grabbed his hands and placed them on my breasts. He made a tortured sound as he closed his eyes.

"I don't want to hurt you," he admitted.

I refused to accept his excuse as I leaned down to take his mouth once more before bringing my hands down his body to release him from his sweats.

He groaned as he fell heavily into my hand. I

gripped him firmly.

"I need you," I begged against his lips before pulling back enough to look him in the eyes. "I love you," I admitted.

He sucked in a harsh breath as my words flowed over him. His hands flexed and released against me as I rose. When I placed him at my entrance and slowly sank onto him, I watched as his face contorted almost painfully.

"I love you," I repeated as I slid all the way down before raising again.

He closed his eyes again at my words and his chest heaved as he breathed deeply. I grabbed his hands as I rode him and pulled them above his head as I laid down on him. He twitched inside of me as I rocked back and forth. I rubbed my lips against him as I repeated myself.

"I love you," I cried softly.

His eyes sprung open as he flipped us so I was below him. He slammed his lips to mine and gripped the back of my neck as he continued at a slow pace. He swallowed down my moans of pleasure as he pulled out almost all the way before plunging back in. When his lips left mine he looked pained.

"I failed you tonight and I don't deserve to hear those words," he whispered. Before I could tell him otherwise he continued as he thrust into me slowly. "*Pero te amo, Roja.* I love you so much I don't think I could ever let you go. Even if it was the best thing for you. Even if you hate me for not protecting you," he admitted with such emotion my chest hurt.

I felt tears leak from my eyes as I looked up at the man I had grown to love. He had opened my eyes so much. Showing me not only how to let other people in, but also how to love myself like I deserved.

"I don't hate you, baby." I wept as he placed his forehead against mine with a shudder. "I think I've loved you for a long time now and I was just too stubborn to admit it. If you want, you can protect me now and for the rest of our lives," I said. His eyes glistened with unhashed tears before he closed them.

"*Siempre, Roja,*" he promised.

He'd kissed me then. A deep kiss that said all the words that were too hard to articulate at that moment. He made love to me and put every bit of his emotion into the act.

We'd found our bliss that morning in each other's arms repeatedly. Only when we had been completely exhausted from our actions did we find rest and solitude. Never escaping the other's embrace.

We both took a few weeks just to be with each other and to heal. Damon coddled me the entire time. During the day, I was the same playful Jill I'd normally been when around him. But during the night, my soul showed me the darkness that lurked beneath.

I'd like to say that my nightmares disappeared after Jason was finally rid from my life. But that would be a lie. I had nightmares for the first few nights but Damon was always there when I awoke screaming. He had become a constant comforting fixture in my life.

Nobody likes to talk about what it feels like after you take another person's life. Even if that was my only way out of the situation, I still felt like scum afterward. It had taken days to stop the nightmares that replayed the moment that knife pierced his heart. I watched over and over again as the light left his eyes.

But after talking with both Damon, my girls, and Dr. Yorker until I was blue in the face, my nightmares had slowed and dwindled until they had become nonexistent.

Although I still missed Fiona every day, I had found a new companion in Boone. He was a little sore for the first few days after Jason, but he turned out to be no worse for wear. And I'd stayed true to my word and bought him the biggest steak I could find.

Damon hadn't grumbled in the slightest when the dog chose me over him time and time again. I think he'd found comfort in the fact that I would always have a protector in the canine.

My house had been cleaned and released to me a few weeks after the attack. Kate, Em, and Lyns offered to clean it out for me and I had taken them up on their offer. I never wanted to step foot in that place ever again. I had put the house up for sale after that and was happy when it sold quickly. Damon had made room for me in his home and we now lived together permanently. A fact we had celebrated almost nightly.

I had almost been sick when the police had shown me pictures of evidence they had found. They hypothesized that Jason had broken into my house the night I found the shattered window. He had immediately taken refuge in my attic where he had been living for the weeks that followed.

The police department had contracted a profiler to pin down why exactly Jason had gone through the hassle to get to me. She explained that he had more than likely fantasized about a fake relationship with me while he had been in prison, and after he was released. Sixteen years is a long time to obsess over the same person. He had spent the weeks after the break-in messing with me to gain my attention. He would move things around after I left for the day, turn on lights after I turned them off, little things that almost went unnoticed.

When I hadn't vocalized my annoyance, he'd escalated his efforts. Like letting the air out of my tires to keep me home. Also using my bed while I was gone. I still got the heebie-jeebies just thinking about him sleeping where I slept.

His last attempt to gain my attention ended violently. The profiler explained that she thought since I had started showing interest in Damon, Jason felt the need to escalate his plans quicker, which was ultimately his downfall. If he had waited it out and planned a little longer instead of rushing, he may have gotten away with kidnapping me.

In the end, she told me I was extremely lucky to have gotten out as easily as I did. She said that she's seen other cases like this not end so well for the victim.

I had been left reeling after I was given all the information, but Damon had helped me back down from the ledge with his unique brand of dominance.

Over time, I'd found my own form of freedom under his careful ministrations. Whoever said you couldn't feel powerful or in control while submitting to the person you loved most, was a damned liar. I never felt freer than I did when I was under Damon's ropes and command.

If that was wrong, then I didn't want to be right.

Some people might say we'd moved too fast, especially after the huge trauma we'd gone through, but I didn't care what other people said. Damon had helped me heal in ways I never thought possible. So, when he got down on one knee on the very dock that started it all, I said yes. A million times yes.

So, now here we were. Sitting on the very couch where I'd spilled my heart and soul, to the woman who helped me all these years. And for the first time in a long time, I had a genuine smile on my face for her.

"I'm doing great, Doc." I grinned as I looked at mine and Damon's joint hands. "And I wanted to tell you that I'm engaged," I admitted as I looked into the eyes of the only man who'd ever held my heart.

His deep-brown eyes glittered at me as he grinned. God, I couldn't wait to start my life with him. These last sixteen years were like I had been asleep and he had just now woken me up.

I looked back at Dr. Yorker and watched her mouth break into a huge smile. She was happy to see me finally happy.

"And how does that make you feel?" she asked with a knowing gleam in her eyes.

I shook my head as I smiled at my future and I left my past behind.

The End

A.E. NALLE

EVERNIGHT PUBLISHING ®

www.evernightpublishing.com

www.ingramcontent.com/pod-product-compliance
Lightning Source LLC
Chambersburg PA
CBHW020937180626
46814CB00013B/568